LEGACY

FIRST COLONY - BOOK 3

KEN LOZITO

ACOUSTICAL BOOKS LLC

Published by Acoustical Books, LLC

KenLozito.com

Cover design by Jeff Brown

Editor: Myra Shelley

Proofreader: Tamara Blain

ISBN: 978-1-945223-16-7

1

(Two hundred years before the Ark reached New Earth)

FLEET ADMIRAL MITCH WILKINSON's stooped form walked the bridge of the battleship carrier *Indianapolis*. Once, this vessel had been the flagship of the NA Alliance Navy, but now it was a solitary life raft for the precious few survivors remaining in the birthplace of humanity. The Vemus had changed everything, spreading across the planet like an untamed plague. But even considering all the destruction wrought by the enemy, humans hadn't been able to overcome certain behaviors of their own that had been consistent throughout their existence—the burning desire for power. Greed and corruption had doomed the human race on Earth.

Twenty years earlier, when he'd smuggled Connor Gates and the rest of the Ghost Platoon aboard the *Ark*, he never would have guessed that mankind's first interstellar colony would be the key to the survival of their entire species. Mitch had been an old man even then. After the *Ark* was on its way, he'd planned on a

quiet retirement while keeping his promise to watch over the son
Connor had left behind. It had been a good plan.

Mitch glanced over at the young man who was speaking with
Dr. Stone. There were times when the light caught his facial
features in such a way that he reminded Mitch of Connor. Mitch
had plucked Sean Gates from Earth before the Vemus had really
begun to spread. He'd brought the boy aboard the *Indianapolis* as
part of an internship awarded to survivors of fallen veterans.
While Mitch knew Connor was very much alive, he'd leveraged
his "death" as a means of keeping Sean Gates close to him.

Sean looked over at him. "We're ready to execute our final
broadcast, Admiral."

Wilkinson turned his slate-blue eyes toward Sean.
"Acknowledged," he replied.

The Vemus had developed an insatiable appetite for humans,
and now there was evidence that they would even venture out
beyond the solar system in pursuit of the last of them. In a final
effort to give the colonists a chance of survival, Dr. Stone was
running some last-minute checks of their most ambitious
undertaking to date.

"Elizabeth," Mitch said, "going back through it for the
thousandth time isn't going to change anything."

Dr. Stone turned her gray-haired head toward him and then
closed down the holoscreen she'd been working from. After
speaking softly to her assistant, she walked over to Mitch.

"It's ready. I just wish . . ." Elizabeth said.

Mitch nodded knowingly. "We all do."

The *Indianapolis* may have been a ship of the wall, but it was
now only a shell of what it had been. The vast stockpiles of
armament once kept there had long been used up and the
weapons they'd managed to keep online were based on energy
beams. They had no missiles and there had been no resupply

missions in the past ten years—not since the governments of Earth had all collapsed and the militaries had splintered into groups that focused on gathering the remaining resources for themselves.

Earth had been lost to them. For a while they'd scraped together an existence on space stations and solar colonies, but those were gone now, too. It had taken thousands of years for mankind to rise from its meager beginnings and—for a brief stint that began during the twenty-first century—had seemed to achieve a golden age of technological wonders. But humanity's fall into barbarism had been swift when the Vemus spread to the solar colonies, taking on a form that none of the survivors had been prepared to face. Mitch had banded together with a faction of the old NA Alliance Navy to try and secure a future, but the Vemus were too strong. They adapted too quickly and there simply weren't enough humans left to fight them. None of those who'd fought the Vemus had even the appearance of being human anymore.

Mitch glanced over at Dr. Stone. She'd found him five years ago, bringing refugees to a space station that orbited Ganymede. Jupiter's largest moon had become a haven. It was there that the brilliant Dr. Stone had eventually convinced him they only had one chance at survival and that all the people in the solar system were already dead, including the two of them; it was just a matter of time.

Mitch had denied the claim at first, believing her to be yet another brilliant scientist who couldn't cope with one of the darkest moments in human history. But shortly after that, remnants of Earth's space navies had begun fighting each other. Men and women Mitch had been friends with had either been killed or given in to despair and made a mad grab for power so their last days could have some semblance of comfort. Then the first Vemus ships from Earth had shown up at the colonies, preying on the survivors. Mitch had taken his most trusted tacticians and tried to come up with a way to survive, but the fact of the matter was that all their projections proved there was absolutely no chance. They could only succeed in delaying the inevitable. The Vemus had adapted and hunted only humans. Mitch didn't understand how a parasitic organism discovered deep in Earth's oceans could have decimated mammalian life on Earth, but that's exactly what had happened. Then it started targeting humans exclusively, and the real fight had begun.

Once he'd exhausted all his options, Mitch sought out Dr. Elizabeth Stone again, wanting to learn more about her far-fetched plan. He'd mistakenly believed that perhaps she had a way to actually help *them* survive. She didn't. What Dr. Stone had in mind was for the survival of those aboard the *Ark*—to update its mission and send it even farther away than they'd originally planned while gathering up whatever resources and people they could and heading out to the fringes of the solar system. It was a death sentence and also one of the biggest leaps of faith Mitch had taken in his entire life.

Dr. Stone had the appearance of a sweet little old lady who had somehow managed to survive, but Mitch had learned that she was one of the smartest and shrewdest people he'd ever met. He and Elizabeth had become mother and father to the survivors they'd taken with them.

Elizabeth had given him a timetable to work with. Updating the *Ark* mission wasn't simply a matter of sending a transmission; they had to enhance their communications array to handle a sustained data burst beyond anything they'd ever done before. And doing so would alert the Vemus to their presence.

Mitch's job was to gather the supplies they needed for the mission. They scavenged anything they could from decimated space stations and unmanned satellites that were the last vestiges of an age now gone. Even though he'd agreed to help Dr. Stone, he hadn't become a true believer in their mission until years later when, on a scavenging mission, they'd found an intact satellite uplink and seen an image of Earth. The bright blue planet was still there but with a cloud cover that could only come from a holocaust the likes of which had only been hinted at during a much earlier nuclear age. Communications from the last space stations had gone dark, but there were plenty of ships still in the system—ships that were patched together and would attack without provocation. Those ships and the people serving aboard them had been absorbed into the Vemus Fleet. Mitch had tried to avoid the Vemus, but they'd become aware of the *Indianapolis* and hunted it. The Vemus had grown in intelligence and complexity in the years since Mitch had first seen their existence appear on mission reports. Some were vaguely humanlike, but there were others that were beyond anything he could have imagined.

Their final mission was such a mundanely obvious thing that Mitch couldn't believe he hadn't thought of it before, but Elizabeth had known. Mitch suspected she'd always known. It was the last piece to the puzzle and it was the thing that would bring the Vemus down on them in full force.

Sean walked the length of the bridge and stood in front of Mitch.

"Credentials to override the *Ark's* mission parameters have been uploaded, Admiral," Sean said.

"Good. What about my other request of you?" Mitch asked.

Sean scowled. "I don't know what you expect me to say. I hardly remember him at all."

Mitch arched an eyebrow. "But you do remember him at least a little bit."

Sean looked away for a moment. "My father left when I was three years old. Then you smuggled him aboard the *Ark*. I have nothing to say to the man."

Mitch regarded the young man. He was beyond his years in so many ways and yet managed to be so young in others. "I doubt that. Your father had no choice. I've told you he had decided to go back to you, to be your father."

"Yeah? Well, he didn't!" Sean snapped, then grimaced. "I'm sorry. You don't deserve that. You've been more of a father to me than he ever was."

"Circumstances made it this way. You don't have to say much. Just tell him who you are. That's all he'll want to know," Mitch said.

There was a quiet buzz on the bridge as the various teams made their final preparations. Mitch watched as Sean glanced at the PRADIS output on the main holoscreen. The Vemus fleet had almost caught up to them.

"Why are you pushing for this? None of it will matter in a few hours," Sean said.

Mitch's gaze hardened. "It matters. Your father didn't deserve what happened to him, just like you don't deserve what's happening to you. We're all in the same boat, but you have a chance to send one final message to someone who cares about you. The rest of us here don't have any family left. We only have each other, and not for much longer."

Sean clenched his teeth. Doing what they'd set out to do wasn't easy for them, knowing that their last efforts would ultimately be for someone else's benefit. Mitch chose to look at it as an investment in a dark future, but there was a lot of bitterness among the survivors on the *Indianapolis* because they knew there would be no escape from the Vemus. They'd exhausted all their resources and this would be their final stand.

Mitch looked at Sean, who returned his gaze. Stubbornness was a Gates' family stock-in-trade. With a slight shrug of his shoulders, the young man finally walked over to one of the consoles and sat down.

"Tactical, put the countdown on the main screen," Mitch said.

He glanced over at the command couch. He was tired of sitting and planning, but most of all he was tired of failing. He wished he could have come up with a way to stop the Vemus, and he supposed that if they'd had more time perhaps they could have found a way together. But that wasn't the case. He was going to die today. They all were. Since these were going to be his last moments alive, he chose to meet his end on his feet.

Elizabeth's hand grasped his. "Thank you," she said softly.

Mitch gave her hand a gentle squeeze. "You were right."

"I know, but it's good to hear you say it," Elizabeth said.

Mitch watched the countdown timer drain away. The main reactor was charging the power relays at the communications array in preparation for the broadcast signal. The signal would reach the nearest deep space buoy and then continue until it reached the *Ark*. Once the colony ship received the data burst, the onboard computers would set upon the task of changing the ship's trajectory and hopefully that of the last humans in the galaxy.

A klaxon alarm sounded, and Mitch glanced over to the woman serving as his tactical officer.

She silenced the alarm. "Vemus forces are aboard the ship, sir."

Mitch swallowed hard. He'd been prepared for this, but when it came down to it, all men fear death when it's their time to go. "Understood," he said and used his implants to begin the powerful broadcast.

The Vemus would be able to follow the broadcast. There had already been evidence that they were amassing ships together for a long journey, and the race for humanity's survival was about to begin.

As the signal went out, the survivors aboard the *Indianapolis* fought a foe that dead scientists back on Earth had determined was of their own making. Those scientists had failed to stop a sickness they hadn't fully comprehended, but the survivors valiantly fought them once more to the last man, woman, and child until they closed upon the bridge. Some of the people there had chosen to take their own lives. Their bodies wouldn't be contaminated by the Vemus, but there were others who fought with weapons in hand until the bitter end—an end for the crew of the *Indianapolis* but the promise of a new beginning for the rest of mankind.

(Sierra – New Earth Colony)

CONNOR STOOD IN HIS QUARTERS, his gaze lingering on a video file he'd selected from the long list on his screen. He wasn't sure whether he could watch it again, but something deep inside him urged him to do it one more time. He pressed his lips together in determination and then pressed play.

"You don't know me at all. In fact, I can hardly remember you. The admiral believes I should record this stupid thing and send it along. Said I should tell you who I am. So who am I? I'm the guy it sucks to be. Hell, I'd have settled for the short end of the stick. Any of us would have settled for *any* part of the stick, but we don't get that. I've fought in a long war with little hope of survival, let alone a victory. Yet *you* get to live. You're the lucky one. By the time you see this message, you'll be alive on some colony world, living your life. Maybe you'll even have a family and be someone else's father—"

Connor stopped the video, his throat thick with emotion at the bitter catch in his son's voice, which came across perfectly preserved. Connor leaned on the small shelf before the holoscreen, momentarily overcome by the weight of regret, but then he reached out and restarted the video so it could disgorge its ancient message into the darkened room.

"I don't know what to say to you. Even though I know what happened, I'm mad at you for leaving. I'm still mad. I'm mad because you left in the first place and I'll never know why. Not really." His son looked away from the camera for a moment. "If my mother knew, she never told me. She died, you know. She was among the first to become ill with what became the Vemus infection. The funny thing is that Vemus isn't . . ." His son's voice trailed off. "The admiral tried to help me find her. We didn't know at the time that it was the beginning of the end for us. Yet it's upon our blood and sacrifice that *you* get to live. *You,* who left . . . left us all behind."

Connor knew what he meant. *You left me behind.* He imagined his son saying it, and it stung like a slap across the face.

"I don't have anything nice to say. I'm not going to say something that will make you feel better about leaving. I don't think you deserve it. If you were here, I might be screaming at you. Maybe we'd even fight," Sean said, glaring at the screen. "I'm good at fighting. Maybe I get that from you. Heh. I can't even imagine you sitting there getting this message. What you must be thinking. Do you even feel anything? The admiral said I should tell you who I am. I'm a soldier, and it sucks. I didn't choose to be a soldier. It chose me. I hate it almost as much as I hate you. That's who I am. I don't think any of this is going to make you feel better. I know I don't feel . . . and I'm long past caring about . . . anything." Sean glanced away from the camera at something off-screen. "They're almost here. I'm surrounded by dead bodies, along with those of us who won't take our own lives. This is all that's left. This is our legacy. We are to make sure that the broadcast signal stays on as long as possible. For you. So you get to live. Who am I? Science says you're my biological father, but I have no father. I'm a soldier fighting on the losing side. It sucks being me. I have nothing left but fury and hate."

The video message from Connor's son had been part of the data cache Reisman had stolen before he died, and the message was over two hundred years old. Connor hadn't known what to expect when he first watched it, but every time he watched his throat became thick with sorrow and regret. He must have watched this video hundreds of times. The bitter man his son had become left Connor smothered with guilt. He should have been there. He'd give anything to change the past, to stay behind and raise his son. Protect him, even knowing what he knew about the Vemus. At least he could have been there to fight at his son's side. Then Sean would have known how much Connor loved him.

He'd thought long and hard about what must have been going through his son's mind in those final moments. The crushing pain he felt at finally seeing Sean and knowing what had become of him struck him like a blow every time he watched the video, but he had to keep watching it. He owed his son that much at least.

With the pain came a sense of pride that his son had fought to the very end. It was a measure of who he'd been. Connor couldn't imagine what Sean had had to endure, the kind of life he'd led. Connor would never forgive himself for not being there. He'd hated Wilkinson for putting him aboard the *Ark*, but those feelings had long since faded away. Connor's choices many years before that event were what had made him leave his family, which had nothing to do with Admiral Mitch Wilkinson. The old admiral knew that, and even Connor's son knew it.

He powered off the holoscreen and rubbed his face. His eyes were puffy and tired. He made himself watch the video of his son as a kind of penance, as if subjecting himself to all the pain would somehow ease Connor's most profound regret. He clenched his teeth and slammed his fist down on the shelf. He hated that video and hated himself for what it represented—a life of regret and a reminder of what he'd left behind.

2

NOAH WAS SURROUNDED BY HOLOSCREENS. Each had data feeds being piped into them that fed several regression-analysis queries he had running. The work he was doing could only be done at CDF headquarters in Sierra. It had been two months since the Vemus attack, and Noah was tasked with data mining everything the late Colonel Wil Reisman had been able to steal from the Vemus warship. More than a few times Noah wished he had Reisman's help. The colonel had been extremely clever and could glean useable intelligence from anything he set his attention on. Noah missed Reisman and had thrown himself at his current project to ensure that Reisman's last action hadn't been for naught.

He was in a large work area where his team was carrying out smaller projects serving the same goal: find anything they could use against the Vemus forces coming for them. Working with scientists for so long had taught Noah that often the best results of a large project came from collaboration with others, so when Connor asked him what he needed to get the job done, Noah had told him he needed a team, a large room, and priority access to one of the CDF's supercomputers. He'd been given all of that, and Noah and his team worked tirelessly. As a result of those efforts, they'd made quite a few discoveries that were being closely examined by subject-matter experts.

As the days passed, Noah kept looking at the clock. They all did. He felt like they were working on borrowed time and at any moment the rest of the Vemus attack force would show up to finish what they'd started.

Someone cleared their throat behind him.

"So this is where they've been keeping you."

Noah turned around and swiped the holoscreen to the side. "Allison, it's so good to see you. Or should I call you Dr. Blake now?" he asked with a smile. The former medic for Search and Rescue had recently become a medical doctor.

Allison gave him a quick hug. She was tall, with long auburn hair and cupid's-bow lips. She peered at him. "You're not getting enough sleep."

Noah snorted. "No one is."

Allison glanced around. "I've heard a lot about what you've been doing. You're an official hero, but I'd love to meet your wife."

Noah felt the skin tighten around his eyes. He and Kara had decided to get married shortly after they returned to New Earth. It had been a quiet ceremony, which was what they'd wanted. "I'd love for her to meet you, but she's at Lunar Base working on . . . I'm sure you can guess."

Allison's eyes drew down in empathy. "I'm sorry. It must be hard being apart like that."

Noah nodded. "I'm sure you're not here to reminisce about our old Search and Rescue days."

"No, I'm not," Allison said.

"What can I do for you?" Noah asked.

"You remember my specialization?" Allison asked.

"Of course. Field biology."

"I've branched out into—" Allison began to say.

One of Noah's analyses finished running and flashed on the holoscreen next to him. He glanced at it, noting the returns.

"What's that?" Allison asked.

"The data cache we got from the Vemus ship. It's over two hundred years old and I'm trying a new regression analysis on the video files. It seems that video logs were the preferred method of recording one's experiences, which makes it difficult to glean useful information," Noah said.

Allison frowned as she read the screen. "What are you trying to find out?"

Noah blew out a breath. "How much time do you have?" he asked with a half-smile. "We needed a quicker way to analyze the information people were recording that didn't require us to watch every video. If we tried to do that, it would take years to get through them all."

"Why wouldn't you focus on the research information and such?" Allison asked.

"That's what we did initially, and I've given that to Connor, but I think there's more to be found," Noah answered.

"Like what?"

Noah pressed his lips together in thought. "Have you ever heard the phrase 'missing the forest because of the trees'?"

Allison nodded.

"I think we're so focused on the facts about the Vemus and what happened to Earth that we're missing key insights from the people who were actually there," Noah said.

"Now you've lost me."

"They fought the Vemus for years, but there was a time *before* the Vemus became as we know them now. I think that's how we can find something in the records we can use against them. Despite everything we've done for the past seven years, we've only really had one encounter with the Vemus, and that was about two months ago. The people back on Earth had years to contend with them. So I'm after those people who had a thought or theory they recorded but didn't have time to fully explore," Noah said.

"I understand. You're looking for a needle in a haystack."

"That about sums it up, but I know you didn't come all this way to hear about what I was doing," Noah said.

"I'm doing something similar—" Allison began.

A comlink came to prominence on one of the holoscreens, drawing their attention. It was a priority message with CDF General Connor Gates' identification on it. Noah opened the channel and Connor's face came on screen.

Connor looked at Noah and then noticed Allison.

"It's good to see you, sir," Allison said, moving to stand next to Noah.

"You as well, Dr. Blake," Connor replied and then looked at Noah. "I need a status update from you."

Before the Vemus attack, Noah had thought of Connor as a friend—albeit a friend who tolerated very little in the way of nonsense—but after their encounter with the Vemus, Noah had noticed his friend becoming increasingly bitter as time went on. He understood why, but he missed the old Connor just the same.

Noah brought up another window on the holoscreen. "I have it right here. I've sent all I found to Sanctuary."

"I'm aware of that, but you were supposed to be looking for more information about the power requirements," Connor said.

"The colossus cannon was theoretical to begin with. I'm not

even sure they actually built it back on Earth . . ." Noah's voice trailed off when Connor speared a look at him.

"Let me guess. You're still mining those video logs," Connor said.

Noah looked away guiltily. "There's good information in there. Things we can use."

"The only thing in those recordings is how the people of Earth were defeated by the Vemus. Wilkinson found plans for an atmospheric weapon, but we haven't been able to produce the power required," Connor said.

Noah felt a flush warm his face. He'd spent a lot of time watching those videos. At first, he'd convinced himself it was just curiosity, but now he couldn't stop thinking about them. Some of them were horrifying, but he found comfort in knowing there were others who had faced what the colony was now facing.

"Noah," Connor called. "All those people are dead. They can't help us, but you can."

"I'm doing my best, sir," Noah replied.

"I know, and I need more from you. I want you to go to Sanctuary and see it for yourself," Connor said.

"I'm not sure I can help them. There are plenty of engineers there who are trying to adapt the power station from the alien city to use with the colossus cannon," Noah said.

"Do I need to make it an order?"

Noah glared at the screen. He wanted Kara with him. She was on the lunar base and the Vemus could attack at any moment. "No," he said and sighed.

Connor's gaze softened. "Thank you," he said.

"Sir, I have a request I'd like to run by you. It will only take a minute," Allison said.

"Make it quick," Connor replied.

"We've been studying the data about the Vemus and its

origins, but in order to figure out how it will affect us here on this planet, we need samples. Living samples, that is," Allison said.

Connor frowned. "We've provided living samples to the research laboratory at the lunar base."

Allison shook her head. "That was the remnant virus. What we're looking for is the parasite. They work together. All the samples contain only the dead virus."

"What is it you're asking for? I won't authorize any of the samples to be brought down to the planet surface," Connor said.

Allison shook her head. "No, that's not what I'm asking. We have a team on the lunar base. They've been requesting permission to try and gather live samples from the larger pieces of wreckage of the Vemus ships in the debris fields before they get too far away."

"I'm not sure that's a good idea—"

"Sir, this is as important as any weapon system we currently have. Perhaps even more so. This thing spread like wildfire across Earth and we're not sure if the same thing is going to happen here on New Earth," Allison said.

Connor pressed his lips together in thought. "Explain it to me then, but keep it brief. I have to give a report to the colonial congress about our readiness status."

"I'll be brief. We're different because we've been living on this planet and making it our home, and it's changed us. Our immune system is different because we've been exposed to this planet. There are mammals of a sort here. We've sent samples of parasites and viruses we've collected to the lab station on the lunar base, but we can't see how they'll interact with the Vemus unless we have live samples to work with," Allison said.

"I thought you've been running simulations," Connor said.

"We have, but they'll only get us so far. What we could learn from a live sample is whether some kind of organism here would make us resistant to the Vemus. The data from Dr. Stone that was found on the Vemus ship said the Vemus exclusively targeted humans *after* Earth scientists failed to find a cure. We suspect that the scientists were trying to modify it so it wouldn't target humans, but, instead, it had the opposite effect," Allison said.

Connor glanced over at someone who was speaking to him off-screen for a moment. "That's a hell of a theory, Blake."

"It's the only one that makes any sense. We know there are viruses on Earth that can rewrite their DNA, but the Vemus represents a much more complex system than a simple parasite and virus pair. This is our chance to gain a better understanding of what we're dealing with," Allison said.

"Okay, you convinced me. I'll authorize a scouting mission. Send me the team leader you want on the mission, and we'll make it happen," Connor said.

"Thank you, sir," Allison said, sounding relieved.

Connor shifted his gaze to Noah. "There will be a transport going to Sanctuary tomorrow morning and I want you on it. Gates out."

The comlink closed and Noah stared at the blank screen for a few seconds before looking away. He rested his hands on his hips.

"He seemed kind of harsh toward you," Allison said.

Noah shrugged. "They've placed the survival of the colony in his hands. How would you be?"

Allison pursed her lips in thought. "All this wasn't real to me until two months ago. Earth and everything about it seemed so far away."

"Trust me, it's real," Noah said. He powered off the holoscreens he'd been working from. "I'm worried about him."

"What do you mean?" Allison asked.

"Some of the things we found in the data cache were for Connor specifically. There was at least one video log," Noah said.

Allison's eyes widened. "Oh god."

"I have no idea what was in the video log or who it was from. The only thing I do know is that after I sent it to Connor, something seemed to break inside him. At first I thought it was because of everyone we'd lost, but this seems different," Noah said.

"Have you told anyone about this?"

"Who would I tell? I'm not sure what good it would do. If it's personal, then shouldn't it remain personal?" Noah asked.

Allison gave him a look that somehow made him feel foolish. "He's grieving, and whatever was on that video log certainly didn't help. Why didn't you look at it before you sent it to him?"

"It wasn't meant for me," Noah said.

Allison arched an eyebrow.

"Fine, I couldn't access it to see what it was. So I sent it to him."

"There must be someone he can talk to about this," Allison said.

The first people Noah thought of were Wil Reisman and Kasey Douglass, but they were both dead. "Diaz might be able to help."

"Maybe. What about that archaeologist, Dr. Bishop?" Allison said.

"Lenora! I'm not sure whether that would help at all. They're not exactly on speaking terms," Noah said.

"I'd try to talk to him, but I don't think he'd listen to me. Frankly, I'm surprised he agreed to my request," Allison said.

Noah nodded, thinking the same thing. Should he contact Lenora and see if she would speak to Connor?

"I have to go," Allison said.

Noah frowned. "You never did tell me what you came to me for."

"Oh, I got what I wanted. I was going to ask if you'd found more information about the Vemus and then I was going to run my request to Connor by you to see if you thought he'd listen," Allison said.

"Glad I could help," Noah said.

Allison left him, and Noah glanced around the room. There were glowing holoscreens active, with several teams of two or three people working together.

Noah brought up a smaller, personal holoscreen and sighed. He really wanted to talk to Kara, but there were comms restrictions to the lunar base. He pressed his lips together, then sat down in a chair nearby. The holoscreen sank down with him. He sent a comlink out, which was immediately answered. He'd almost hoped it wouldn't be.

"Hello, Lenora. Do you have a few minutes to talk? I need your advice about something. It's about Connor."

3

CONNOR STEPPED off the personnel carrier onto the landing pad on the roof of the congressional building. His security detail followed him, and Connor glanced over at the rooftops of the tall buildings nearby. Rail-cannons were mounted on them for Sierra's defense. CDF soldiers were stationed throughout the city and were on alert. With the imminent threat of invasion, some people were reluctant to leave their homes, but a familiar face met him at the rooftop entrance to the building.

"Major Quinn. I was expecting to encounter a different Quinn before the meeting," Connor said.

"She's already inside, so you're stuck with me, sir," Sean answered.

They went inside and entered the stairwell.

"Not a huge group of people in the congressional committee, but they're all expecting you to give them an update on the state of our defenses," Sean said.

"They want much more than that," Connor said and quickened his pace.

They left the stairwell and quickly made their way through the building to the main hall. Sean stopped just outside the meeting room. "Director Mallory wanted me to inform you that Parish is part of the committee," Sean said.

Connor's chest tightened. Stanton Parish had tried to have Connor killed before the Vemus attacked them, but he couldn't prove it. Connor and Tobias had managed to remove Parish from the office of governor, but they couldn't be completely rid of him. Like it or not, Parish was an elected official, but he was unfit to deal with the current threat to the colony. There had been a push from Parish's supporters for him to remain in an advisory role on the defense committee, and in the interest of a smooth transition of power, Tobias had agreed. Connor hated the man. Parish had reallocated resources away from the defense of the colony and denied multiple requests to finish the defensive projects they'd begun, and the result was that the CDF had had to face their enemy at half their fighting capacity. Too many lives had been lost due to the actions of Stanton Parish. Removing Parish from office seemed like a slap on the wrists compared to all the CDF soldiers who had died defending New Earth.

"Alright, I've been informed," Connor replied.

Sean eyed him for a moment and then opened the door. The interior chambers were mostly empty except for the committee that sat at the meeting table. Defense of the colony was everyone's priority now that the Vemus had finally shown up.

Tobias Quinn was speaking, and Connor went to the empty seat next to Frank Mallory. Sean stood off to the side. Sitting across from Connor was Dr. Ashley Quinn, who had retained her post as chief of staff for all things medical in the colony. She regarded Connor knowingly. He knew that, being the gifted doctor she was, she could just glance at him and know he hadn't been taking care of himself. Connor looked away and glanced around at the others on the committee. Like himself, they were all lacking sleep and working long hours. Thanks to Connor's implants, he only needed two hours' sleep. It had taken the scientists here years to reverse-engineer Connor's NA Alliance military-grade implants that had been cutting edge when the *Ark* left Earth space. The CDF, given the nature of their work, were given top priority for the new implants. Colonial scientists had managed to improve on the design so that a person was less likely to reject them, but they were in short supply, and they could only outfit about five percent of the colony, or fifteen thousand people.

More than one committee member shifted their focus to Connor while Tobias was speaking. Many of them had doubted Earth had been lost, thanks to the efforts of Stanton Parish. Now they looked to Connor to protect them, and the fact that he couldn't weighed heavily on him.

"I've asked General Gates to come to this meeting to provide a status update on our readiness for the Vemus threat," Tobias said.

"Excuse me, Governor, I'd like to raise a question for General Gates that I believe those of us on this committee would like to hear his opinion on."

"Dr. Mendoza, why don't we hold all questions until General Gates has provided his update," Tobias said.

Connor looked at the woman who had spoken. She was tall, even when seated, and had long features. Her bony shoulders drew up toward her ears, giving her the appearance of a hawk's wings right before it was about to fly. Dr. Gabriela Mendoza was a staunch supporter of Parish and had been his scientific advisor.

"What is it you'd like to know?" Connor asked the astrophysicist.

"The Vemus signal you discovered during the battle two

months ago—has it been detected since the battle?" Dr. Mendoza asked.

"No, it has not," Connor answered.

"Are you certain, then, that the Vemus have another attack force coming here?"

"Yes, I am," Connor said and addressed the rest of the committee. "You've all read the reports from that attack. The source of the signal was away from the attack force and we have no idea where it was actually coming from. The signal went dark after the attack."

"Isn't it possible that the source of the signal could have been from one of the ships that was destroyed?" Dr. Mendoza asked.

Connor shook his head and reminded himself that they were scared. "Look, we've been down this road before. You doubted the attack was coming in the first place and that didn't work out so well. Now you're wondering: if there *is* another attack force out there, why haven't they come yet?"

There were several head-bobs around the conference table.

"I don't have a good answer for you. I just know they're out there. The fact of the matter is the Vemus learned as much about us as we did about them during our encounter. They quickly adapted their tactics during our battle with them. We know from the data cache taken from one of their ships that when the Vemus left Earth, they had a massive fleet of ships—more than what we've faced. Our engineers believe the Vemus signal was coming from outside this star system. That's all we know. We've scanned the area where we thought the signal was coming from and haven't detected anything, but it could be that we don't have the ability to detect them with our scanners. What I believe is that the second Vemus attack force changed their tactics and will enter this star system from a different point of entry," Connor said.

"Why?" Dr. Mendoza asked.

"Because we're dangerous. We've proven that much. They'll be cautious on their second attempt, but make no mistake; they're coming here because this is where *we* are."

"We can't possibly scan all vectors of the sky," Dr. Mendoza said.

"You're right, we can't. We're doing the best we can. It's been two months since the attack. Every hour we get is a gift. More time to prepare. The Vemus aren't going to blunder into the star system again. Every able-bodied person is going to be called upon to fight, and it still might not be enough. Our orbital defenses aren't going to be able to stop another attack force like what we faced before," Connor said.

"What do you need then?" Dr. Mendoza asked.

"Five more years and the full effort of the colony to build our own fleet of ships and orbital defenses. That's what I need, but it won't be what we'll get. We'll be lucky if we get another five days," Connor said.

There were several gasps.

"What the general is saying," Mallory said, speaking up for the first time since Connor entered the room, "is that there's no way we can know when the Vemus will attack again. It could be at any moment. We have bunkers set up and we've been identifying archaeological sites that could be used as shelters," Mallory said and inclined his head toward Connor.

"Yes, we've done all that," Connor said. "The fact of the matter is that when the Vemus attack us, we're not going to be able to stop them in space. There's a high probability that an invasion force will land on this planet."

There was a long silence in the meeting room. If the Vemus were able to land an attack force, they could also spread themselves to mammalian life on New Earth.

Stanton Parish cleared his throat, and Connor swung his powerful gaze at the man.

"What about the colossus cannon?" Parish asked.

"We're reviewing the schematics for it," Connor said.

"But with all the resources being devoted to Sanctuary—"

"As I said before, we're reviewing the schematics for it," Connor said. Not wishing to disclose the current status of the cannon, he looked over at the other committee members. "We're doing everything we can, and it still might not be enough."

Many of the committee members focused on the area in front of them. They'd wanted Connor to come in here and give them hope, but there very well might not be any hope for them to survive. He instinctually believed the Vemus attack was imminent, but even he was at a loss as to what they were waiting for, and the anticipation of attack was wearing away at all of them.

"We still don't know why they're coming," Dr. Mendoza said.

"That's not entirely accurate," a man said, and Connor's internal heads-up display showed that the man's name was Dr. Fritz Kramer.

"We know from the data cache and the video logs that the Vemus spread themselves across mammalian life on Earth. This is unprecedented in any organism that has come before. The Vemus started infecting sea mammals—whales and dolphins—before it started spreading on land," Dr. Kramer said.

Connor remembered the Vemus soldiers they'd fought on the *Indianapolis*. They had thick, dark skin, were massive in size, and were extremely strong.

"The Vemus are, in fact, two separate organisms that have formed a symbiotic circle. They depend on each other to thrive. Many scientists believed that the Vemus didn't show up until they were exposed," Dr. Kramer said.

"Exposed?" Tobias asked.

"Disturbed is perhaps a better word. Earth scientists weren't sure, but they couldn't find a credible theory as to how the Vemus spread so rapidly. This leaves us with two or three possibilities. First is that the Vemus are a biological weapon that was created in a lab and simply grew out of the control of its creators. The second is that chance brought the two organisms together and it spread itself through the food chain to the point that by the time people became aware of its existence, it was already too late," Dr. Kramer said.

"And the third?" Connor asked.

"The third is the most far-fetched. One or both of the organisms are not Terran based. A meteor crashed into the Pacific Ocean and brought one or both of the organisms to Earth," Dr. Kramer said.

"And we can never be sure," Connor said.

"No, we can't," Dr. Kramer said.

"Even if we knew the origins of the Vemus, why would they come all this way for us? That's a tall order for a disease," Dr. Mendoza said.

"We modified it," Connor said.

"No, that can't be right," Dr. Kramer said.

"It *is* right," Connor said, pressing on. "When the Vemus started spreading to animals on land, there was a tremendous loss of life. In a panic, our scientists tried to modify a strain of the virus so it would avoid humans. I have no idea what they did, but I do know that after they modified the virus, it seemed to seek out humans exclusively."

"You're oversimplifying what happened," Dr. Kramer said.

"Am I? I don't think so, because that's what the records say happened. You said it yourself. The two organisms depended on one another. One of those organisms was a virus that was capable of rewriting its DNA, but after the scientists got through with it, they had augmented its ability. Instead of simply being able to rewrite its DNA, it could store DNA from any infected host. I can give you a firsthand account of how the Vemus are highly adaptive to situations. I saw them change forms to get us as we left their ship," Connor said.

Ashley cleared her throat. "The basis for any living organism is to reproduce as part of its life cycle. When the Vemus started targeting humans to the exclusion of all else, it found a species of more than twenty billion throughout the solar system."

"This doesn't explain how the Vemus were able to track us over sixty light-years. How does an organism fly spaceships, use weapons, and plan attacks?" Dr. Mendoza asked.

There was a heavy silence throughout the meeting room.

"Like I said, we modified it. Made it stronger," Connor said.

More than one committee member's face became ashen.

"Stronger, yes," Franklin Mallory said, "but some of their tactics denote a lack of imagination. They can execute basic attacks, but they haven't done anything complex as far as strategy goes. That's why we were able to stop them before."

Mallory gave Connor a pointed look, and Tobias steered the discussion to the preparations being made. Connor had already drafted what he thought was the best strategy for when the Vemus invaded, and it hadn't been well received. He felt as if Wil and Kasey were standing behind him, judging everything he said and did, and he didn't think they approved either.

4

AFTER THE MEETING ENDED, Tobias asked Connor and Frank to stay behind for a few minutes. Connor glanced at the clock on the wall. He just wanted to get out of there. He'd had enough of being around these people for the time being.

When the room cleared, Tobias regarded him for a moment. "When I asked you about the state of our readiness, I didn't think you'd dash all hope of our survival."

Connor sighed. "That's reality. I can't spread false hope."

"I wasn't asking you to, but we need everyone to keep working. We're barely holding together as it is, but if you take away all hope, they'll just give up . . ." Tobias paused for a second. "What's going on with you? You don't need me to tell you all this."

Connor looked away. The image of his dead son came to his mind and he could hear his son's bitter words in his mind, twisting him up in knots. "It's been a rough few days."

"I'm sorry, did you say days? How about months or years? We need you focused," Tobias said.

"I'll be fine. I just need to get out of here and get some air," Connor said.

He hastened toward the door and was out of the meeting room before anyone could reply. He hardly saw the faces of the people he passed as he fled down the hall. There were too many faces, all looking to him to protect them. Everywhere he went people looked to him to give them hope, but deep inside he was hollow. He felt he had nothing left to give. He would fail them all and then his life would be over.

Connor rounded a corner and nearly collided with another person. The exit to the building was within sight and he hastened toward it, muttering an apology. He knew his security detail was likely closing in on him, but he just wanted to be alone for a while.

Connor shoved his way through the side exit of the congressional building and took several deep breaths of fresh air. He was greeted by the scent of freshly mown lawns, sliced by paved paths that led throughout the campus. The sun gleamed and the blue sky overhead had hints of green to it that were unique to New Earth. He jogged down a path through the gardens.

He was well away from the building when he heard his name being called, and something in the voice penetrated his angst. Connor spun around and saw Lenora running toward him, her long, thick hair trailing behind her. The sight of her made his pulse quicken, but the respite was short-lived. Connor glanced in the direction she'd come from and saw the personal transport ship she must have used to fly here.

"Is that your ship?" Connor asked.

Lenora frowned. "Yes," she said.

"I need to get out of here. Can you take us somewhere?" Connor asked.

Lenora eyed him for a moment.

"Please, I just need to get away from here," Connor said.

"Yeah, sure. Let's go," Lenora answered.

They hurried toward Lenora's ship and climbed aboard. Connor glanced out the window and saw Sean Quinn, along with Connor's security detail, racing toward them.

"Should we wait for them?" Lenora asked.

Connor shook his head. "No. Just take off," he said, his voice sounding strained.

Lenora engaged the thrusters and the ship lifted off the ground. Once they were above the buildings, she flew them away from the city. Connor used his implants to shut down the transponder inside the craft.

An alert appeared on the heads-up display, and Lenora glanced at him. "What's going on?"

"They'll track us through the transponder. I just need to get away for a while," Connor said.

"It's not going to fool Sean," Lenora said.

"I know," Connor replied.

He'd trained Sean well, and he had the makings of a great leader. Too bad he might not get the chance.

Lenora took them away from Sierra, and after a few minutes she set them down in an open clearing surrounded by trees. A hundred kilometers away from Sierra and New Earth looked as if it had never been inhabited by humans.

Connor's heart was racing as he hastily climbed out of the seat. He opened the hatch and his shoulders brushed against the sides as he went out before it fully opened.

"Where are you going?" Lenora asked, following him.

Connor stepped out onto the grassy field, and the soft ground yielded to his heavy footfalls. His breath came in gasps. He kept thinking about how they were all going to die and it was all his fault. He hadn't fought hard enough for what they needed. Perhaps *he* had even started to doubt that the Vemus were coming for them, and he'd bought into what Stanton Parish had been saying. He felt so small and insignificant compared to the vastness of everything around him. They were still so new to this world that there would be nothing to mark their passing if everyone in the colony died.

Lenora's brows drew up in worry. "You need to calm down."

Connor swallowed hard. "I can't."

Lenora placed her hands on his shoulders. "Look at me. Look into my eyes."

Connor did as she asked.

"Good. Now just take slow, deep breaths. Do it with me."

Lenora took a deep breath and Connor tried to follow along, but he couldn't feel his hands and he was becoming dizzy. His chest tightened and he pushed away from Lenora. He backed away, his gaze darting back and forth as if he were about to be attacked.

"It's okay. You're fine. It's just the two of us here," Lenora said soothingly.

Connor just wanted to run. He needed to run. He spun around but felt something jab into his back. There was intense heat, the strength went out of his muscles, and he collapsed to the ground. Lenora caught him and eased him down. His vision faded and he blacked out.

HE HEARD Lenora speaking as he began to wake up. There was something soft under his head. He opened his eyes and found that he was lying on the ground in the same field she had taken him to. He drew in a deep breath and blew it out. His heart was no longer racing.

Lenora put her comlink away and came over to him.

"What did you do to me?" Connor asked.

"I used my stunner on you. You were having a panic attack and weren't thinking straight," Lenora said.

"A panic attack?" Connor repeated, frowning. "That can't be right."

"Why? Because you're the great Connor Gates? The CDF general who singlehandedly defeated the Vemus?"

Connor didn't reply. He knew she was baiting him. Instead, he sat up. "How long was I out?"

"A few hours. I called Ashley and she told Sean I took you somewhere to rest," Lenora said.

Connor stood up and rolled his shoulders. "You stunned me?"

"You were about to go running off. So it was either stun you or chase you through the forest and *then* stun you."

"And you left me on the ground?"

"You needed the rest," Lenora said.

He could think more clearly, but he still felt tired. "How'd you even know where to find me?"

"Noah called me. He's worried about you."

"I'm fi—"

"Don't you dare tell me you're fine! You're not fine. Having panic attacks and telling everyone they're going to die is not fine," Lenora snapped.

Connor clenched his teeth and sighed. "I don't want to fight with you."

"That's because you know I'm right. Everything that's happened is exacting a toll on you. You can't compartmentalize everything no matter how hard you try," Lenora said.

"What's that supposed to mean?" Connor asked.

"Wil and Kasey. They were your closest friends. You have to grieve."

"They're dead. There's nothing I can do about that."

Lenora's gaze hardened. "They deserve better than that."

Connor threw his hands in the air. "What do you want from me?"

"All you're stating is facts—they're dead. What you're refusing to admit is that they mattered to you. That their loss means so much to you that you can hardly stand it," Lenora said.

"I'm sorry. Roaming around Sierra weeping isn't going to help anyone," Connor replied.

"God, you can be such an ass. You could teach a rock about being stubborn, and when it graduated from the Connor School of Stubbornness, you'd still have more to teach it. Why is everything black and white with you? It's either hot or cold. I'm not telling you to run around crying uncontrollably, you idiot. I'm telling you to acknowledge their loss. Accept that they're gone. You don't have to be okay with it. In fact, you shouldn't be," Lenora said.

Connor looked away from her. He knew he was keeping everything locked up inside. He felt it all pushing against the walls he'd built, but he was afraid that if he let it out, there would be nothing left.

"Wil was right there in front of me. I should have been able to save him. If I hadn't left him in the computing core . . ." Connor's voice trailed off.

Lenora came over to his side and stood next to him, rubbing his shoulder with one of her hands.

"He was dying and he was still concerned with the data he'd found on the ship," Connor said.

"He knew it was important," Lenora replied.

Connor's shoulders slumped.

"What's the video log you keep watching?" Lenora asked.

Connor's shoulders stiffened, and he wheeled away from her.

"Noah told me you keep watching something that was retrieved from the *Indianapolis*," Lenora said, leaning toward him.

A wave of fury washed over Connor. How dare that little shit pry into his personal logs! "Did he say what it was?"

Lenora shook her head. "No, just that you watch the same ten-minute video multiple times a day and have been doing so since he gave you the files. What's on it?"

Connor balled his hands into fists, thinking how he'd like to pummel Noah for poking around where he shouldn't. But that would be stupid because it was those same instincts in Noah that Connor had come to count on over the years.

"What's on it?" Lenora asked again.

A long moment passed before Connor spoke. "It's my son," he said softly and looked away from her.

"Your son?" Lenora muttered in disbelief. She walked in front of him.

"He died on the *Indianapolis*. Our team made it to the bridge of the *Indianapolis* two months ago and there were signs of a battle having been fought there before. I think that's where he—" Connor said, his voice cracking.

Lenora looked at him, her brows drawn up in concern. "That's awful, Connor. I'm so sorry. Why didn't you tell anyone?"

Connor felt as if he were standing on the edge of a cliff and all it would take was a slight breeze to push him over it.

"Who would I tell? You? The last time we spoke we ended up screaming at one another," Connor said.

Lenora's face reddened. "I would have listened," she said. After a few moments, she continued. "What was he like?"

Connor swallowed hard as sorrow tried to close up his throat. "Young. He looked strong and bitter, with eyes that had seen too much. He didn't want to record anything. Wilkinson asked him to do it. He was more of a father to him than I was."

"You can't do this to yourself."

"What? Admit the truth?"

"That's not fair and you know it. You didn't leave him behind. You were forced onto the *Ark* against your will. You didn't leave your son behind. He was left behind because of what Wilkinson did. You want to punish someone, punish him," Lenora said.

"Wilkinson was just trying to protect me."

"Fine, then just accept that none of this was fair and there's nothing you can do to change anything," Lenora said.

Connor's eyes became misty. "My son hated me, blamed me for leaving him."

"You're not to blame—"

"Aren't I? I was the one who volunteered to lead the Ghosts, to do my duty."

"Why does anyone have to be blamed? It doesn't make any sense. His memory of you is that of a small boy who missed his father," Lenora said.

"That's right. A father who should have protected him."

"You can't do this to yourself. This guilt you've been carrying around is eating you up inside. It's not right. It happened. You made your decisions and then life happened. You can dwell on it and keep punishing yourself for everything that's out of your control or you can move on," Lenora said.

"Move on," Connor sneered. "Just like that. Brush it to the side and pretend it didn't happen?"

"That's not what I meant and you know it."

Connor looked away from her and shook his head. "I have to take responsibility—"

"That's crap. You're trying to make yourself feel better because you regret how everything turned out. You're not doing this for your son. You're doing this as a way to atone for leaving. You're feeding your regrets. That's not how it works. Give yourself a break. You can't live your life based on hindsight. No one can," Lenora said.

Connor pressed his lips together. "It's not right," he said.

"There *is* no right and wrong. He was about to die. He must have been angry and scared. Did you even consider that?"

"Of course I did, but . . ." Connor said, his voice dying off. The words just wouldn't form in his mind.

"Mitch Wilkinson was a manipulative son of a bitch. You have this unshakable perspective that everything he did was to protect you, right?" Lenora asked.

Connor jutted his chin out and then nodded.

"In that case, he didn't have your son record a message so he could yell at you. Wilkinson knew it would cause you pain, but if you're right about him, I think he just wanted you to *see* your son. See the man he grew up to be. He wanted you to know that he did look after your son just like he promised you. He didn't send the message so you could torture yourself. So stop it. You can't fight the Vemus if you're weighed down by guilt," Lenora said.

Connor stood there, allowing himself to come to grips with what Lenora was saying. His brows pushed forward and he felt his body sag. He was so tired.

"Stop pretending you're in this fight alone."

Connor was about to deny it, but she was right. How had he come to be so lost?

"I don't know if we can survive," Connor said at last.

"Then we'll die, but it won't be because we didn't fight. If Wil and Kasey were here, they'd be telling you the same thing," Lenora said.

Connor felt his mouth hang open. There was so much he wanted to say. He wished he could be the person Lenora deserved, but he wasn't.

He heard the high-pitched whine of a combat shuttle's engines flying toward them, and a data link came to prominence on his internal heads-up display, identifying the CDF shuttle.

5

THE HANGAR BAY of Lunar Base was a buzz of activity, and Captain Jon Walker glared at the power conduit he'd been struggling to replace on his ship for the past few hours. Being stationed on the Colonial Defense Force moon base was a new post for him. He'd only been there for six months. What had started out as a tech platform for building missile defense platforms and ships had become a full-blown military base. Since the Vemus attack, personnel had been working tirelessly to conceal the base. Aboveground installations were either hidden away or relocated to belowground facilities per General Gates' orders. There was so much work going on that he couldn't wait on a flight engineer to fix the power conduit on the combat shuttle.

The connectors for the conduit wouldn't meet. He grabbed one end of the connector and pulled. Straining to get the pieces closer together, his hand slipped off and he banged it against the sidewall.

"Piece of shit!" Jon shouted, about to kick the damn thing.

"That ought to do it," someone said from behind him.

Jon spun around to see his brother, Brian, laughing at him. Brian glanced at what Jon had been working on.

"What the hell did you do to this thing?" Brian asked.

"Not me. Something from that damn debris field out there tore into the rear of my ship," Jon said. He noticed that his younger brother had a pale orange EVA suit on. "What's going on? I didn't think they let you scientists come topside, where the real work's done."

"Salvage run in the debris field," Brian replied.

Jon frowned. "Salvage for what?"

Brian regarded him for a moment. "We're looking for an undamaged section of a Vemus ship."

Jon frowned. "You've got to be kidding me. Why would they have you do that?"

"They're not having me do that. I volunteered," Brian said.

While Jon had chosen to join the Colonial Defense Force and become a soldier, his younger brother had gone in a different direction. Brian worked at a level of intelligence that was a cut above the norm. It was for this reason that Jon and Brian had gotten to come on the *Ark*. Jon's aptitude scores were high, but Brian's were definitely pretty far to the right of the bell curve that measured such things.

"What are you doing?" Jon asked.

"I told you, I'm—"

"I don't mean that. This is a field mission. Aren't you supposed to be in a lab somewhere trying to figure out a way to stop the Vemus?"

Brian jutted out his chin. "We need samples, living samples, in order to figure out how this thing works."

Jon eyed him for a moment. "Can you wait a couple of hours? I'll take you out there myself."

Brian was about to reply when someone came around the rear of the shuttle.

"What's going on here?" Colonel Hayes asked.

Jon immediately stood straight and snapped a salute. "Nothing, sir."

Colonel Hayes looked at Brian. "Walker, you and your team are to report in on *Explorer II*."

"Sir," Jon said, "permission to go on the salvage mission."

Colonel Hayes frowned and then looked at the state of Jon's ship. "Your ship isn't flight-ready."

"Sir, I can have it fixed and ready in an hour," Jon said.

Colonel Hayes glanced at the power conduit Jon was trying to get installed. "Those conduits are always a pain in the ass. After that, you've got to get the couplings on the right or the actuators won't pivot the pad properly. You've got more than an hour's work here, Captain."

Jon tried to think of a reply, but everything the colonel had just said was right. Damn it! If he'd just left it alone he could have flown Brian and his team out there. *Explorer II* was piloted by Davis, who wasn't the best pilot for the job.

"Dr. Walker, get on over to *Explorer II*. They're waiting for you, son," Colonel Hayes said.

"Yes, sir," Brian said.

Jon watched as his brother left. "Stay sharp, kid," Jon called out.

Brian turned around and gave him a wave.

"He'll be alright," Colonel Hayes said.

"I'm sorry, sir."

"I know he's your brother," Colonel Hayes said.

"Yes, sir."

Colonel Hayes called over a flight engineer and ordered him to get Jon's ship ready.

"Where am I going, sir?" Jon asked.

"Another run to the *Phoenix*. We've got HADES IV-Bs fresh off the line that need to be delivered ASAP," Colonel Hayes said.

Jon sighed inwardly. Delivery runs were about the only thing they got to do these days. He understood the necessity of it, but that didn't make it any less boring.

"We'll get it done, sir," Jon said.

"Carry on, Captain," Colonel Hayes said.

The flight engineer examined Jon's work and then called a couple of his crew over while Jon set about helping them repair his ship. They couldn't afford not to have all of their birds flight-ready. He glanced over at *Explorer II* as it flew out of the hangar. He'd promised his parents he'd watch out for Brian, which hadn't been so easy since they normally weren't at the same place. The Vemus were dangerous. He'd heard stories from the survivors of the *Vigilant* and the *Banshee*. What they'd faced on the Vemus ship was enough to give anyone nightmares, but he knew Brian didn't see them that way. He was too analytical. He thought of the Vemus only in scientific terms and not as an enemy to be destroyed. If his ship hadn't had a damaged engine pod, he could have flown Brian out there. Now his brother was out there with Davis, who wasn't the worst pilot on the lunar base, but he wasn't the best one either. He'd seen the debris field full of the remnants of Vemus ships. It was dangerous space to fly through, and with only one ship that could be spared for Brian's mission, a rescue if things went wrong would be long in coming.

Brian had wanted a mission of his own and now he'd gotten it. Jon just hoped it wasn't too exciting for him.

6

NOAH HAD SPENT the remainder of his day prepping his team before he left for Sanctuary. He knew Lenora had spoken to Connor, but he hadn't heard anything else since then. He hadn't seen Connor either. He thought of opening a comlink to Sean, but since Sean was always within earshot of Connor, he didn't think that was his brightest idea.

Lars Mallory waited for Noah to power off the holoscreens. "Why are they sending you to Sanctuary?"

Noah left his work area, and he and Lars walked out into the hallway.

"They want me to look at the alien power station there," Noah said.

"Last I heard about that was that they weren't able to get it to generate a significant amount of energy," Lars said.

"Yeah, the preliminary report I saw was that it's early fusion tech. Looks like the alien species that lived here was developing their own fusion reactor," Noah said.

"They said it was a few hundred years old," Lars said.

"Yup, and no one knows where the species that built it actually went."

"That's probably a blessing," Lars replied.

"Why do you say that?" Noah asked.

"Because they also genetically altered some of the species here."

"Like the ryklars and the berwolves?"

"Precisely. They're way more intelligent than we expected from a predator," Lars said.

"Maybe we should convince them to fight with us when the Vemus get here," Noah said.

Lars stopped walking and pursed his lips. "That's not a bad idea, you know."

"I was kidding," Noah said quickly.

"I know, but it really isn't that bad an idea," Lars said and started walking in the opposite direction.

"Where are you going?" Noah asked.

"I'm going to talk to my father. Have fun in Sanctuary, and try not to blow the place up," Lars called back as he hastened down the hall.

Great, Noah thought. He'd just become responsible for the CDF putting animals in their war against the Vemus. He'd better get to Sanctuary quickly before he accidentally gave anyone else ideas of questionable moral implications.

7

THE COMBAT SHUTTLE flew toward Phoenix Station, and Connor brought up the optical feed onto his personal holoscreen. Sean shifted in his seat next to him, and Connor noticed him looking at the holoscreen.

"She would have made a beautiful ship," Connor said.

"It would have been something to see her fly, sir," Sean said.

The *Phoenix* was supposed to be the Colonial Defense Force's first battleship carrier, but Connor had scrapped that plan after the Vemus attack. Instead, he'd challenged his engineers to come up with something the CDF could use in defense of New Earth, and this was their answer. They'd presented Connor with the option of having a battleship carrier that could be combat ready in six to eight months or a slower-moving space station with a comparable combat arsenal in just two months. Thus, the *Phoenix* became Phoenix Station, whose combat readiness increased with each passing day. On the surface, it was an easy decision to make, but it had meant forgoing any type of mobile combat units beyond New Earth's immediate vicinity.

"There are only a few sections I recognize from the *Ark*,"
Sean said.

Connor nodded.

Phoenix Station was an elongated cylinder with a massive
section of it covered by the Montgomery III construction
platform. Instead of a grouping of massive magnetic drive pods
in the rear of the ship, they'd put smaller MDPs in subsections of
the station.

Connor watched as Sean brought up his own holoscreen and
zoomed in on one of the subsections.

"Looks like they've completed sections seven and eight,"
Sean said.

Phoenix Station was like a heavily armed mobile wall
positioned at a point in space where the gravitational pull from
New Earth and the star in this system were equalized.
Positioning Phoenix Station here made maintaining its orbit
relatively easy, but the downside to the smaller MDPs was that
the behemoth combat station was slow to reposition.

"Two more sections to be brought online," Connor said.

They'd had to cut some corners to get Phoenix Station
operational, which meant that not all the sections were equal in
their capabilities. Each section had a wide array of weapons
capabilities, but not all sections had the same complement of
sensor arrays. The sections without sensors were dependent on
those that had them. Sections that were comprised primarily of
missile tubes just needed targeting data, which could be
uploaded from any sensor array. Connor knew the ingenuity that
had gone into Phoenix Station was enough to make any NA
Alliance general proud, and since he was the CDF's only general,
he was quite pleased with what they'd been able to accomplish in
a short span of time.

"We only need ten or twenty more just like it," Connor said.

"Well, if we're wishing for something, how about a universal override for Vemus ship navigation systems so they fly right into the star and we don't have to worry about 'em." Sean said with a snort.

Connor nodded. He'd noticed that Sean and others who served close to him were paying more attention to Connor's own readiness. He couldn't blame them. He'd let himself go. He didn't take care of himself, and his performance suffered severely for it. Sleep helped. Ashley had prescribed him meds to help him sleep. He still felt compelled to watch the video log of his son though. He could recall every moment of it with startling clarity. He hadn't watched it today, but he couldn't promise himself that he wouldn't watch it later on, believing that once he made the promise he would soon break it.

"Sir, Noah has reported in. He's arrived at Sanctuary," Sean said.

Connor glanced over at Sean, arching an eyebrow. "Planning to apprise me of each CDF's individual location, Major?"

"No, sir, I just thought you'd want to know about this particular instance," Sean replied.

"I guess this is where I could tell you to lock it up and command you to silence," Connor said.

Sean calmly met Connor's gaze.

"I'm not angry with Noah," Connor said. *At least not as much,* he thought to himself.

"Yes, sir," Sean said.

"Is that a 'yes, sir' or an 'if you say so, sir'?"

A small smirk snuck onto Sean's face. "Yes, sir," he replied mildly.

The smirk reminded Connor of Ashley. "Well played, Major. Your mother would be proud."

"I've learned from the best, sir."

Connor looked back at his holoscreen. They were on final approach to the main hangar. He was overdue to inspect Phoenix Station, and Connor suspected the reason for Tobias and Franklin suggesting it was due in part to the lengthy travel time out to the station. Mandatory downtime, as it were.

"Colonel Cross will meet us in the hangar, sir," Sean said.

Connor nodded and closed down the holoscreen. His stomach tightened as the combat shuttle entered Phoenix Station's gravity field. The main hangar was designed to be in a permanent vacuum, which conserved resources by not requiring the hangar to be depressurized every time a ship needed to land. The pilot flew the shuttle to the landing pad, and the auto-dock extended to the rear hatch. There were several knocks as the auto-dock sealed against the hatch and the indicator light went from red to green.

Connor exited the shuttle first. CDF personnel in full dress uniforms lined the way forward to where Colonel Savannah Cross waited to greet him. The lines of soldiers saluted Connor as he took his first steps onto Phoenix Station. Connor returned their salutes.

"Welcome to Phoenix Station, General," Colonel Cross said.

She stood ramrod straight and had a burning intensity to her gaze. Savannah was like Connor in that they were both workhorses. Shortly after the Vemus attack, he'd assigned the *Banshee's* commanding officer to Phoenix, and she hadn't disappointed him in the slightest.

"Thank you, Colonel," Connor replied.

Connor glanced at the CDF officers near Colonel Cross and noted that her XO was nowhere in sight. He made a mental nod of approval. No doubt Colonel Cross had kept Major Elder on the main bridge of the station. Though they were at Condition Three, maintaining combat readiness was paramount to their survival. Connor had browsed the station's records on the way here and knew that Colonel Cross dedicated a significant amount of time to combat drills. She was determined to be as prepared as humanly possible for the next engagement with the Vemus.

"General, if you will follow me, I'm prepared to give you a tour of our primary systems for the main section of the station," Colonel Cross said.

"Excellent, Colonel. I'm looking forward to it," Connor said.

They kept to the main section of the station because it would have been impractical to tour the other eight subsections. He was here to check that operations of the station were running smoothly, not to visit every nook and cranny of the station, which would have taken him weeks.

For the next several hours, Savannah led Connor through Phoenix Station, meeting the crew. Some of them had served on Titan Station and, having survived, pushed to be part of this station. The former Titan Station soldiers knew what was at stake. They'd faced the Vemus before. In all Connor's years in the military, he found that the CDF soldier showed a level of dedication normally reserved for an elite few he had observed in his military career.

He was reminded of Wil and Kasey throughout the tour. He remembered doing a similar inspection of Titan, and while Wil and Kasey had been completely professional, there'd been an underlying camaraderie that Connor missed. Kasey had been his second in command since his days with the Ghosts. Wil had been an outstanding intelligence officer who had a singular talent for finding his way around almost any obstacle. Connor was at home around people in uniform, be it the NA Alliance Military or, as now, the Colonial Defense Force, but there were so many missing faces that he would have liked to see.

Colonel Savannah Cross was an exemplary military officer. Given that there were only about three hundred thousand colonists, Connor hadn't been sure what caliber of military personnel he'd be able to find among them, especially since one of the driving forces for the *Ark* program had been to limit any military presence in the colony. Circumstances had changed all that, and Connor was struck by how well the colonists had risen to protect their future. A strong will to survive was embedded in human nature, along with the tenacity to overcome obstacles and become what they needed for survival. It was both awe-inspiring and concerning how quickly humans could go from being civilized to adapting to war in a short span of time.

"We dedicate this part of the station to weapons engineering and development," Colonel Cross said.

Most of Phoenix Station's mass was to support weapons systems, so when they went into the open area, Connor was surprised at the extensive amount of activity.

Connor looked at Colonel Cross. "What's going on here?"

"We had a number of soldiers who had ideas for our current weapons systems to simply repurpose what we've already got. It started out as a small group of soldiers collaborating in their off-duty hours," Colonel Cross said, and there was no mistaking the pride in her voice.

The CDF soldiers began to notice they had an audience, and one of them detached himself from the group. He was a bull of a man, which had inspired the designation Connor had given him when he'd been part of Search and Rescue.

"Captain Randle," Connor said and glanced around at all the construction bots that were in various states of retrofit.

"General," Captain Wayne Randle said. "I'm glad you made it here."

"What are you doing to the construction bots?" Connor asked.

A hungry gleam appeared in Randle's eyes. "We had a surplus of machines that were part of the drone workforce, so I thought I'd make use of them. These construction bots were built for salvage, and since we're not doing much of that anymore, I'm fitting them with a one-meter storage bay," Captain Randle said.

Connor took a closer look at one of the bots. The storage bay extended from the back and the robotic arms were tucked away for extra storage. Realizing the potential of what Randle had created, Connor smiled.

"They can penetrate the hull of a ship and deliver their payload. They're not reusable, but they can get into some pretty tight places that would be hard to detect," Captain Randle said.

"What's their range?" Connor asked.

"Two hundred thousand kilometers. As long as we paint the target, they can do the rest," Captain Randle said.

Connor glanced at Colonel Cross. "You authorized this?"

"Yes, General," Colonel Cross said.

"How many more projects like these have you got going on?" Connor asked.

"We have a few others like this. Mostly, the crew is dedicated to the established weapons systems, but for these rare gems I thought it prudent to allow some good old-fashioned ingenuity, sir," Colonel Cross said.

Connor nodded. "Excellent work."

Captain Randle looked relieved.

"I mean it. It's efforts like this that will help us the most in the long run," Connor said.

He heard a chime from the nearby speakers.

"Colonel Cross, please report to the bridge," a computerized voice said.

Colonel Cross frowned and then sent her acknowledgment. "General, we were going to end our tour at the bridge, but something must have come up."

"Indeed, Colonel. Let's get to the bridge," Connor said.

Colonel Cross's face suddenly became ashen, and she pressed her lips together.

"Are you feeling alright?" Connor asked.

Colonel Cross's cheeks reddened for a moment. "I'm fine. Just felt a bit of nausea for a second."

They proceeded to the bridge of the main section of Phoenix Station. Though Phoenix Station was comprised of the last major section of the *Ark*, the bridge was entirely new construction. Workstations were being manned for all the major systems that would be found on a ship. Major John Elder stood in the command area that was slightly elevated above the workstations.

Connor glanced at the main holoscreen and saw a PRADIS scope on the screen. On the edge of the star system was a detected anomaly. The anomaly was in a quadrant far away from where Titan Station had been.

"Situation report," Colonel Cross said.

"The anomaly just appeared, ma'am. PRADIS indicates that it's over twenty kilometers across. We're repositioning tactical drones to get a better reading of it," Major Elder said.

"Could this just be a large asteroid?" Connor asked.

He didn't believe it was but needed to ask the question just to be sure.

"We're not sure, General. We're double-checking this anomaly against the known large asteroids already mapped in the system," Major Elder said.

"It's not an asteroid," Major Quinn said.

Connor looked over at Sean.

"It just changed course as of the last PRADIS sweep, so

either it hit something large that forced it to change course or someone is flying it," Major Quinn said.

Connor glanced back at the main holoscreen. Sean was right. Connor felt his stomach sink to his feet. Their time was just about out.

COLONEL NATHAN HAYES sat in his office at Lunar Base and glanced over at the cylindrical aquarium that used to belong to his commanding officer on the *Vigilant*. Ian Howe had loved the aquarium, which was home to several species of brightly colored fish, and Nathan kept the aquarium as a tribute to his friend and mentor who had died aboard ship. To help him unwind at the end of a long day, Nathan would turn out the lights in his office and leave on the interior lights of the aquarium. The small bands of reflected light and soft sounds of churning water provided a taste of being planet-side, and it helped keep him anchored.

Nathan left his office and began to make his way toward the residential modules at Lunar Base. New Earth had one moon that was in orbit three hundred and twenty thousand kilometers away from the planet. They'd been able to tunnel into the softer sections of the crust and currently housed over two thousand people on base. They'd already been expanding the base before the Vemus attack, but since then Nathan had been tasked with minimizing base operations on the surface.

He came to the elevator that would take him to the residential modules, where a shower and a warm meal would be waiting for him, but he had a thought that caused him to hesitate before pushing the button. Instead, he used his neural implants to check the duty roster for the Command Center and saw that Major Shelton was on duty. Nathan sighed. Major Shelton was new to Lunar Base and Nathan wanted to see how she was settling in. He also liked to observe all his officers on duty. Nathan retreated from the elevators and started to make his way to the Command Center.

As Nathan entered the room, Major Vanessa Shelton acknowledged his presence by standing up from the command chair. She glanced at her workstation, and Nathan noted that her worried expression had nothing to do with him being there but with the alert on her screen.

"Sir, I was about to contact you. Blackout protocol has been authorized. We're to cease all surface activities immediately and restrict communications to direct laser communications only," Major Shelton said.

Nathan frowned. DLC was old technology that could be used over long and short distances but was highly susceptible to being intercepted and spoofed. Nathan wasn't sure whether the Vemus could detect a DLC beam, but the concept was simple and they needed to be very careful. He leaned in so he could see Major Shelton's screen, quickly using his implants to confirm that the message from CDF COMCENT was authentic. DLC would limit their comms capabilities, but it also minimized the risk of their base being detected by the Vemus since they weren't broadcasting a communication signal.

"Set Condition Two, Major," Nathan ordered.

Nathan looked at the main holoscreen while Major Shelton

sent out a base-wide alert. There was an incoming data dump from Phoenix Station.

"Colonel, Dark-Star status will be achieved in twelve hours," Major Shelton said.

"Understood," Nathan replied.

In twelve hours, they would have virtually no presence on the lunar surface, which was a vast improvement when compared with the drills he'd run when he'd first assumed command of the base. Coming from a warship command, twelve hours seemed like a lifetime, but Lunar Base was comprised of more than just CDF personnel. They were essentially a small conclave of soldiers mixed with scientists and construction workers in their munitions factory. They were stocked with supplies that would last for six months.

"Major, we need the current status of all teams deployed. And start checking them off as they report in," Nathan ordered.

Orders for blackout protocol could only come from CDF command, and Nathan knew General Gates would not give the command unless he had credible evidence of an imminent threat to New Earth.

Major Shelton went to the auxiliary workstation so Nathan could take command. It seemed that he and Major Shelton would become better acquainted over the next few hours after all.

Lunar Base was vitally important to New Earth's defenses, and General Gates had changed their mandate to a purely passive presence until they were authorized to engage. Rules of engagement for Lunar Base could be given from COMCENT or, in the absence of the chain of command, by the commanding officer. Connor had gone over his strategy for how Lunar Base would be used when the Vemus arrived. They would lend support to Phoenix Station if called upon or, in the worst-case scenario, as a secret base from which to engage the enemy. They were to keep their presence hidden for as long as possible.

"Colonel, we have an overdue salvage team. It appears they were on a deep salvage mission in the debris field," Major Shelton said.

Nathan brought the specs to his personal workstation. Captain Davis's team had missed their check-in. They were escorting Dr. Brian Walker's science team, who was trying to capture living samples of the Vemus.

"What are your orders, Colonel?" Major Shelton asked.

"That's a high-priority mission. We're going to send in a second team," Nathan said.

"Colonel, once we're in Dark-Star status, if the second team runs into trouble we won't be authorized to respond."

"Understood, Major," Nathan said, knowing Major Shelton was just doing her job. "I want Captain Walker's squad on point for the second team. They're authorized to assess the current status of the first team and assist with their mission. If there's evidence of Vemus infection, then they're to use containment protocols."

"Yes, Colonel," Major Shelton replied.

Nathan hoped Davis's team was just experiencing some kind of communications issue due to the fact they were in the debris field rather than having encountered any trouble. Captain Jon Walker was an exemplary pilot and could effect a rescue mission if it came down to it. Besides that, if Nathan had a brother, he knew he'd be out there looking for him if he could.

"Tactical, keep our PRADIS updated with the data dump from Phoenix Station and continuously update it for as long as they send their feeds to us," Nathan said.

"Yes, Colonel," the tactical officer replied.

Lunar Base going dark meant that any active scanning of the

star system must stop and they would become reliant upon sensor feeds from Phoenix Station. As their PRADIS was updated, Nathan began to understand why General Gates had put him in command of Lunar Base. He'd seen combat and knew that it would be a waiting game. The real test of Nathan's resolve would come when the first shots were fired and those at the base could only watch the engagement from afar. Even if Phoenix Station were to become compromised, Nathan could not reveal their presence unless they could decisively destroy the Vemus invasion force. And as of this moment, they still didn't know what was coming for them.

9

Almost twenty-four hours had passed since they'd first detected the anomaly, and Connor was returning to the Command Center on Phoenix Station. He'd just finished briefing the defense council, and the cities of New Earth were on high alert. There had been no further course changes from the anomaly, and after careful analysis of its apparent change of course, Phoenix Station's operations team was almost evenly divided on whether the anomaly had, in fact, changed course. The change had been so slight that there were credible arguments to be made that this was just a natural occurrence for objects in deep space. Connor had decided to err on the side of caution and ordered Phoenix Station to Condition Two, which set a series of actions into motion, including Lunar Base going dark. Lunar Base was their failsafe if Phoenix Station was destroyed, and it would not be an easy thing for Colonel Hayes to carry out his orders should the worst happen, but Connor had the utmost faith in him.

"Sir, Dr. Allen is requesting to speak with you at your earliest convenience," Sean said.

Connor checked the time. "Tell him I'll follow up with him in a few hours."

Dr. Allen had been the *Vigilant's* chief medical officer and Connor knew Allen wouldn't reach out to him if it wasn't important. On the other hand, if Dr. Allen had an urgent matter, he would have said so.

They reached the corridor to the Command Center.

"Sir, there's something I need to bring to your awareness," Sean said.

Connor stopped walking and glanced at his security detail. "Give us a minute."

The armed soldiers walked farther down the corridor, giving them some privacy.

"What is it?" Connor asked.

Sean frowned. "This may be nothing, but it's just something I've noticed. I think Colonel Cross is hiding something."

Connor's eyebrows rose. Even in the CDF, it was no small thing to accuse a superior officer of hiding something, but Connor knew Sean Quinn had good instincts.

"Go on," Connor said.

"I'm not sure, exactly. She seemed a bit distracted, like she had something else on her mind. Don't get me wrong. Colonel Cross is good at her job and I don't think she's being negligent in her duties, but there's something on her mind," Sean said.

Connor frowned. "We're all under a lot of pressure. If this anomaly is the Vemus, it's enough to unsettle anyone."

"That's just it, sir. I noticed it while she was giving us the tour before the anomaly appeared on PRADIS. I just wanted to make you aware. Perhaps she'll . . . I don't know . . . tell you about it," Sean said.

Connor pressed his lips together. "Alright, I'll keep an eye out for it, but if you notice something while we're in there," Connor said, jabbing his thumb in the direction of the Command Center, "you need to either let me know or ask Colonel Cross about it."

"Yes, sir," Sean said.

Connor suppressed a frustrated sigh. It wasn't Sean's fault. Connor blamed the former governor, Stanton Parish, for this development. In addition to facing their next encounter with the Vemus, his officers were keeping a close eye on everyone Connor came into contact with. It was Captain Alec Toro's failed attempt to assassinate Connor aboard the *Vigilant* that had prompted this response. While Connor didn't doubt Colonel Cross's loyalty, the fact that Sean had raised the concern was a symptom of the repercussions of their dreadful experience aboard the *Vigilant*, which had cost the life of the ship's commanding officer.

They entered the Command Center, and Connor looked over at Colonel Cross, who had her blonde hair pulled back into a tight bun. She spoke to her operations officer and looked as Connor expected—completely focused on her duties.

Colonel Cross looked over at him as he approached.

"Phoenix Station will be in the direct path of the anomaly in the next six hours, General," Colonel Cross said.

Phoenix Station was big and moved as slow as molasses, not having been built for speed. They'd thought that anything detected would be far enough out to give them ample opportunity to reposition.

"Understood. What's the status of Lunar Base?" Connor asked.

"Dark-Star status. They have one overdue salvage mission. Colonel Hayes has dispatched a second team to investigate, sir," Colonel Cross replied.

"Any change from the anomaly?" Connor asked.

"Slow and steady as she goes, General," Colonel Cross replied.

They couldn't afford to sit there and wait for whatever the hell this thing was to show its teeth, so Connor had ordered that stealth recon drones—or as they were commonly referred to, SRDs—be deployed. Stealth was a bit of a misnomer because the drones worked by using a tremendous burst of speed that put them on an intercept course. The engines would then cut out and the drone would only make slight course adjustments. What they got was a very fast flyby of the anomaly, and the drones would transmit scan results and high-res images.

Connor looked at the PRADIS scope and saw that the SRDs were on a staggered approach from different vectors. They were moving at the ultra-high speeds that could only be achieved by unmanned spacecraft. Only a human presence aboard a ship necessitated that the ship slow down so people didn't die.

"The SRDs' preliminary scans don't reveal much," Sean said.

"That's why we equip them with high-res optics so we can get actual eyes on the target," Connor replied.

"If that *is* the Vemus, they could have their fleet flying in a tight formation to fool PRADIS into thinking it's one large astronomical body. Either way, we'll know in a few minutes," Colonel Cross said.

She stepped away as a call came to her personal comlink. Connor glanced over and noticed she was speaking in hushed tones.

"Is everything alright, Colonel?" Connor asked when she came back over to him.

"It's fine. Just a report in from one of our weapons R&D engineers, sir," Colonel Cross said.

Connor nodded and looked back at the main holoscreen.

Sean was right. Colonel Cross was definitely hiding something. R&D engineers normally didn't have a direct line to the commanding officer. They would go through proper communications channels. The question remained: what was Colonel Cross hiding, and would it impact her ability to carry out her duties?

Connor decided to wait. They were about to receive an update from the first SRD to pass the anomaly. The remaining four SRDs would be close behind.

"We have an incoming transmission from the SRDs," Lieutenant Daniels said.

Connor turned toward the comms officer. "Put what you've got on the main screen."

They waited while the incoming transmission completed and then images began to appear on the main holoscreen. The first series of images showed a circular object the lead SRD had photographed from farther out on its approach. The cyber warfare suite then analyzed and grouped the images together from all the drones they'd sent. As the SRDs came closer to the anomaly, the images had the appearance of a large asteroid over twenty kilometers across. Connor peered at the images, looking for some indication that the celestial body was something other than a naturally occurring piece of space rock.

As the SRDs drew closer to the anomaly, the computer system grouped images by the drone designation. SRD-1 was the first to fly and provide images of the rear of the anomaly. The back of the asteroid seemed to have been cut off, and it appeared as if they were looking into a deep, dark cave. There was no light, so they couldn't see inside.

"Which SRD had the full scanner array?" Connor asked.

"SRD-3, sir," Colonel Cross answered.

"Prioritize the SRD-3 feed, Lieutenant," Connor said.

Lieutenant Daniels entered a few commands and the SRD-3 feed came to prominence.

Connor kept his eyes on the main holoscreen. Everything in his gut told him that this was the Vemus, but he wouldn't do anything until he had undeniable proof. They were resource-stricken as it was, and he couldn't afford to send any missiles out there until he was sure it was the enemy.

The SRD-3 feed cut out. Rather than start barking out orders, Connor waited for Phoenix Station's crew to do their jobs.

"SRD-3 is no longer transmitting. Putting the partial transmission up on the screen, sir," Lieutenant Daniels said.

SRD-3's sensor sweep had been about to give them a view of the dark side of the anomaly when it suddenly cut out, but there was no indication that the SRD had been fired upon.

"Tactical, show me where our remaining SRDs are in relation to number three. Is there any overlap so we can see what happened to it?" Connor asked.

He knew there was no chance to change the SRDs' approach because there was already a significant delay in the data transfer from the edge of the star system, not to mention the speeds with which the SRDs were moving away from them. No, they were essentially looking at a window into the past. Whatever had happened to the SRDs had already happened.

"I believe I have something, General," Lieutenant Daniels said and showed them the feed from SRD-4. "It's in the upper left quadrant of the feed."

The feed showed a close-up view of the rocky asteroid surface, and Connor could barely see something small flying through the edge of the camera feed. Lieutenant Daniels replayed it and zoomed in on the spot. Connor watched the grainy image of something flying past that seemed to slam into something invisible. There was no flash. The SRD simply broke apart.

"What happened to it?" Sean asked.

"Were there any spikes detected in the scanner array?" Colonel Cross asked.

"No, ma'am," Lieutenant Daniels said.

"There wouldn't be," Connor said, drawing their attention back to him. "It was destroyed before the array could have detected anything in the first place."

"How do you know that, sir?" Sean asked.

"It's the Vemus. They used some type of X-ray laser to take out the SRD. The drone didn't actually hit anything, but a focused shot could easily disable the drone," Connor said.

Colonel Cross frowned. "If that's true, why wait for the SRD to get so close? Why not take it out sooner?"

"They didn't want to show their hand. A short high-power pulse is all it would take. It likely didn't target the other SRDs because they were just taking pictures. Number three was actively scanning it when it passed," Connor said.

"So when the drone got to something the Vemus didn't want us to see, it had to take action," Sean said.

"Correct. We forced their hand. Now we know they're coming," Connor said.

"How do you think they'll react, sir?" Colonel Cross asked.

Connor drew in a deep breath. "They're still pretty far out in the system, but my bet is they're going to speed up."

"Look at the size of that thing. Twenty kilometers across. How many of them could there be?" Sean asked.

"Work with tactical. I want to find out all we can about them. We run the numbers and devise firing solutions based on what we get. Remember, we've got to be smart about this. There's not a single weapon that can take out something of that size. We need to wear them down layer by layer until there's nothing left," Connor said and then looked at Colonel Cross. "Call in your reserves. We need all hands for this."

"Yes, General," Colonel Cross said.

"Comms, send a preliminary report to COMCENT, along with all SRD data," Connor said.

Connor swung his gaze back toward the main holoscreen. The Vemus had tracked them to this star system, sent in an invasion force, and collected data about the colony. Now they were coming. He hesitated to even think of what they'd seen on the images as a ship, but he didn't know what else to call it. The Vemus ship was larger than any city they had on New Earth, and it was heading right for them.

10

CAPTAIN JON WALKER had only just returned from a Phoenix Station supply run when he got the call from Major Shelton. The deep-salvage team led by Daniels had missed two check-ins. His brother was part of that team and was now among the missing CDF crew. Colonel Hayes had specified that Jon was to lead the rescue team and go in search of the overdue salvage team. Jon wasted no time calling in key members of his squad to be part of the away team. The combat shuttle was stocked with the extra supplies required for a rescue mission and headed out almost immediately.

Six hours later, they still hadn't found a trace of the missing salvage team.

"Nothing on our scope, not that it would do much good here," Lieutenant Chester said.

Daron Chester had been assigned to Jon's squad shortly after Jon arrived on Lunar Base. The two of them had become fast friends.

"We're following the path Daniels took," Jon replied.

"Yeah, but why don't we just head to their last known check-in point and start searching there?" Lieutenant Chester asked.

He gave Daron a sideways glance. "You really don't know?"

"No, I just love the sound of your voice. Just brightens my day," Lieutenant Chester said mockingly. "No, I don't know. That's why I asked . . . sir."

Jon snorted. The tacked-on formality was a nice touch. "We follow the path they took. If we skip around, we run the risk of missing something vitally important."

"Like what?" Lieutenant Chester asked.

"What if they were returning to Lunar Base and had an issue? Or their ship was damaged somehow? Or anything else you can think they'd encounter in the middle of a debris field like this? We'd miss them while we just skipped ahead," Jon replied.

Daron thought about it for a minute. "I guess you're right."

"I am right, and if I'm not, we can continue moving forward with our search knowing for a fact that we didn't miss them rather than just hoping we didn't," Jon replied.

They'd been following the path Daniels had taken through the debris field, and there was so much enemy-ship wreckage that Jon wondered how Brian could hope to find anything. They flew amidst the ruins of battleship carriers and heavy cruisers, which were on a slow but steady course away from New Earth in a field of space known as no-man's-land. The salvage team had staggered their flight path through this wreckage.

"Explain to me again what they were doing out here," Lieutenant Chester said.

"They were looking for live Vemus samples. My brother's a field biologist, and the team that's studying the Vemus needs live samples for analysis," Jon answered.

Lieutenant Chester shivered. "The whole situation gives me

the creeps. This thing took out all the people back home and then traveled sixty light-years to get to us here. And your brother wants to get up close and personal with one?"

"I wouldn't say that. He just needs a sample. They want to understand how the Vemus work so we can protect ourselves," Jon said.

"Really think we can do that? Protect ourselves, I mean," Lieutenant Chester asked.

"No idea. I don't know how any of that stuff works, but I hope there's something our scientists can find that was missed," Jon answered, craning his neck back. "Sims!"

A few moments passed and Corporal Sims came to the cockpit.

"You wanted me, sir?" Corporal Sims said.

"Yes," Jon said. "Chester is wondering whether we can really protect ourselves from the Vemus."

Sims' narrow eyes peered at him for a moment. "You mean the infection that leads to becoming the Vemus?"

"That's the one," Jon said.

"Sir, I'm not sure—"

"I'm not asking you to answer me definitively. I know you're not a biologist, but you *are* a medic. So what's your opinion?" Jon asked.

Corporal Sims swallowed. "I really don't know. The write-ups they sent out about it say the Vemus is a parasite that uses a virus to spread itself. You have to come into direct contact with a parasite to be affected by it."

Lieutenant Chester frowned. "What does the virus do?"

"No idea. My suggestion is not to let it touch you if we find ourselves in the presence of any Vemus forces," Corporal Sims said.

Daron swung around in his chair to look at the medic.

"Don't let it touch you," Daron said with a hint of sarcasm. "You're a big help."

Jon snorted and Sims shrugged.

Chester grumbled. They were all worried about the Vemus. Sims's advice was as good as any. A few minutes later, an active response to their scans appeared on the combat shuttle's heads-up display.

Jon adjusted their course and headed for it. They flew toward a large piece of wreckage that was the size of a CDF heavy cruiser like the *Vigilant*. As he studied it, he couldn't begin to guess what part of a ship the wreckage could belong to, but it must have been from a battleship carrier.

They found the salvage team's shuttle attached to the hull.

Jon decreased their velocity.

"Looks like they found an exterior hatch left intact," Lieutenant Chester said.

The salvage team's shuttle was located near an airlock. Jon tried to open a comlink to the shuttle, but he didn't get a response. He switched over to the personal comlink channel and still didn't get a response.

"This is the place. Now, do we go inside or do we fly around this thing and see if there's anything more to learn?" Jon wondered aloud.

Sergeant Roger Lee came to the cockpit and looked at the heads-up display. "I'm not sure if flying around the outside will tell us that much, but you never know. It shouldn't take long to make a quick sweep."

Jon nodded in agreement. He decided to play this by the book and do a bit of recon by flying around the outside of the Vemus ship wreckage. Specialist Hank Horan attempted to reach the salvage team as they went, but there was no response.

Their previous approach had showed that the wreckage was

the size of a heavy cruiser, but as they circled it they learned it was significantly larger. The broken innards of a battleship carrier came into view on the HUD. Glowing lights were strewn from the twisted metal framework where the ship had been ripped apart.

"They still have power," Sergeant Lee said.

"And judging by the size, there should be several intact layers to explore," Jon said.

"You say that like it's a good thing," Lieutenant Chester said.

Jon frowned at him.

"Not to worry, Captain. That's what the big guns are for," Lieutenant Chester said.

"Alright. Suit up. We're going inside," Jon said.

They finished their circuit around the wreck and still couldn't raise the salvage team.

"Sir," Specialist Thoran said, "since there's still power in the wreckage, whatever the Vemus are using to suppress communications must also be active."

"Understood, Specialist," Jon said.

What the specialist didn't say was that there might not be a reply because the salvage team members were all dead. He glanced at Daron, who bobbed his head. Jon wasn't going to leave until he found out.

He flew the shuttle back to the salvage team's ship and engaged the landing gear. Metallic spikes drilled from the metal skids, holding the shuttle in place. Jon set the shuttle's systems to standby and climbed out of the pilot's chair, then walked to the back of the shuttle and stepped into his Nexstar Series Three combat suit. He slipped his arms into the open sleeves, which closed upon feeling his presence. Jon activated the combat suit's systems, bringing them online, and the rest of the suit closed up, sealing him inside.

"Final gear check!" Jon called. "Check yourself and the person in front of you." There was a flurry of activity as they all did one final check on all the joints and fittings of their equipment, along with those of the people around them.

Jon depressurized the shuttle, and the hatch popped open and swung down into position. They all quickly moved to the edge and hopped off. They engaged their magboots, which kept them attached to the hull of the ship. At least this section of the exposed hull was original and not that Vemus exoskeleton crap.

Jon led the five-man team toward the airlock and saw that the salvage team had used the manual override to gain access to the ship.

"Once we're inside, we go slow and steady. Check your corners," Jon said.

He opened the airlock. They stepped inside and closed the outer door.

Lieutenant Chester stepped to the inner door, and Jon stood ready with his AR-71. There was a faint flickering of light beyond the small round window. Lieutenant Chester hit the door controls and stepped to the side. Jon went through first and entered a dark corridor. His HUD compensated for the low light, so he could easily see the features of the corridor.

Jon shuffled a few steps away from the door to allow the others to come through.

"No comms chatter, sir. Shall I try to reach the salvage team?" Specialist Thoran asked.

"Not yet. They have to be somewhere inside here. No need to draw unwanted attention until we have more of an idea of what we're dealing with," Jon replied.

"What we're dealing with . . ." Lieutenant Chester muttered.

Jon spun around. "Do we have a problem, Lieutenant?"

Daron Chester sucked in a harsh breath. "Sorry, Captain. Won't happen again."

"Alright. Stay to the back and guard our flank," Jon said.

Daron was a good man, but there was no way to know how someone would react to imminent danger until they found themselves in harm's way. Jon needed his whole team.

Sergeant Lee moved up to take Chester's place. Jon kept a slow pace as they made their way down the deserted corridor. Emergency systems lit the way, but the rooms they passed were all dark and abandoned.

Jon's suit sensors indicated there was minimal atmosphere being maintained. It had been over two months since the battle, and Jon was confident that the section they were in was as well sealed as they could have hoped.

As they moved forward, they hit a few dead ends and had to backtrack, but they soon settled into a routine as they delved further into the wreckage. They checked all the rooms they came across and then moved on.

"I think we're in one of the aft sections of the ship," Sergeant Lee said.

"How do you know?" Jon asked.

"This part of the ship would have been reinforced to compensate for the main engines. It's likely the missile that took this ship out hit near the forward sections. This area is relatively intact," Sergeant Lee replied.

"Intact and a strong possibility for contact with the enemy," Jon said.

He activated the comlink in his combat suit and began sending out a series of pings, waiting for a reply. None came.

"Captain," Lieutenant Chester said, "the IR spectrum shows an increase in temperature down the corridor to the right."

Jon peered down the corridor. "Any idea what's down this way?"

"Hard to say. If Lee is right, this could be part of the munitions factory they had on board the ship," Lieutenant Chester said.

"Makes sense. That area of the ship would be heavily shielded," Jon said.

They headed down the corridor, and Jon felt a shudder coming through the floor. It quickly stopped and then there was a loud chafing of metal grinding along. Each of them moved to the side and braced themselves against the wall.

"Impacts along the outside of this thing," Sergeant Lee said.

Jon nodded. The wreckage they were in, while large, was still in the middle of a vast debris field. He wondered what they could have hit that would be felt throughout the area they were in.

They continued but Jon brought the team to a halt when he heard a knocking sound echo through the corridor. The repeated cadence was too regular to be a simple impact from wreckage outside the ship. This came from within. Jon motioned to the rest of the team that he'd heard something.

Jon pressed onward, thinking about how much he'd like to have the layout of this place. The farther they went down the corridor, the louder the knocking became. The emergency lighting became brighter as they came to a wide doorway. There was a long window that had years of dust along the edges, and there was also the periodic flashing of light from inside. This must be the munitions factory, but why would the equipment be operating?

Jon crept toward the window and eased himself up to get a better look. Beyond the wide doors was a vast space with long pieces of machinery.

"What do you see?" Lieutenant Chester asked.

"I'm not sure. This has got to be the munitions factory, but I don't—"

Jon ducked back down, and the others backed away in response to his sudden movement. He'd seen something and it had caught him by surprise. Jon slowly rose again and peered through the window. He adjusted the visual spectrum of his helmet and zoomed in on the far end. There was a dimly lit room where he saw several objects moving in the shadows.

Jon swallowed hard and sank back down below the window. "We found them."

"Good. Let's get them and get out of here," Lieutenant Chester said.

"We can't," Jon said and looked back at his squad. "There are Vemus forces inside. They're clustered around a particular area."

Damn it, Brian. Why did you have to volunteer for this? Jon thought. The salvage team was in serious trouble, and Jon wasn't sure if he could get them out.

Sergeant Lee crept by and peeked through the window, then came back to him. "I saw the salvage team. They're pinned down in a room on the far end, but . . ."

Jon shook his head. "There are a lot of Vemus soldiers."

At least that's what he thought they were. Even with the enhanced display, it was difficult to make out the details from this distance.

Daron looked at him pointedly. "There are only five of us," he said.

"I know. I just need a minute to think," Jon replied.

His brother was trapped and there was no way he was going to walk away. He just needed to figure out how to get him free.

11

CONNOR WASN'T sure if the initial shock of what they were going to contend with could ever wear off, but they got to work nonetheless. The SRDs had long since stopped sending transmissions. By their best estimate, only two of the SRDs had made it past the massive Vemus ship. The remaining three all went offline while they were sending their data back to Phoenix Station. All three SRDs going offline in virtually the same fashion was a strong indication that they had been shot down. They had images of one of them being destroyed, which was evidence enough of hostile intent.

Connor had called in his tactical officers and separated them into groups. Each of the groups was tasked with coming up with a firing solution that would destroy the enemy. They were clustered together in nearby work areas while Connor remained in the command area.

Colonel Cross came to stand at his side. "We were expecting another fleet," she said.

"So was I. Instead we got . . . *that*," Connor said while

gesturing toward the main holoscreen. "Even if we'd been able to resupply the missile defense platforms, I'm not sure it would've been enough to destroy it."

"The tactical groups are divided as to when we should fire the weapons we've got," Sean said.

Connor pressed his lips together in thought. "If we fire now, they'll know we see them coming and it'll give them ample time to take out the incoming missiles."

"What if we waited until they were close to our relative position?" Sean asked.

"How close? Give me a distance," Connor said.

"Within Sagan's orbit," Sean said.

Connor frowned in concentration while weighing the possibilities. Sean hadn't just now come up with this idea. He was pitching his own agenda. Sagan was the fifth planet in this star system and relatively close to New Earth.

"You think we should wait until they're within Sagan's orbit before we fire our missiles? Why would we wait that long?" Colonel Cross asked.

"Our previous engagements with the Vemus showed that they limit themselves to basic strategy, but if we send out our missiles now, they stand a greater chance of taking them out. Even though the HADES IV-Bs with Noah's enhancements were designed to overcome fleet ship-point defenses, we don't have to deal with that here. What we need is to maximize the effect our weapons have on them, and I think if we wait until they're much closer to us, we'll stand a better chance of doing the most damage," Sean said.

"But if we attack now, we could soften them up before they come in range of our short-range weapons," Colonel Cross said.

"I don't think that's going to be enough," Connor said and realized he agreed with Sean's proposal. "We'd do some damage, but they could just slow down and repair their ships before coming the rest of the way. If we wait, they're committed."

Colonel Cross glanced at Sean as if seeing him in a new light. "I can see why you keep Major Quinn close at hand."

"He still surprises me sometimes. Remind me to tell you how he first came to be in my service," Connor said.

Colonel Cross laughed. "No need. I've heard the story before. He snuck into a storage crate not knowing you intended to do a low-altitude drop."

Sean grinned. "The general dumped everyone out of that Hellcat as a welcome-to-basic-training gift."

It had been seven years since that first Search and Rescue platoon was formed, and Connor had become as fond of those recruits as he had of the Ghosts. Most had moved on to join the CDF, but some had chosen other pursuits. Those had been much simpler times, when only a few thousand colonists had been brought out of stasis.

Connor glanced at the image of the Vemus ship on the main holoscreen. "They're not very imaginative, are they?" he said.

Sean frowned. "I'm not sure what you mean."

"The Vemus. They fight and move toward an objective with an almost singular purpose. Throughout our entire engagement with them aboard the *Vigilant* they never once slowed down or retreated. They hunted us, but only because we kept coming at them. We kept attacking," Connor said.

"We blocked their signal so they couldn't coordinate their efforts," Sean said.

"True, but even when we went aboard the *Indianapolis,* there were only a few hundred Vemus aboard," Connor said. He had to keep referring to them this way because he didn't want to think of them as having been human before they were infected. "So we wondered where the rest of them were."

Sean's eyes widened. "They held the bulk of their troops in reserve for this attack. At twenty-two kilometers across, there would be room enough for millions of them aboard that ship."

"But why send a fleet of ships ahead? Wouldn't they have kept some in reserve? Now we can just focus our efforts on the one ship," Colonel Cross said.

"Like I said, not very imaginative. They could have ships hidden away. We didn't get a good look at the back of their ship," Connor said.

"We can send in more recon drones and see if they can sneak up behind them, sir," Colonel Cross said.

"I think they'll just shoot them down before we can get any usable intelligence. Instead of sending the drones, let's position our recon drones out near Sagan's orbit," Connor said.

"If we're going to do that, why not a minefield?" Sean said.

Connor nodded. "We keep them dormant with a periodic check-in so they're powered off while the Vemus ship approaches. Then, during their periodic check-ins, we broadcast the signal for the mines to go active."

"We can coordinate that with our missiles then," Colonel Cross said.

"Why don't you go inform the tactical teams that we've decided on a direction and see what else they can come up with," Connor said.

"Yes, sir," Colonel Cross said.

After Cross walked away, Connor looked at Sean. "Any more bright ideas you'd like to share?"

Sean scratched the stubble of his beard. "I need to shave this thing. It itches something fierce."

"Now you sound like Diaz," Connor said.

Sean smiled but then it slipped away. "I wish I could think of something I knew would blow that ship out of the sky."

"You and me both. I know we can do some serious damage to it, but I'm not sure we can stop it," Connor said.

He quickly glanced around. He hadn't meant to say so much, but Sean had been with him for a long time. The kid was smart enough to be a true general one day, not like Connor, who had the position because there was no one else with enough combat experience to effectively do the job.

"I don't think anyone heard you, but I agree. Have you considered adding Lunar Base as part of our resources for facing the Vemus?" Sean asked.

The question alone spoke volumes about Sean's natural leadership ability. Most officers were siloed into their specific area, whereas Sean saw the whole playing board.

"I have, but I'm not convinced it will change things," Connor said.

"Why not?"

"Well, we could use their resources and weapons and list them among our assets. But we don't know what else the Vemus are capable of. I'm trying to account for things we haven't thought of yet. If the Vemus defeat us here, Lunar Base is our last line of defense in space. They'll be that much more of a threat to the Vemus if they don't know we have a base there," Connor said.

Sean nodded in understanding. "It's a gamble either way. If the Vemus detect Lunar Base somehow, Colonel Hayes will engage them. Otherwise, he'll stay there and continue to do a tactical assessment."

"Those were his orders. Nathan wasn't thrilled about them, but he's the best man for the job," Connor said.

"I know *I* wouldn't like watching someone else fighting while I just sat on the sidelines," Sean said.

"Yeah, but you'd do it if it meant saving everyone back home. We need to grind the Vemus down," Connor said.

Sean glanced at his PDA. "Dr. Allen is still waiting to speak with you."

Connor frowned regretfully. "I know, but he'll just have to wait."

12

NATHAN WAITED for PRADIS to update on the main holoscreen. They were about to get another data dump from Phoenix Station. He glanced at the series number for the incoming data and felt a weariness creep into the small of his back. The Lunar Base Command Center had settled into a routine since achieving Dark-Star status. Every two hours they received a new data dump from Phoenix Station and had been doing so for the past twenty-four hours.

Major Shelton joined him in the command area, and they watched the PRADIS screen in silent anticipation. It had been over twelve hours since General Gates had given the anomaly heading for them the designation Alpha with a subheading of Vemus. The data points on PRADIS refreshed, showing the Alpha moving significantly closer to New Earth and increasing its speed by thirteen percent.

"They still haven't fired any of their missiles," Major Shelton said.

The Vemus Alpha was still quite far out in the star system,

only now coming within range of the sixth planet's orbit. Gigantor was a gas giant that had blue bands and out-massed Jupiter by more than eighteen percent. Nathan had only seen pictures of it. For over seven years, the colony had been devoted to settling on New Earth and preparing for a threat that turned out to be the Vemus. They simply hadn't had much time to explore their surroundings. They were aware of similarities with the Sol System, which was part of the reason New Earth was similar in size and composition to their former home. Nathan would have liked to explore their new planetary system more, but as he watched the Vemus Alpha on the screen, he wasn't sure he'd ever get the chance.

"Colonel," Major Shelton said, her tone tight with tension, "the Alpha is within range of the HADES IV-B missiles. Why hasn't General Gates fired any of them yet?"

"One minute, Major," Nathan replied.

He walked toward the main holoscreen and studied the details of the PRADIS output, pressing his lips together while considering his response. He turned back to Major Shelton and noticed his tactical officer, Lieutenant LaCroix, waiting for his response as well. Other CDF soldiers craned their necks toward him as if sensing something.

"Some of you are wondering at the lack of response toward the Vemus Alpha heading toward us," Nathan began and waited a moment. "Why hasn't Phoenix Station taken any offensive action against our enemy?"

There were several head-bobs from the CDF soldiers in the command area.

"This will be among our greatest challenges because of our orders. We're in a communications blackout, with our only updates coming through the PRADIS system. This is necessary to conceal our presence from the enemy. There's no way to know for sure what strategy General Gates and his staff at Phoenix Station have decided on to address the Vemus threat. We've been expecting another fleet and suspected it would be bigger than what we faced over two months ago," Nathan said and flung his arm back toward the main holoscreen. "That is something different, something we *didn't* anticipate, and we're in the dark as to how Phoenix Station plans to engage the enemy. The fact that they haven't opened communications with us indicates that our orders haven't changed. We remain in communications blackout and observation status," he said and allowed his gaze to take in his staff. "It's a shit job, and it's ours. We're the last line of defense for New Earth. We're the Trojan horse if Phoenix Station fails. Our forces *will* engage the enemy and you can be sure that General Gates will do his utmost to stop the Vemus. So, instead of wondering why Phoenix Station hasn't fired their missiles, we'll be working on our own plan for engaging the enemy. I want teams divided up and focused on separate theaters for engagement. The first will be based on how we can assist Phoenix Station with the attack on the Vemus Alpha. The second will be how we'll engage the Vemus Alpha should Phoenix Station be destroyed."

The CDF soldiers became grim-faced and determined.

"We focus on what we *can* do, and don't be afraid to think of the worst scenarios you can come up with as long as you concentrate on the solution to those scenarios. The Vemus are bringing an invasion force. Given the sheer size of the enemy ship, we have to find the weak spots. We have to be smarter than our enemy. That's the only way we're going to survive," Nathan said. He waited a few moments. "Now get back to work. The colony and our fellow CDF soldiers are depending on us. We will not let them down."

The soldiers in the command area returned to their posts, and Major Shelton came over to stand by his side.

"Sir, I must apologize. If you want to relieve me of command I will understand," Major Shelton said.

"I'm not relieving you, Major. We have a job to do. All of us. As commanding officers, the burden is on us to remain steadfast and hold to our orders even when we don't have all the information," Nathan said.

"I won't let you down again, Colonel," Major Shelton said.

Nathan leaned toward her so no one else could hear him. "I'm just as scared as you are," he admitted.

A small smile appeared on Major Shelton's face. "I'm glad you're here, Colonel. With your permission, I'd like to broadcast what you've said to the rest of the base. I think it will be good for them to hear it."

Nathan considered the request for a few moments. "Permission granted."

Major Shelton left him and went over to the ops station.

"Colonel, I've just received a message from Captain Walker," Sergeant Boers said.

Nathan walked over to the comms workstation. "What have you got, Sergeant?"

"They've found the salvage team, but there are Vemus forces keeping them pinned down. Captain Walker is requesting backup-team deployment, sir," Sergeant Boers said.

Nathan's eyes widened. The fact that they'd found the salvage team in all that wreckage was a monumental feat, but Vemus soldiers being aboard one of the wrecks was a sobering thought. He'd thought they'd all be dead by now.

"Sir?" Sergeant Boers asked.

"Acknowledged receipt of the message, Sergeant. Do not send a reply," Nathan said and hated having to say it.

"Yes, sir," Sergeant Boers said, her voice sounding thick and constrained. "Sir, can't we send Captain Walker backup?"

Nathan's mouth went dry. "No," he replied solemnly.

Sergeant Boers opened her mouth to speak.

"You have your orders, Sergeant," Nathan replied sternly.

"Yes, sir," Sergeant Boers muttered and turned back to her workstation.

Even though Nathan was following orders, he still couldn't escape the feeling that he was abandoning soldiers under his command. It would be such an easy thing for him to order another combat shuttle with reinforcements. There would be no shortage of volunteers should he ask for them. Nathan glanced over at the operations work area with an almost wistful urge to do just that, but he squelched the urge almost as suddenly as he felt it. He would not disobey his orders. Captain Walker and his crew were on their own. He hated it, but given what they were about to face, he had to believe it was the right call.

13

THE CDF SOLDIERS on Phoenix Station worked at an accelerated rate, preparing for the Vemus Alpha. Authorization for the use of stimulants had been given, but it was a narrow line to walk. Connor had sent out an advisory to all officers reminding them to rotate their crews, allowing a soldier to work only two extra shifts before rotation was mandatory. It was difficult for any of them to rest, even when off duty.

Connor entered a small conference room where Colonel Cross and Major Elder were already sitting. Connor went to one of the unoccupied chairs and sat down with Major Quinn, who came to sit at Connor's side.

A holoscreen was powered on in the middle of the conference table, and a comms channel was opened that connected them to CDF headquarters in Sierra. They were greeted with a view of a small conference room occupied by Governor Tobias Quinn, Director of CDF Operations Franklin Mallory, Director of Field Operations Damon Mills, and Captain Juan Diaz of the CDF Infantry Division.

Connor was glad Tobias hadn't brought the rest of the colonial defense committee into this meeting.

"Just so we're on the same page," Connor began, "this will be our final meeting before we engage with the Vemus Alpha ship. From here on out we'll send data bursts that will contain any intelligence gathered about the enemy, as well as our own analysis of our engagements with the enemy."

"That's clear, Connor. Just one question. Why isn't Colonel Hayes patched into this meeting?" Tobias asked.

"Lunar Base remains in comms blackout," Connor replied.

"But shouldn't—" Tobias began and then stopped himself. Franklin Mallory leaned over and spoke into Tobias's ear, and the governor nodded. "Never mind. Franklin has just reminded me. Please continue."

Over the next hour, Connor laid out the plan they'd come up with for engaging the Vemus Alpha. Connor couldn't remember planning a more complex operation in his entire career, nor could he remember learning about one in history. The militaries of Earth hadn't had to face a singular enemy like what the colony was about to.

Connor watched the holoscreen and saw Tobias take a sip of his coffee before responding. "I just want to make sure I understand this on a high level. Once this Vemus Alpha crosses Sagan's line, you'll begin firing our missiles at them?"

"This is not a simple point-and-shoot exercise. That's only one facet of the plan—"

"I trust you, Connor," Tobias said. "I know you've picked over this plan of yours eight ways till midnight . . . or is it Sunday?" Tobias frowned. "I can't remember. What I want you to know is that we're not going to pick apart your plan. You have our support and gratitude."

"On behalf of Phoenix Station, we appreciate it," Connor

said. They'd traveled a long road to get here, and on the eve of what would ultimately become the defining moment in human existence, they had to trust each other.

"I would like a few moments to speak with you alone," Tobias said.

Connor nodded and looked over at the others, but they had already risen from their seats and were starting to leave the room. Sean paused to take one last look at the holoscreen. His father gave him a firm nod, and Sean followed the others out.

Connor saw that the committee members had left the conference room on New Earth and Tobias was also alone.

"What's your state of readiness?" Connor asked.

Tobias sighed. "We're still moving people to various bunkers throughout the continent and to Sanctuary. Anyone who can hold a gun has been armed, and we've been training them as best we can."

"But they're not soldiers," Connor said.

Tobias shook his head. "No, they're not, but they have a right to fight for their survival."

"You're right; they do," Connor said and debated in his mind whether to be completely honest with Tobias about their chances.

"I need you to do something for me," Tobias said.

"What do you need me to do?" Connor asked.

"Level with me. What are the odds of this plan of yours stopping the Vemus?"

Connor drew in a breath. "We'll hit them hard. We'll make them bleed, but I don't know if we can stop them. That ship is the biggest thing we've ever seen. We're not even sure how it works. In theory, the Vemus are able to absorb other spaceships and this could be the result of that, but without knowing how thick the exoskeletal hull is, we can't be sure exactly how much damage our weapons will do. That's why we hope to hit them by surprise."

Tobias nodded. "With an extremely narrow margin of error."

"Some of the things we're doing here were only theoretical in the NA Alliance military—things like completely replacing how we do secure communications and command-and-control units that make even the thought of targeting missiles flying at point-four c's of light-speed possible. I could keep going, and I know you could do the same," Connor said.

Tobias leaned back in his chair. "The *Ark* was supposed to be our escape from Earth, a way to begin anew without all the historical conflicts dogging our footsteps. We brought the best and the brightest with us. Admiral Wilkinson snuck you and the rest of the Ghosts aboard the *Ark* in order to escape injustice, and I understand his motives for doing so. What I didn't anticipate was how essential you and Wil Reisman and Kasey Douglass would be to our survival. Given what I know now, I believe none of us would even be here if it weren't for you. We'd have fought and cobbled something together for our defense, but it wouldn't have been the Colonial Defense Force. That was your gift to this colony, and no matter how this turns out, I thank you. My son has become his own man in no small part due to your influence. I'm proud of him . . . and of you."

Connor felt a small lump growing in the back of his throat. The path that had led Sean Quinn to join the CDF had always been a point of silent contention between Connor and Tobias.

"Sean earned his place. He's proven himself time and time again," Connor said.

"I know he did," Tobias said knowingly. "I think that's one of the reasons he's stuck by you—the fact that he's my and Ashley's son held no sway with you."

Connor nodded and watched as Tobias seemed to be

deciding whether to say something else. It was a question Connor had anticipated and was something any parent had a right to ask, knowing their child was going to be in imminent danger.

The moment passed and Tobias didn't ask Connor anything.

"I'll send Sean in to speak with you," Connor said at last.

Tobias swallowed hard. "Thank you," he said, his voice sounding thick.

"Good luck. Send my love to Ashley," Connor said.

"I will. You take care, Connor."

Connor rose from his seat and headed for the door. Once outside the conference room, he motioned for Sean to go back inside. Connor closed the door, having no desire to hear what father and son had to say to one another. It wasn't that he didn't care; it was that he cared too much. Connor only knew what his own son looked like and had a sense of the man he'd become. But thoughts of his son still brought a deep, powerful pang of guilt. He didn't think he'd ever forgive himself no matter what anyone said. Connor glanced at the conference room door for a moment before walking away.

Colonel Cross and Major Elder walked with him back to the Command Center, where they entered and went to their stations.

"General," Captain Caleb Thorne said, "we're ready to execute operation *Tip of the Spear* on your command."

Connor looked up at the PRADIS screen. The Vemus Alpha was approaching Sagan's line and would cross it within the next few hours. They had to launch now to get their missiles and command-and-control units in place.

"Do it," Connor said and used his neural implants to send his authorization codes.

Phoenix Station had secondary and tertiary computing cores, and the station was designed to be able to maintain operational effectiveness even if the subsections broke apart. Connor watched as Captain Thorne executed Connor's orders. HADES IV-B missiles were launched from missile tubes along Phoenix Station's superstructure. The missiles would cluster into groups, going to their preconfigured coordinates before heading to the main objective.

Connor's mind raced as he thought of all the possible outcomes of his actions. They'd come up with this plan as a team, but Connor was the one who gave the order. The responsibility fell squarely upon his shoulders. He had trouble believing their attack would simply do nothing to the Vemus Alpha, but it was a possibility. The best-case scenario was that they would soften up the Vemus Alpha's outer layers so when it attacked them, the remaining weapons on Phoenix Station would continue to tear apart that ship until there was nothing left.

A countdown timer appeared in the upper right corner of the main holoscreen. The pieces were moving into place and soon the attack would begin. The colony was as ready as it would ever be. Anyone left in the cities was there to fight. Noncombatants had been moved to secure locations.

"Tactical, prep data dump for broadcast," Connor said.

"Yes, sir. Ready to send on your command," Captain Thorne replied.

"Send it, and I want the scheduled dumps to occur more frequently now that our missiles are in the air," Connor ordered.

"Yes, sir," Captain Thorne replied.

At least they could keep Lunar Base in the fold as much as possible. Connor knew Nathan Hayes would follow his orders, but being kept in the dark would wear away on anyone's resolve, and the fact that they were fighting for their very survival would only compound the tension. He'd put Nathan in command of

Lunar Base because Nathan believed in the mission. He wouldn't blindly follow orders, and it would take someone with a strong belief in what they were doing to carry out the difficult task Connor had set out for them.

Major Quinn entered the command area and walked toward Connor, coming to a halt at his side.

"Thank you, sir," Sean said.

"You're very welcome, Major," Connor replied.

Together they watched as the CDF soldiers who manned their posts in the various work areas of Phoenix Station executed their duties, all while the Vemus Alpha drew steadily closer, coming toward them like some inescapable leviathan with a purpose none of them really understood. Connor looked around at the CDF soldiers performing their duties. They were rolling the dice. What happened afterward they would deal with, but right now they were committed to a course of action. Connor's gaze came to a stop on the Vemus Alpha image on the PRADIS screen, and he clenched his teeth.

"Sometimes you have to roll the hard six, sir," Major Quinn said, speaking so only Connor heard him.

"You've got that right," Connor said.

There was no turning back now.

14

NOAH HAD ONLY BEEN at Sanctuary for a few days and he hated it. He was supposed to help with the alien power station they had here and somehow adapt its output for the colossus cannon. A short while ago he'd received news that Lunar Base was in comms blackout, which meant he couldn't communicate with his wife. The last he'd heard from her was a prerecorded message that was to be sent down from Lunar Base personnel if Dark-Star status was authorized. Well it was, and now he was out of touch with the most important person in his life. He hated this. Maybe he should steal a ship and head to Lunar Base.

Sanctuary was the largest refugee camp for colonists to hide from the Venus threat. Its location on the continent put it far more remote than any of the small cities they'd built. Sierra was the only true city, and was the most heavily populated, but Haven and Delphi were a distant second and third. The colony government had put time and resources into building bunkers and temporary housing away from population centers. They'd targeted areas that were naturally fortified against New Earth predators but could also be hidden from an invasion force. Since Sanctuary was a large alien city built mostly underground, it could easily accommodate tens of thousands of people.

He was working in one of the topside temporary work areas the archaeological teams had put there when it was just them way out in the middle of nowhere. It was one of the few quiet places he'd found where he could get some work done. Adapting an alien power source to their equipment was a simple concept, but it wasn't easy to actually do.

The door burst open and Lenora stormed inside, her face contorted with lines of anger.

"What's wrong?" Noah asked.

Lenora swung her gaze toward him, seeming surprised to find him sitting there. The fury in her eyes gained the intensity of one of the tornadoes that used to blaze through this area of the continent until they'd put a couple of storm satellites in the area that used focused microwaves to prevent the tornadoes from even forming.

"All the damn people here, contaminating the site. We had an area cordoned off because we haven't had the chance to catalog the artifacts or really study the area. We just marked their locations. And I just found people moving into a group of habitats because they felt crowded in the designated areas and wanted extra space. Kids were running around, playing with artifacts, if you can believe that. Who lets their kids run around and play with things we barely understand?" Lenora said, her tone shrill.

Noah regarded her for a moment, arching his eyebrow.

Lenora glared at him. "Don't you say it."

"They're scared, Lenora."

Lenora blew out a frustrated breath and shook her head. "I want my dig site back."

"Yeah, well I want my wife back. We should tell the Vemus to stay away because they're inconveniencing our lives," Noah said.

Lenora crossed her arms in front of her and looked away from him. For a few moments, neither said anything.

"I'm sorry. It's just . . ." Lenora said and then growled in frustration. "How can you be so calm?"

Noah's eyes widened. "Calm! Trust me, I'm not calm. I'm just trying to focus on my work."

"That would be nice." Lenora rolled her eyes. "I have a hundred thousand people here interfering with *my* work. Can you tell them to go away?"

"A hundred! I thought they capped it at fifty thousand," Noah said.

"No, we've got a hundred now. One of the major bunkers failed. The area was unsuitable because of seismic activity or some such. Those people were moved here," Lenora said.

"It's only temporary—" Noah began, and Lenora glared at him.

"Don't give me that. And it's not the people being here . . . Well, maybe it is, but it's just . . ." Lenora's voice trailed off.

Noah looked at her. Lenora was like a big sister to him. She'd taken him under her wing when they'd first woken up after being in stasis for two hundred years. But he'd never seen her so agitated. She usually had a tighter rein on her emotions. She was a born leader. Once set upon a task, just get out of her way. It was no wonder she and Connor had had some of the most heated arguments he'd ever seen. In some respects, they were two sides of the same coin, but in others they were polar opposites.

"I can't even figure out where the aliens that built this place went. They're all gone. No remains, nothing. Nothing but these structures to even say they existed, and if the same thing happens to us . . ." Lenora said, her voice becoming thick.

Noah's instinct was to give her a hug and tell her that everything would be alright, but he knew that wasn't something Lenora wanted. "There really is no sign of what happened to the aliens that built this place?" Noah asked instead.

"Nothing but theories. We don't even know what they looked like. We know they manipulated the genetics of some of the species that live here now and that they were quite advanced in some ways and primitive in others," Lenora said.

"So they didn't get on a spaceship and fly away from here?"

"There's no evidence of them being able to fly in the atmosphere, much less in outer space," Lenora answered and pressed her lips together. "Do you think they're alright?" she asked and gestured upward.

Noah swallowed hard. "Right now they are. They haven't engaged the Vemus yet."

"How do you know that?"

"Well, for one, we would have heard about it. Dark-Star status is a protocol that essentially hides the fact that we have a lunar base. It's part of Connor's overall strategy," Noah said.

Lenora looked away. "Connor," she muttered as if the name were a blessing and a curse. Noah heard a tinge of longing in it. "But he wouldn't order that protocol unless they had found the Vemus."

"He wouldn't have done it unless he was absolutely sure," Noah agreed.

Lenora's shoulders drew upward and he watched her body stiffen. "Damn it."

This time Noah did give in to his instincts. He rose out of his chair and hugged Lenora. She was trembling, and after a moment she clung to him, burying her face in his chest. Noah didn't say anything, and after a minute she let him go, quickly wiping her eyes.

"He was never really here. Once we learned about the threat coming from Earth seven years ago, he stopped being here. He threw himself into his work, building the CDF. Then he lost Wil and Kasey . . . and that message from his son. This fight has been more personal for him than it's been for anyone else. I'm worried about him. I'm worried he's going to throw his life away to balance all the loss as if he had no other choice but to sacrifice himself," Lenora said.

Noah's mouth hung open. For as long as he'd known her, she'd never spoken to him about Connor.

"Connor would trade his life for a chance to stop the Vemus from coming here," Noah said.

Lenora shook her head. "I'm sure he thinks he would. It's what he'll convince himself he's doing. But you didn't see him before he left for Phoenix Station. He wants to die. He thinks that if he sacrifices himself, it will make up for all his regrets," Lenora said.

Noah's brows pulled together. "That's not true—"

"Yes, it is. He blames himself for not being there for his son. He blames himself for not being able to save Wil and Kasey and all the other soldiers who've died fighting the Vemus. He refuses to see the fruits of all his efforts and only focuses on what was lost," Lenora said.

"I thought he was doing better. Didn't you speak to him?"

"I did. He seemed like he started to listen, but I'm not sure. You know him; he can teach a boulder about being stubborn," Lenora said.

"Yeah, but—"

"If he really thought he was going to live, don't you think

he'd be here fighting or coordinating the attack instead of being on Phoenix Station?" Lenora asked.

"You don't understand just how fast things can change up there. He's right where he needs to be," Noah said.

"Which just happens to be the perfect place for him to perform his heroic sacrifice," Lenora said bitterly.

Noah sighed, becoming irritated. "He may carry all that guilt, as you say. You're probably right about that, but what you don't see is that he wants to protect *you*."

Lenora snorted. "Don't you dare say he's doing this for me."

"It's part of it, whether you want to admit it or not," Noah replied.

Lenora stomped away from him. "If he wanted to protect me, he should have stayed."

Noah's shoulders slumped. "Come on, Lenora. That's not fair."

"No, it's not, and neither is him throwing his life away. Neither is it fair that your wife is holed up on Lunar Base. Nor is it fair that people had to leave their homes so they can hide because otherwise they might die. None of this is fair!" Lenora shouted and stalked out.

Noah took a deep breath and couldn't stop his mind from racing. They were both right, and that worried him more than making Lenora see reason.

He powered off his workstation and went outside. There were makeshift roads worn by all the traffic—be it people on foot or vehicles moving equipment. Work crews were hustling about, relocating into the ruins and off the surface. They needed to mask their presence here as much as possible, but as Noah looked around at all the temporary tents and buildings, he didn't see how that was going to be possible.

Noah glanced around, looking for Lenora, but she was nowhere to be seen. Instead, he heard a high-pitched, piggish voice giving orders while coming closer to him. Noah started walking away but he heard the shrill voice calling after him and turned around.

"Captain Gibson, what can I do for you?" Noah asked.

Captain Raeburn Gibson was a tall man with unusually long arms and torso. His thin dark hair was cropped and his glassy eyes were framed too close together, giving him the appearance of someone who was constantly glaring, although in Raeburn's case that might be true.

"Captain Barker, my PM has informed me that we're behind schedule with the power converter," Gibson said.

Gibson was part of Field Operations and Security and not part of the CDF, so Noah didn't have to report anything to him. Though their ranks were similar, Gibson was in charge of security, but he'd taken it upon himself to meddle in other work that didn't concern him. He was just supposed to keep the peace and run evacuation drills. Noah was convinced that Gibson had been assigned to Sanctuary just to get him out of the hair of whoever sent him here. He had no idea who, but he was sure that was the reason.

Gibson cleared his throat. "Aren't you supposed to be working on that this morning?"

Noah frowned and shook his head. "This doesn't really concern you."

Gibson's sidekick was an imposing man named Barnes. If Gibson was the brains, then Barnes was the muscle. Barnes glared at Noah, and the rest of the security detail waited to take their cue from him. They were all armed with shock sticks.

"You're mistaken, Captain," Gibson insisted.

"Really," Noah replied. "You're not part of the CDF, and

Field Ops doesn't have any authority over what I do with my time."

Gibson nodded and pursed his fat lips together as if agreeing with what Noah had said. "Ordinarily you'd be right, but in this state of emergency, Field Operations and Security is granted special authority. Sanctuary is a civilian installation and anyone within its boundaries, including CDF soldiers, are under my jurisdiction," Gibson said.

Noah couldn't believe it. This idiot thought he could actually strong-arm him. "That's crap and you know it. If you think you can stroll around here, throwing your weight around, you're sorely mistaken."

Sergeant Barnes took a step toward him, glaring menacingly, but Gibson placed a hand on his shoulder and pulled him back. Much to Noah's surprise, the large man actually stepped back. What kind of hold did Gibson have on the man to make him so obedient?

"If I find that you're bullying these people, I'll have a squad brought in here so fast you won't know what hit you," Noah said.

Gibson's eyes narrowed dangerously. "Tread carefully. Things won't always be this way. Change is coming, and you'll need friends if you want to survive."

"Go bother someone else," Noah replied.

"Get back to work, Captain Barker. If you don't get the power converters online, Sanctuary is defenseless," Gibson said and walked away, leading his team.

Noah glared at them in disgust. The colony's finest, but fear made people do stupid things. Some people froze and were unable to take action, while others seized the opportunity to grasp at anything to make themselves feel secure.

Noah did need to check with the engineering teams working on the power converters. They couldn't just connect their equipment to the alien power station. They needed a relay to convert the power so it would work with colony equipment, which was easier said than done since the alien power station was prone to overloads and they couldn't figure out why. Noah glanced up at the sky. He bet Kara could have figured it out.

15

CAPTAIN WALKER WAITED for Specialist Thoran and Lieutenant Chester to return. Sending them back to their shuttle to deploy a comms drone had been the right call. Meanwhile, the Vemus soldiers continued to devote all their attention to the trapped salvage team.

"Shouldn't they be back by now?" Corporal Sims asked.

"Let's give them a few minutes more," Jon replied.

Lieutenant Chester had strongly suggested that they send in a request for backup from Lunar Base, and while Jon was anxious to save his brother, he had to concede Lieutenant Chester's point. It should only take an hour to return to the shuttle and deploy a drone. Jon glanced at the time on his heads-up display and saw that they were rapidly approaching the hour mark.

He'd taken the risk that most of the Vemus soldiers were inside the munitions factory area trying to get to the salvage team. Some of the Vemus soldiers continued to slam their fists on the wall, but the bulk of their group waited. Having carefully observed them for the past hour, Jon had the feeling that the

Vemus weren't trying to get into the room where the salvage team was trapped so much as keeping an eye on them.

Sergeant Lee squatted down next to Jon. "What do you think of the plan?"

Jon looked over at him. "Once we start, it's not like we get a do-over. They'll know we're here."

They'd been running reconnaissance around the area, looking for a safe way to extract the salvage team. Jon had even considered using the weapons on the combat shuttle to poke a few holes in the area nearby. He'd hoped to draw the Vemus soldiers away, but Sergeant Lee pointed out that it was a terrible idea. Blowing more holes in the wreckage of the ship could make this place even more unstable than it already was. When Jon had pressed Lee to go along with the plan, Lee reminded him that if he persisted with it, they ran a greater risk of killing the salvage team rather than saving it. Instead, they'd placed explosive charges in the adjacent tunnels, hoping that it would draw the Vemus away from the salvage team to investigate.

"Are you sure we can't try opening a comlink to the salvage team?" Corporal Sims asked.

"Too risky. The reports from when the *Banshee* was captured were that the Vemus are able to detect comlink signals, so if we use them, we'll give away our position," Jon answered.

He'd read the reports released by CDF intelligence. They'd disseminated the debriefing from the soldiers involved and sent out useable intelligence throughout the CDF. Jon remembered reading it and thinking it was interesting, but he hadn't expected to use that knowledge. Combat suit-to-suit communications in close proximity didn't require a comlink broadcast, so they were safe from the Vemus detecting them for now. The range wasn't that extensive or else they'd be able to speak with Lieutenant Chester and Specialist Thoran back on the shuttle. Jon wanted to go back to the munitions factory door and look through the window but decided against it. Why tempt fate at this point? They knew what was there. A few combat drones would have come in handy at this point, but they didn't have any.

A few minutes later their overdue team members made it back to them.

"Run into any trouble?" Jon asked.

"No, sir. But we got no response from Lunar Base," Lieutenant Chester said.

Jon frowned. "Not even an acknowledgment?"

"Nothing. We sent out a comms drone and waited for it to get beyond the Vemus jamming signal and return. No response, Captain," Lieutenant Chester said.

Jon looked at Specialist Thoran. "What do you think it means?"

"They should have gotten our transmission. Unless the Vemus can somehow travel at the speed of light and are attacking right now, I think Lunar Base has been ordered to go into communications blackout and couldn't respond even if they wanted to, Captain," Specialist Thoran said.

Jon grimaced. "Dark-Star status. I didn't even think about that."

The other members of the team considered it for a moment.

"It would explain their lack of response," Lieutenant Chester said.

"Yeah, but that means there's another Vemus attack force out there," Corporal Sims said.

"It also means we're on our own. It's safe to assume that they got our transmission but weren't able to respond," Jon said.

"Would they send another team anyway, even if they couldn't respond, sir?" Sergeant Lee asked.

Jon looked at them all and shook his head. "No. Not with

another attack force on its way. The priority is New Earth and keeping Lunar Base's location a secret."

Specialist Thoran's face became pale. "We have to get out of here."

"We're not leaving without the salvage team," Jon said firmly. He looked around at all of them. "We can't leave our people behind. They'd do the same for us, and they might have learned something important."

Sergeant Lee nodded grimly.

Lieutenant Chester nodded as well. "We're with you, Captain."

Jon felt the muscles in his chest loosen. "Thank you. You're all heroes. Now let's get this done."

Lieutenant Chester snorted. "Let's just get them so we can get out of here in one piece, sir."

"Alright, enough with the pep talks. Lee and I did some recon while you were gone. We've placed concussive charges . . ." Jon went over the plan he'd laid out with Sergeant Lee. It didn't take long to explain since it was relatively simple. Too bad it wasn't going to be easily executed.

"Were you able to bring what I asked you?" Jon asked.

"We only had one on board," Lieutenant Chester replied and gestured over to the heavy case he'd been carrying.

Jon must have been getting tired because he'd completely missed the fact that Lieutenant Chester had brought the case.

"And the ammunition chest is over there, sir," Lieutenant Chester said and frowned. "Are you sure you're alright, Captain?"

Jon nodded. "I'm fine. I just didn't see that you had the case. We need to place the heavy turret at the far end of this corridor."

He was counting on the Vemus to investigate the concussive blasts, only to walk into the path of their only heavy turret. It should rip them to shreds, giving them time to get the salvage team out of there.

A violent shudder spread from the floors and down the corridor. Power lines inside the walls began to overload, sending showers of sparks until fire control systems cut them off. At least the safety systems were still operational.

"That was another impact," Lieutenant Chester said.

Jon nodded. "We've got no time to waste. Let's get moving."

The five-man rescue team left the area. They'd set up the turret and then observe the Vemus soldiers before executing the plan.

16

CONNOR SAT in his office aboard Phoenix Station. The cup of coffee Corporal Faulkner had brought sat untouched, having long since gone cold. He'd lost the taste for coffee since his time on the *Vigilant* when someone had tried to poison him. While he didn't believe that anyone here would be trying to murder him, he just couldn't look at a cup of coffee the same way anymore. Perhaps he should try tea, but what he really wanted was something a lot stronger.

"General," Dr. Richard Allen said, sitting across from Connor. "I realize the timing of this news is delicate, but with all that's been happening, I wasn't sure when a good time to disclose the information would be."

Connor drew in a breath and sighed. "And you're certain this is accurate?"

"Quite certain, General," Dr. Allen said, meeting Connor's gaze.

"Are there any others in the same condition?" Connor asked.

"Yes, General," Dr. Allen answered, and Connor's eyes

widened. "With a crew of ten thousand, there's bound to be more than one. I have a list prepared."

Connor leaned forward in his chair and shook his head. "The ones who're unaware is one thing, but for the people who knew and didn't report it—that's another."

"Sir, these are extraordinary times we live in. We're all coping with the threat the Vemus represent in our own ways—" Dr. Allen said.

"I understand," Connor said and rose from his seat. "I appreciate you bringing this to my attention. Send your list to Major Quinn and we'll get it sorted out. I'm due to return to the Command Center," he said and left his office with Dr. Allen following.

"Good luck, General," Dr. Allen said.

"Good luck to us all," Connor said.

Sean was standing a short distance away with his security detail and walked with Connor on his way back to Phoenix Station's Command Center.

Sean eyed him for a moment. "I take it the news from Dr. Allen was significant, sir?"

Connor nodded. "Let's just say you were right about Colonel Cross."

They walked into the Command Center, where the CDF soldiers on duty were actively working at their stations. The countdown timer on the main holoscreen was mirrored on Connor's own internal heads-up display, but he glanced at it anyway. The first salvo of HADES IV-B missiles would be in target range soon.

Connor headed to the command area where Colonel Cross waited. She met his gaze and something unspoken passed between them. Her eyes narrowed and she glanced away for a moment. Then her shoulders slumped before she squared herself away.

Connor stood next to her with his hands clasped behind him. He could feel the tenseness coming off of her in waves. He glanced at the barely perceptible pooch in her midsection. "You should have told me," Connor said quietly.

Colonel Cross looked at him and was about to reply.

"Alpha missile group closing in on target. Command-and-control units have the target marked," Captain Thorne announced.

Connor looked at the main holoscreen. The alpha missile group was the farthermost away from the Vemus ship. They'd been modified to maximize their speed, reaching forty percent relativistic speeds, which meant that as the Vemus Alpha crossed Sagan's line, the fifty-four-million-kilometer distance would be covered in under eight minutes. Twenty of their modified HADES IV-Bs were carrying fusion warheads.

Connor and the rest of the CDF soldiers on Phoenix Station waited.

"Detonation signal received," Captain Thorne said. "Confirmed detonation of all twenty missiles," he said, unable to keep the excitement from his voice.

Millions of kilometers away from them, the Vemus Alpha ship was blindsided by the CDF missiles. Layers of the exoskeleton sloughed away almost immediately, burning away in chunks. Large gaps began to appear on the hull of the massive ship where the CDF missiles had delivered their powerful payloads.

"Bravo and Charlie missile groups are closing on the target," Captain Thorne announced.

Connor knew those missiles moved much slower. That was

why they'd waited to send the alpha group until the other missile groups were in position. A subgroup of Bravo and Charlie were targeted to hit the rear of the Vemus Alpha. Connor's gaze was fixed on the main holoscreen. Those missiles had to reach their target. Since there were no visible engines on the massive ship, they had to be in the rear, hidden away in the cavernous mass. He planned to blindside the behemoth and then continue to hit the ship, chopping away at it and hopefully crippling it in the process.

"Confirm all HADES active," Captain Thorne said.

The breath caught in Connor's chest. The command-and-control units would provide updates for as long as they were active. They didn't have thousands of missiles, so every one of them counted.

The command-and-control units beamed back their updates, but it still took the data over three minutes to make it to Phoenix Station, where the computing core immediately put it into their cyber-warfare suite. The whole process from the time the command-and-control units sent an update to when it appeared on the main holoscreen in Phoenix Station's command area was three-point-two minutes. That didn't sound like a lot of time, but it could make all the difference in a war such as this. There was nothing else for them to do. They were committed to this engagement, just as the Vemus Alpha was.

"Missile groups going offline," Captain Thorne said, his voice rising.

"Can you confirm detonation?" Connor asked.

"I'm trying to . . . negative, General. They must be taking out our missiles," Captain Thorne said.

Connor watched the long list of HADES IV-B missile statuses. Some were getting through the countermeasures the Vemus were using, but not nearly as many as they'd hoped. As more and more missiles went offline without delivering their payload, Connor's gut clenched.

"Sir, command-and-control units are now offline. Switching to PRADIS," Captain Thorne said.

Connor clenched his teeth. Without the command-and-control units, they couldn't know what sort of damage they'd done. He looked away from the main holoscreen, but the officers in the command area still watched with grave expressions.

"PRADIS is online," Captain Thorne said. "Sir, we have three hundred marks on the plot—make that four hundred. Speed and mass readings indicate NA Alliance Condor class heavy missiles."

"Set Condition One," Connor said. "Ready station defenses. We have incoming missiles."

"Action Stations. Action Stations. Set Condition One." Lieutenant Daniel's voice was broadcast throughout Phoenix Station.

"Time to impact—one hour at their current speed, sir," Captain Thorne said.

"Thank you, Captain. Any change in their speed, I want to know about it immediately," Connor said.

"Yes, General," Captain Thorne answered.

"Major Elder, you have the con. Colonel Cross and Major Quinn, follow me," Connor said.

"Yes, General," Major Elder said, giving them a curious glance as they left.

Connor led them to the nearest breakout room and told Sean to wait outside. Colonel Cross went inside, and Connor closed the door.

"What do you have to say for yourself, Colonel?" Connor asked.

"Sir, I was going to tell you—" Colonel Cross began.

"You were *required* to tell me the moment you found out. How far along are you?" Connor asked.

"Not that far—"

"How far along!" Connor shouted.

"Eight weeks. Just over eight weeks, sir," Colonel Cross said finally.

Connor's eyes widened. "Eight weeks," he muttered in disbelief. "You must have known you were pregnant for over a month and didn't report it."

Colonel Cross looked away.

"We have protocols to follow. You were required to report this to me as your commanding officer within seventy-two hours of finding out," Connor said, his voice lowering in volume but no less stern.

Colonel Cross glared at him. "Permission to speak freely, sir."

"Granted."

"I know the damn protocol and the regulations," Colonel Cross said.

"Then why didn't you tell me?"

"Because I wanted to fight! I have a right to fight. My pregnancy doesn't in any way impede my ability to command," Colonel Cross said.

"This is about more than just you, Savannah. 'No pregnant woman shall serve in an active combat zone,'" Connor replied.

"Are you going to arrest me?" Colonel Cross challenged.

"No, I'm not going to arrest you. But I am sending you back to New Earth," Connor said.

"No, don't!" Colonel Cross pleaded. "Let me stay. Let me fight. You need me."

Connor's eyebrows drew together, furrowing over his eyes. "Absolutely not. This isn't just about you anymore. There's another life at stake."

"All of our lives are at stake! What difference does it make whether I stay here and fight or go back to New Earth and fight there?" Colonel Cross said. "Tell me, what difference does it make?"

"All the difference in the world, but you can't see it now. What is the Colonial Defense Force motto?" Connor asked.

Colonel Cross sighed heavily. "Defend the colony and all its people," she said softly.

"Your baby, even at this stage, is part of this colony. The regulations on this are clear," Connor said.

Colonel Cross gritted her teeth, and the edges of her eyes reddened.

"Who is the father? And does he know?" Connor asked.

"Where are you going to send me?" Colonel Cross asked.

"Answer the question, Colonel," Connor said.

"It's Colonel Hayes," she said, and her shoulders slumped.

"Does Nathan know?" Connor asked.

Colonel Cross's lips trembled and she shook her head.

"Understood," Connor said. "For the record, I understand why you did what you did, but I can't condone it. We have these regulations for a reason. You think that fighting here at Phoenix Station is no different than on New Earth, but I say you're wrong. You might hate it, and you might hate me for enforcing the regulations even in times such as these, but I intend to give your and Nathan's baby the best chance at life I can."

Colonel Cross looked away from him.

Connor opened the door. "Major Quinn, have two members of your security detail escort Colonel Cross to the hangar bay. She's been relieved of duty. She, along with several hundred nonessential personnel, are returning to New Earth. See that she's assigned to Sanctuary, then come inside."

"Right away, General," Major Quinn said.

Colonel Cross began to walk out of the breakout room, but stopped before the threshold. She turned around and stood up straight, with her shoulders back. She raised her right hand to her brow and saluted.

Connor brought his heels together and saluted back to her in kind, then gave her a firm nod, and she left.

Connor rested his hands on his hips and sighed heavily. He looked up at the ceiling, still thinking about what Savannah had done. He kept thinking about whether he should inform Nathan that he was going to be a father but decided against it. News like that should come from the mother, but Lunar Base was in a communications blackout. Would it affect Colonel Hayes's ability to command Lunar Base? Would the news of him becoming a father affect his judgment and make him prone to rash decisions? Connor pressed his lips together while he considered. He'd put Nathan in command of Lunar Base because of his commitment to their strategy for fighting the Vemus. While the news of his becoming a father would come as a shock, Connor believed that, of anyone under his command, Nathan could handle that news, but he'd leave it up to Savannah to tell him.

The door to the breakout room opened, and Sean stepped inside, closing the door behind him.

"You wanted to see me, sir," Sean said.

"You were right about Colonel Cross. She's pregnant," Connor said.

Sean nodded. "It makes sense now, sir."

Connor snorted. Savannah and Nathan were hardly the first officers to survive an ordeal like their first engagement with the Vemus and wind up sleeping together. Regardless of the status of their relationship, they both had something to consider.

"Your keen observation skills continue to impress me, Major," Connor said.

"Thank you, sir. I aim to please," Sean said with a smile.

Connor sighed. "You won't like your new orders."

Sean frowned. "New orders, sir?"

"Yes," Connor replied. "I'm sending you back to Sierra. You're to take command of the city's defenses. I'm giving you full authority over all CDF forces on the ground."

"But, sir, I thought I'd be at your side for the duration," Sean said.

"Plans change. You and your entire team will go to Sierra," Connor said.

Sean's mouth hung open. "Is this because . . ."

Connor knew what he was about to ask, and Sean let the question go unfinished. "If you need to ask that, I haven't done a very good job of not giving you special treatment all these years."

Sean clamped his mouth shut. "Permission to speak freely, General."

"Keep it quick." Connor glanced at the clock.

"Why are you sending me back to New Earth? We have soldiers and commanding officers there already," Sean said.

"Let me tell you something. We're not all the same, commanding officers included, but there are some who are born with a certain instinct that either makes them die young or enables them to rise through the ranks. The fact of the matter is, Sean, you're one of the best officers I've ever served with. And that includes Wil and Kasey. They both commented on more than one occasion about your abilities as an officer," Connor said.

Sean swallowed hard. "Thank you, sir. I'm glad you believe in my abilities, but I don't have the rank to take command of Sierra's defenses."

Connor smiled. "A CO once said to me that titles are cheap. People will follow those who do the work. Damon Mills is bullheaded, but he's a good man. He'll listen to you. I'm giving you operational command authority for the CDF ground forces. I'm sending my authorization to your PDA. You're to report to Sierra at once."

"But, sir, I don't know if I can do this."

Connor put his hand on Sean's shoulder. "I know you can. I firmly believe that when the Vemus reach the city, it will stand a much better chance at surviving with you in command. Remember what you've learned and trust your instincts."

"You said *when* the Vemus reach the city. You don't think you can stop them here?" Sean asked.

"You've seen it for yourself. We'll slow them down and do whatever damage we can against them so you'll have fewer to face on the ground. Very little will change that," Connor said. He'd been thinking it for so long that to finally admit it aloud was somewhat freeing.

He watched as a range of emotions crossed Sean's face, but the young man was smart enough to know the answers. Instead, he hardened his gaze. "I'll do my best, General."

"Good luck," Connor said, and his throat became tight.

"You too, sir," Sean said.

They left the breakout room, and Connor watched the young man he had helped shape into a fine young officer walk away from him. He'd always looked at Sean as a son, and he was filled with fatherly pride in the man Sean Quinn had become. He wondered if Admiral Wilkinson had had the same thoughts when he looked at Connor's own son. Connor felt a heavy weight lift from his shoulders. The video recording of his son was painful for him to watch, but he now had a better understanding of why Wilkinson had asked him to record it. Connor had spent a lot of time hating Wilkinson for the actions he'd taken and how Connor had to live with the results. It wasn't a perfect world by a long shot, and if Connor could find it in his heart to forgive Mitch Wilkinson for setting him on this path, then perhaps he could finally forgive himself for his own actions that had put him on this same path.

Connor swallowed those thoughts away. He wished he could tell Lenora that he finally understood what she'd been trying to tell him.

"General, they need you in the command area," a CDF soldier said.

Connor nodded and headed there. This fight was far from over and he intended to make the Vemus bleed as much as he could before the end.

17

NOAH WALKED among the ruins of the alien city the colonists called Sanctuary. He'd been working with a team of engineers to convert the alien power station into something they could use for the colossus cannon. The problem was that the technology was hundreds of years old. The aliens had tapped into geothermal energy deep in the planet's crust. Since the colonists didn't have the resources to build a power plant of their own, they'd taken the option of leveraging what was already there. The plan was simple, just not easy. Noah had finished running a series of tests, and the power output seemed stable enough for further testing. But if the Vemus somehow found this place, he wasn't sure how long the colossus cannon would remain operational.

He'd decided to take a walk to clear his head. He wanted to find Lenora. She'd been pretty upset, and wasn't that what little brothers were supposed to do? A member of the archaeological team had told him she'd gone into an area of the city that was cordoned off from refugees. The soldiers securing that area took one look at his uniform and rank, then let him pass.

The aliens that built this place hadn't constructed anything like stairs. Instead, they preferred ramps that made traversing to the lower levels of the city seem like he was walking along a winding road. It would have been nice if they'd built elevators, but they apparently hadn't had any need for them either. He came to a subterranean level of the city where the only lighting came from some of the temporary light fixtures they'd set up. Noah peered ahead and noticed that the lighting became brighter in the distance. The source of the light came from a building whose large circular door was partially open. Some unseen mechanism must have pulled the door into the wall because there was no way Lenora could have opened it herself.

Noah called out and heard Lenora answer him from inside the building, but her voice echoed and sounded distant. Noah went inside and followed a corridor that circled into a large cavern. There were glowing amber lights along the smooth walls. Noah walked deeper into the cavern and noticed that there were even more levels beneath the one he was on.

He saw Lenora standing a short distance away, in front of a curved screen that showed some type of alien writing scrolling past, going from left to right.

"What is this place?" Noah asked.

"I think it's some kind of archive," Lenora said in hushed tones, as if they were in a church.

"An archive! That's amazing. How'd you find it?" Noah asked.

Lenora gave him a sidelong glance. "A group of refugees wandered down here and said they'd found something. They described this room."

"Maybe having the refugees here isn't such a bad thing after all. You could put them to work," Noah said.

Lenora blew out a breath and looked at him regretfully. "About before. I'm sorry."

"You don't need to apologize. None of this is easy."

"That doesn't mean I didn't mean what I said. I'm just sorry I yelled at you," Lenora said.

Noah glanced at the alien symbols scrolling past on the antiquated screen. It wasn't made of glass but was constructed of some kind of tightly knitted flexible mesh.

"If you really feel that way, then why don't you send Connor a message?" Noah said.

Lenora frowned. "I'm not going to send him some final message professing a bunch of emotional crap. He doesn't need that."

Noah laughed. "No, of course not, but would it hurt for you to tell him you'd like him to come back home?"

"We're not together," Lenora replied firmly.

"I know that, but you still care about him," Noah said, thinking that Lenora could also teach a thing or two about being stubborn.

Lenora regarded him for a moment. "Maybe."

Noah's comlink chimed, and he tapped the receiver near his ear. "This is Noah."

"We need you back topside, sir. Captain Gibson is ordering a test-fire of the colossus cannon," Corporal Johnson said.

Noah jerked back a few steps. *Idiot!* He sucked in his bottom lip in frustration. "I'm coming. You have to stall him. If he fires that weapon, he could overload the entire system."

"Yes, sir," Corporal Johnson said.

The comlink closed.

"God, please save me from idiots like Gibson," Noah said.

"I'll come with you," Lenora said, "in case God is busy."

Noah snorted and, together, they ran out of the alien archive. He contacted members of the engineering team, informing them of what was happening. Three work crews were on their way to the mobile Command Center.

They ran through throngs of refugees, and Noah shouted for them to make a space. Most didn't recognize him, but they did recognize the Colonial Defense Uniform and had come to respect it. A few minutes later they were within sight of the mobile Command Center. There was a crowd gathered, with more than a few work crews. Field Operations and Security personnel had established a perimeter just outside the Command Center, and Captain Gibson was standing just behind the line, red-faced, with a wild look in his eye. His left cheek was swollen. Noah saw Corporal Johnson on his knees. He looked disoriented, as if he'd just had a shock-stick used on him.

Noah pushed his way through the workers, and the line of Field Ops and Security forces held their shock-sticks ready.

"Gibson! What the hell are you doing?" Noah shouted.

Captain Gibson swung his angry gaze toward him and sneered. "Your man attacked me."

Noah looked over at Corporal Johnson and scuttled over to him. "Get away from him," Noah snapped.

The Field Ops agent standing over Corporal Johnson glared at Noah.

"Back off," Lenora said, coming to stand next to Noah.

The Field Ops man glanced back at Gibson.

"This is ridiculous," Lenora said and stepped forward, helping Corporal Johnson back to his feet. Surprisingly, the Field Ops team let her do this.

Corporal Johnson was hunched over, holding his middle.

"Are you alright?" Noah asked quietly.

"You did say to stall him, sir," Corporal Johnson said and grimaced.

Noah motioned to some members of the work crew to take Corporal Johnson, and they led him off to the side.

Noah turned back toward Captain Gibson. "You can't test-fire the colossus cannon. You'll overload the system."

"I had my own people check the latest reports for the power converter. The energy levels are constant. We can test the weapon," Captain Gibson sneered.

Noah took a moment to calm down. He needed to defuse the situation, not exacerbate it. "You don't know what you're doing—"

"I've had about enough of your smug comments. You come here, strutting around, thinking you're so superior. People actually believe you're some kind of hero. The people are scared. They need to know they can be protected here," Captain Gibson said and glanced at a Field Ops person next to him. "Ready the cannon for test-firing."

Noah stepped forward and felt Lenora grab his arm, holding him back. "You're such an idiot. Yes, the power levels are constant, but if you fire that weapon, you'll overload the system and destroy our only means of defense."

"Rubbish," Captain Gibson spat.

The line of Field Ops and Security forces stood ready, almost inviting Noah to try and push his way through.

"I don't know what your tech expert told you, but the power requirements for the colossus cannon are not comparable to the mag-cannons that were installed in Sierra. The power draw is much more taxing on the system and is prone to spikes," Noah said.

Captain Gibson narrowed his gaze. "You would have accounted for that," he said and glanced behind him. "Proceed with the test-fire."

"No," Noah muttered, stepping closer.

One of the Fields Ops and Security agents jabbed the shock-stick into Noah's middle and unleashed its fury. Noah dropped to the ground, crying out in agony.

"Don't do it," Noah screamed.

There was a loud pop, and for a moment Noah thought the colossus cannon had fired, but it hadn't. Captain Gibson glanced up toward the sky in surprise. A few moments later, Noah heard the high-pitched sound of a combat shuttle's engines coming toward them. The colossus cannon hadn't fired. What he'd heard was the sonic boom of a ship reentering New Earth's atmosphere.

Three CDF combat shuttles flew overhead and landed nearby. Noah regained his feet, and Lenora helped to steady him. He glanced over and a slow smile crossed his face. CDF soldiers were pouring out of the shuttle, their dark blue uniforms appearing like a godsend. A group of them were making their way toward them.

Noah straightened and saluted. "Colonel," he said.

Colonel Cross returned his salute. "Sitrep, Captain."

The Field Ops and Security forces lowered their shock-sticks but stayed in formation. Noah was sure this had everything to do with the armed CDF soldiers that stood behind Colonel Cross.

Captain Gibson pushed his way through his men, his piggish eyes glaring. "Captain Raeburn Gibson, ma'am, and I'm in charge here."

Colonel Cross regarded Gibson frostily. "I wasn't speaking to you, but since you're here, are you the one who assaulted men under my command?"

Captain Gibson glanced at the armed CDF soldiers and then back at Colonel Cross. "It was your soldiers who assaulted me first."

"We'll see about that," Colonel Cross said and turned toward Noah. "Captain Barker. Front and center."

"Yes, ma'am," Noah said and noticed Lenora smiling at him in a big-sisterly way. "Field Ops Captain Gibson was trying to test-fire the colossus cannon. We've been adapting the alien power station here. I informed Captain Gibson that this would overload the system, but he decided to use Field Ops to force us to bring the cannon online."

Colonel Cross swung her gaze back to Gibson, who flinched. "Explain yourself, Field Ops Captain."

Colonial Defense Force authority superseded any authority the Field Ops captain had, and he knew it. "The people are scared. I was trying to demonstrate our ability to protect them."

Colonel Cross arched an eyebrow. "Forcibly?" she said, and Gibson stubbornly met her gaze. Colonel Cross glanced to the soldier on her right. "Captain Gleason, take the Field Ops team into custody. Find somewhere to hold them, and I'll deal with them later."

"Excuse me, Colonel," Lenora said, "but I know of a place you can use."

"Thank you—" Colonel Cross said and stopped.

"Dr. Bishop," Lenora said.

Colonel Cross frowned. "Lenora Bishop?"

"You can't do this!" Captain Gibson cried while struggling with a CDF soldier.

"That's about enough of that, Captain," Colonel Cross snapped. "If you don't get yourself under control, I'll order my soldiers to gag you. Is that understood?"

Captain Gibson's face paled.

Colonel Cross leaned forward. "And just because I'm feeling a bit indulgent, I'll tell you another reason why firing that cannon as a way to make everyone feel better for a few fleeting moments is a bad idea. The Vemus are coming. Long-range scanners detected the discharge of orbital defense weapons. In other words, your pitiful attempt to get your gun off would have painted a great big target in the one place we don't want the Vemus to find. Does that clear up any misgivings you might have had?"

Captain Gibson's mouth made a wide circle, but no words came out.

Colonel Cross looked at Captain Gleason. "As you were, Captain."

Noah watched as the Field Operations and Security team was escorted away from the mobile Command Center.

"Dr. Bishop, would you join me inside?" Colonel Cross said. "And you too, Captain Barker."

Noah followed them inside and went to the nearest terminal to make sure the startup power sequence for the colossus cannon had been properly shut down.

"Please, call me Lenora."

Colonel Cross nodded. "And you can call me Savannah."

Noah stepped away from the terminal and looked at Colonel Cross.

"Go ahead and ask, Captain," Colonel Cross said.

"I thought you were in command of Phoenix Station, ma'am," Noah said.

He watched as the colonel pressed her lips together to suppress a sneer.

"Ordinarily, I would dress you down for asking that kind of question of a superior officer, but General Gates and a few others have warned me of some of your eccentricities," Colonel Cross said.

Noah felt his cheeks redden. "Apologies, Colonel."

Colonel Cross glanced at Lenora. "It seems that General Gates is a bit of a stickler for certain rules and regulations."

Lenora snorted. "When it wins him an argument."

Colonel Cross chuckled. "You *are* the Lenora I've heard about."

"I'm not sure what you mean."

"It's not important," Colonel Cross said. "General Gates has sent me to Sanctuary, and I need to know our state of readiness."

Noah still didn't understand why Connor would send someone as capable as Savannah Cross to Sanctuary when the Vemus were coming, but he didn't need to understand to follow his orders. Colonel Cross had a reputation for not tolerating nonsense.

"One hundred thousand refugees are at Sanctuary. The colossus cannon is operational, but we've been experiencing power fluctuations from the alien power station, ma'am," Noah said.

"Can you fix it?" Colonel Cross asked.

"The power station is hundreds of years old. If I had enough time, I'd say it would be better to put our own reactor here, ma'am," Noah said.

"Break it down for me. Can we fire the cannon or not?" Colonel Cross asked.

Noah frowned. "We can, but—and this is a strong but—we can't predict the power fluctuations. The power converter we've installed attempts to manage them, but there's a significant risk that when the colossus cannon is fired in earnest, it could overload the entire system."

"So you're saying we have a gun that we can fire a few times, but if we sustain a high rate of fire the system will fail?" Colonel Cross asked.

"Yes, ma'am."

"What happens if the system fails?"

"It depends. The power converter could burn out, or if there's enough of an overload, we could lose the entire system in an explosion," Noah answered.

Colonel Cross blew out a breath and regarded him for a moment. "You have quite a reputation, so I know you've been working this problem for as long as you've been here."

"Thank you, ma'am," Noah said.

"I can tell you with absolute certainty that the Vemus are on their way here right now. We've engaged them at Sagan's line, and General Gates evacuated all nonessential personnel from Phoenix Station," Colonel Cross said.

Noah swallowed hard. "What happened?"

Colonel Cross leaned back against one of the desks. "We used your modified missile design and sent everything we had against them."

"Did it work?" Noah asked.

"At first. Then the Vemus launched countermeasures and were able to take out a high percentage of the HADES IV-Bs before they could reach their targets," Colonel Cross said, glancing at Lenora. "I'm not sure how much either of you knows."

"We haven't had any news," Lenora said.

"The Vemus are heading here in one massive ship, and the hull is made from the exoskeletal material we faced two months ago," Colonel Cross said.

"How big is the ship, Colonel?" Noah asked.

Colonel Cross looked at them grimly. "Twenty-two kilometers across."

Noah's eyes widened and he gasped. "That's not a ship. That's a flying city."

"We know the Vemus can absorb other ships. We think they've massed together somehow," Colonel Cross said.

"But why would they do that?" Lenora asked.

Colonel Cross shrugged. "This is likely their answer to our defenses. Together in one massive ship, they represent a single overwhelming force."

Noah's mind raced as he did the calculations. "We don't have enough missiles."

"No, we don't," Colonel Cross confirmed.

"What about the rest of the soldiers at Phoenix Station?" Lenora asked.

"They couldn't confirm the amount of damage we'd done. Phoenix Station still has other close-range weapons that will make the Vemus pay for every kilometer closer they get to New Earth," Colonel Cross said.

"What are their chances?" Lenora said, her eyes wide.

Colonel Cross looked at her solemnly and sighed. "I'm going to be honest with you. I'm sorry, but the chances of survival for anyone on Phoenix Station are virtually nonexistent."

Noah watched as Lenora's breath caught in her throat. Then her eyes flashed. "Connor has survived overwhelming odds before."

"I know. I was there. I wish I could tell you something different to give you some hope, but that would be a disservice to you," Colonel Cross said.

Lenora turned away from them. "I need to get some air," she muttered and fled the Command Center.

Noah looked at the colonel, and she nodded for him to speak.

"What do you need me to do, Colonel?" Noah asked.

"You have a little bit of time. I need that cannon operational for as long as you can give me. What we cannot have is blowing ourselves up in the process. You tell me what you need and I'll try and get it for you," Colonel Cross said.

Noah nodded, feeling suddenly lighter because Colonel

Cross was there, but then he was dragged back down by the impending invasion. He began with what anyone solving complex problems should do, which was to start by listing their assets. Then they could come up with a plan of action. Noah and Colonel Cross got to work. He didn't know why Connor would have sent her here, but he was glad he had.

18

CAPTAIN WALKER WAITED outside the dull gray doors to the munitions factory aboard a large chunk of Vemus warship wreckage. He'd been watching the Vemus forces through the small window. Their skin was a deep, dark purple that glistened in the light. Their rounded heads angled to a pointed snout with lighter-toned oval shapes where Jon expected the eyes would be. They were clustered at the far end of the room. One of the Vemus towered above the others and pounded against the door while the others tried to beat their fists against the wall.

I'm coming, Brian, Jon thought. He could barely see the salvage team trapped in the room on the far side of the munitions factory floor. He checked his rifle and set the nano-robotic ammunition to incendiary. The high heat rounds worked best at disabling Vemus, according to his combat suit computer. Sergeant Lee and Lieutenant Chester hastened down the corridor. They'd just finished setting up the heavy turret, leaving the ammunition box attached. Jon accessed the heavy turret's camera and controls through his combat suit's systems. All systems were ready.

"Locked and loaded, Captain," Sergeant Lee said.

"Check your weapons," Jon said.

There was a flurry of activity as they all did one final check of their equipment, along with that of the people around them.

"We're ready, Captain," Lieutenant Chester said, giving him a determined look.

"Go ahead, Sergeant Lee, if you please," Jon said.

"Detonating the first group," Sergeant Lee said.

Jon heard the faint pops of the concussive charges and watched to see if the Vemus had heard anything. The Vemus soldiers ceased all activity and became rigidly still.

Sergeant Lee held up two of his fingers. There were more pops even louder than before. The Vemus soldiers began moving off to the side and out of sight—a few at a time at first and then more and more.

"It's working!" Jon said.

All the Vemus had run off, leaving the area. Jon slapped his palm against the door controls and the age-old contraption sputtered as the gears pulled the doors apart. They went inside. Jon kept the heavy turret's camera feed in the upper right corner of his heads-up display. There was still no sign of the Vemus.

"Blow the third group," Jon said.

He didn't wait for Sergeant Lee to respond but kept moving forward. They crouched as they ran, using the munitions factory lines as cover. Tall metal racks stood along the left side of the factory where two-hundred-year-old mag-cannon projectiles were secured in place. There were countless tips of two-meter projectiles perfectly aligned where the NA Alliance Navy had left them. Jon focused in on the room at the far end, and an IR channel opened to his combat suit.

"Jon, is that you?" Brian asked in disbelief.

"We've lured them away. This is your chance to get out. Come on, let's go," Jon said.

Jon heard someone shouting over the comms channel. They were yelling for Brian to open the door.

"What are you waiting for?" Jon asked.

"Jon, please stop," Brian said. "It's not safe for you. Take your team and get out of here."

"What are you talking about?" Jon asked.

He noticed some movement from the video feed of the heavy turret. The Vemus were making a sweep of the area. Jon and the others reached the end of the line of racks and stopped. He held his AR-71 ready and peered around the corner. The Vemus were gone. They hadn't left anyone to guard the prisoners. Jon crossed over to the door where Brian waited. The door control panel was broken and charred.

"Stop. We've been infected. We can't go back with you even if we wanted to," Brian said.

Jon heard more shouting and saw Captain Davis screaming for his brother to open the door.

Brian was pointing a pistol at Captain Davis. "Stay back," Brian said. "I'll shoot."

Another IR channel connected to Jon's combat armor.

"Walker, your brother is crazy. We're not infected. Tell him to let us go," Captain Davis said.

"Brian, you've got to calm down. We can figure this out. Come with me," Jon said.

He heard Lieutenant Chester mention they were running out of time.

Brian turned back toward the window. "Trust me, Jon," Brian said.

Jon felt as if he were hearing an echo of every time Brian had asked him to trust him. They were only a year apart in age, and no matter what they were doing, his younger brother was always there for him. Even after Jon left, Brian was always there when it counted.

Captain Davis screamed for Jon to open the door.

"Sir, the Vemus are at the turret," Sergeant Lee said.

"Activate the turret," Jon ordered.

He looked back through the window, trying to find some sign that the people inside the room were infected.

"You don't look sick," Jon said.

Brian swallowed. "We are. We've all been exposed. First comes the virus and then the parasite, except it works like nothing we've ever seen before. The virus alters the DNA of the host, allowing the parasite in, which takes over the host. It causes genes to express at an astonishing rate—never mind that. We're already dead."

Jon felt his throat become thick. "What if you're wrong?"

Brian glared at him. "Do I tell you how to fly a ship? Shoot a gun? No, because you know what you're doing. I'm *not* wrong."

"How did you even get exposed?" Jon asked.

Brian shook his head. "No time. There's more, much more I learned about them. Things the CDF can use. They're like nothing we've ever seen."

An uplink registered with Jon's combat suit computer using an active comlink. Jon's eyes widened. The Vemus could detect active comlinks.

"What are you doing? You'll bring them right to us!" Jon said.

"It's the only way to transfer the data fast enough. IR bandwidth is too narrow and the transfer will take too long," Brian said.

Jon slammed his fists against the metallic door. "What if you're wrong?"

Brian was watching Davis, who looked as if he were about to charge forward, pistol or not. Jon's gaze narrowed. Where were the salvage team's weapons? How did they only have a pistol? An alarm appeared on his internal heads-up display. The heavy turret was nearly out of ammunition. The video feed showed a corridor littered with the bodies of Vemus soldiers. There was a moving shadow along the ceiling, and the feed cut out. The heavy turret was offline.

"Captain—" Lieutenant Chester cried.

"I know," Jon said and looked back at his brother behind the smudgy window. A series of high-pitched whistles and clicks came from the corridor.

"Contact!" Sergeant Lee shouted.

Jon swung his rifle up and fired his weapon at a Vemus soldier. He took cover by the nearest rack, and the rest of the team did the same. They kept the Vemus pinned in the corridor. Dark liquid burst from their bodies. White bolts flew by as the Vemus returned fire.

Jon heard a startled cry from the IR channel and then heard the pistol go off from inside the room. Jon called out for his brother. The door opened, and Brian stumbled out of the room. Jon went to take a step toward him and then stopped. He couldn't risk it since Brian was infected.

Jon glanced at the grisly mess inside the room. "What have you done?" he said. Brian had killed the surviving members of the salvage team.

"They captured us. Caught us by surprise," Brian said.

Jon looked at the splatter of blood on Brian's EVA suit. He wasn't wearing a helmet, and there was a layer of thick black mucus ringed around his neck.

Brian threw his pistol down. "Give me your rifle. I'll hold them off for as long as I can."

"Captain, we can't stay here. We have to leave. Now!" Lieutenant Chester said.

Jon looked over at his team as they continued to lay suppressing fire toward the Vemus.

Brian rushed toward him and tried to grab his rifle. Jon spun away.

"Go, Jon. Get the data to CDF command. The key to stopping them is in there," Brian said.

Jon gritted his teeth and growled. He turned and fired his weapon at the Vemus. They were clustering in the doorway and were about to charge. A white bolt slammed into the end of the rack and knocked Jon off his feet. Hands grabbed him and he was pulled back. Jon regained his feet and saw that Brian was holding his rifle. Brian roared and then charged the Vemus, firing the AR-71 at full auto.

Jon cried out as his team pulled him away. He heard Brian screaming in rage until he was suddenly cut off.

"He's gone. We have to go, Captain," Lieutenant Chester said and took point, leading them away.

Sergeant Lee pushed him forward and Jon followed Lieutenant Chester, stumbling in a half daze. They reached another door and Jon withdrew his pistol. White bolts slammed into the door as it opened. They returned fire and hastened through the exit. There was movement to the right, and Jon fired his weapon. The Vemus charged toward them. Jon and the rest of the team ran away, firing a few rounds before retreating more. They came to the end of the corridor, and an explosive force slammed him against the wall. This place was coming apart. Jon and the others scrambled to their feet and headed for the ship in an all-out run. High-pitched whistles and clicks from the Vemus followed them. Jon glanced behind him and saw the Vemus closing in on them, propelling themselves on all fours and quickly eating up their small lead.

Jon tripped over something and dove to the ground, sliding down the corridor. He heard someone cry out as he quickly regained his feet. Specialist Thoran was sprawled on the ground behind him. He was climbing to his feet when the Vemus reached him. Jon watched in horror as a Vemus grabbed Specialist Thoran and hauled him back into the mass of soldiers as if he weighed nothing at all.

The big Vemus soldier turned back around, and its pointed snout revealed a line of sharp teeth. Jon fired his weapon, hitting it in the chest and muscled shoulders. The Vemus went down and then struggled to rise.

Sergeant Lee grabbed him. "He's gone. We have to go."

They turned and ran, heading for the airlock. Jon was the last one inside and they quickly shut the door. Jon looked through the window and saw the Vemus soldier he'd just shot rise to his feet and charge toward the airlock doors.

They ran into the combat shuttle.

"Cover that door," Jon said and ran toward the cockpit.

The combat shuttle was on standby and quickly came to full power. He heard something slamming against the shuttle's airlock doors. He disengaged the docking clamps and used the maneuvering thrusters to get away from the wreckage. Outside the shuttle's windows he saw dark shapes pouring out of the airlock into the vacuum. Jon didn't wait around. He engaged the main engines and sped away. Once they reached a safe distance, he fired a pair of hornet missiles, targeting the wreckage. There was a bright flash as the large chunk was blown apart.

"Captain, we have to follow decontamination protocols," Corporal Sims called out.

Jon inputted the coordinates for Lunar Base and set the navigation system on auto. It would be slow going since they were in a debris field, but he wasn't in a rush to go anywhere.

Jon climbed out of the chair and headed to the rear of the shuttle. He heard Sergeant Lee arguing with Corporal Sims.

"Captain, tell him to remain on his own life support. We have to follow emergency decontamination protocols, which now includes the shuttle," Corporal Sims said.

Jon looked over at Sergeant Lee, who was rocking back and forth, not making eye contact with anyone. He kept muttering about needing to get out of his combat suit.

"Roger, look at me," Jon said.

Sergeant Lee looked up at him.

"I need you to stay in that suit just a little longer. Can you do that?" Jon asked. His head was pounding and he felt like everything was trying to push its way out, but he tried to appear as calm as he sounded. "Alright. Just sit tight for a moment. We need to make sure we're not contaminated," Jon said.

Sergeant Lee gave a slight nod and continued to rock back and forth.

Jon looked back at Corporal Sims. "He'll be alright. Remind me again what we need to do."

Corporal Sims swallowed hard. "We need to vent the shuttle for a few minutes. The exposure should take care of anything that might have gotten on our suits."

Jon nodded. "Lieutenant Chester, prepare to vent the shuttle. Once we're vented, we'll open the rear hatch."

"Yes, Captain," Lieutenant Chester said and went to the rear of the shuttle.

There was a loud hiss as their atmosphere was sucked out of the shuttle. Auto-tethers attached to the back of their combat suits. Jon knew it was just a precaution, but he wouldn't want to risk being sucked out of the shuttle without a tether attached.

"Atmosphere vented. Opening the hatch and shutting down the heaters," Lieutenant Chester said.

The rear hatch opened and the debris field spread out before them. They waited the allotted time for the extreme cold to kill any microorganism they'd been exposed to on the Vemus ship.

Corporal Sims scanned them with the bioscanner. "We're clear, Captain."

"Close it up, Lieutenant," Jon said.

The rear hatch closed and they pressurized the shuttle. The heaters quickly brought the shuttle's interior up to acceptable temperatures and they were able to get out of their combat suits.

Sergeant Lee came over to him. "I'm sorry, Captain. Not sure what came over me. It was as if everything was closing in on me."

"It's fine, Sergeant. You stayed in control and followed orders," Jon said.

Jon felt his chest clench. Brian was gone. His brother was dead and they'd lost Specialist Thoran.

"We need to talk about what happened, Captain," Lieutenant Chester said.

Sorrow closed up his throat for a moment and Jon swallowed hard.

"Captain?" Lieutenant Chester asked softly.

"I'm alright. I just need a second, Daron," Jon said and looked away.

He squeezed his eyes shut and rubbed his forehead, feeling the stinging behind his eyes. "Damn it, Brian! Why did you have to go on that mission?" he said and looked at the others. "He should have been in the lab, not out on some salvage recon mission."

Lieutenant Chester regarded him for a moment. "What did he say happened?"

"He said they'd been captured. They were infected," Jon said.

Lieutenant Chester frowned. "I saw the room. He shot all of them."

Jon winced, remembering the sight of the dead salvage team members. "He said they were already dead."

"You knew him best. Could he have just lost it? You know, cracked under the pressure of being captured?" Lieutenant Chester asked.

Jon thought about it and shook his head. "Brian never lost his temper or anything like that. He was strong. He knew what he was doing. He was—"

Jon winced as a wave of grief slammed into him. He forced it back. "He wasn't crazy."

"What do we do now?" Corporal Sims asked.

Jon sighed. "We go back to Lunar Base."

"Empty-handed. We couldn't even rescue them," Sergeant Lee said.

"Not empty-handed. Brian learned something while they were on that wreckage. He said it was something we could use to stop the Vemus. We have to get the data he uploaded to my suit back to Lunar Base," Jon said.

"What's in the data?" Lieutenant Chester asked.

"I don't know, but I think it's time we have a look and see what was worth them dying for, don't you?" Jon replied.

19

CONNOR SAT in the commander's chair at Phoenix Station's main Command Center. Despite taking massive amounts of damage, the Vemus Alpha had increased speed after the Colonial Defense Force's surprise attack. They'd had the high-res optical array focused on the Vemus Alpha ship, and the images showed massive impacts to the colossal ship. Deep chasms were revealed in the exoskeletal hull that hadn't started to regenerate, but the ship hadn't altered course either.

Phoenix Station was directly in its path.

"General," Lieutenant Daniels said. "I have Captains Mason and Saunders from the Bravo and Charlie sub-Command Centers on comms."

"Put them through to my station, Lieutenant," Connor replied.

The holoscreen flickered on, and Captain Wade Mason and Captain Evelyn Saunders appeared on his screen.

"Station separation is just about ready. Can you confirm your status?" Connor asked.

"Bravo station is ready for separation from the main, General," Captain Mason said.

"Charlie station is ready as well, General," Captain Saunders said.

"Very well. We'll stay networked for as long as possible so our attacks can be coordinated, but I'm going to level with both of you. At some point it won't be possible. In that moment, your only mandate is to fire your station's weapons at the enemy for as long as possible. Is that clear?" Connor asked.

"Yes, General," the two captains said.

Connor looked at the station sub-commanders on his holoscreen. Beneath the brave facade were two officers as green as anyone else untested in combat. He'd considered reassigning Major Elder to one of the substations but decided to keep him at Phoenix Station Main with him. One went into battle with the army one had.

"This is what we trained for. Remember your training. We have an objective to achieve. It's as simple as that," Connor said.

"We won't let you down, General," Captain Mason said.

"I know you won't. Now, the second wave of our attack will begin once we reach our target coordinates. Good luck to you both," Connor said.

Both captains repeated the sentiment. They knew the stakes and thought they knew what it was going to be like when the end finally came. But Connor had been in enough dangerous situations to know that when death does finally claim you, it's when you least expect it. He cut the comlink, and the holoscreen powered off.

Phoenix Station was made up of ten large sections. Each of the sections could be self-contained and operate autonomously, though there were only three Command Centers. Connor had decided to break Phoenix Station up into three primary sections, with the central section containing four subsections while the two remaining groups were comprised of three subsections. He thought that the Vemus Alpha having multiple targets would enable the CDF to strike another devastating blow. Over sixty-five percent of the HADES IV-B missiles had reached their target before the Vemus unleashed their countermeasures that took out the command-and-control units. If all the Command Centers were to become inoperable, the burden of engaging the enemy would fall to individual gun-battery commanders.

"At least the wave of Condor missiles is over," Major Elder said. He sat in the executive officer's station next to Connor.

"I think they fired them just to give us something to do," Connor said.

"They fired thousands of missiles at us to occupy us until they could get here to finish the job? I'm not sure I understand those tactics," Major Elder said.

"Condor missiles are the NA Alliance Military's design for long-range engagements. Our HADES IV-Bs have better targeting systems," Connor said.

"Thank god for that," Major Elder said.

Connor agreed. In addition, their point-defense lasers were able to confuse the Condor missiles' guidance systems enough that they could disable them completely. Once compromised, the fact that the Condor missiles didn't retarget reaffirmed Connor's conclusion that those missiles weren't the real attack. It had been a bullying tactic by an enemy that knew the superiority of its position and attack force.

"Ops, has there been any detection of the Vemus control signal?" Connor asked.

"Negative, General," Lieutenant Rawn said.

"Alright," Connor said. He strongly believed that the Vemus had other ships tucked away in that Alpha, but they hadn't detected them. "You're a go to disengage station sections three and eight," Connor said.

"Confirmed, General. Disengaging sections three and eight," Lieutenant Rawn said.

Connor looked at the main holoscreen, which showed a live video feed of the locking clamps that held Phoenix Station together. There was a brief flash that simultaneously appeared on all the video feeds.

"Station sections disengaged, General," Lieutenant Rawn said.

"Acknowledged," Connor said.

He watched as the maneuvering thrusters pushed the two sections away from them. He glanced over to his left and noted the empty space beside him. It had been nearly fifteen hours since he'd sent Colonel Cross and Major Quinn back to New Earth, but he still found himself looking for Sean. He didn't regret his decision to put Sean in charge of the CDF ground forces, but he did miss him.

"General," Major Elder said.

Connor looked up and saw Captain Randle walking toward the command area. Standing at six feet, seven inches tall, Wayne Randle was a giant among men. The working CDF soldiers seemed to part ways, allowing the big man to pass.

"Good of you to join us, Bull," Connor said, using the designation he'd given Captain Randle in Search and Rescue all those years before.

"Wouldn't miss this, General. I've come to inform you that most of the drill-mines have successfully sent in return statuses," Captain Randle said.

"So they made it to the Vemus Alpha," Connor said.

"Yes, they should be drilling beneath that exoskeleton of theirs, sir," Captain Randle said.

"Should? We don't know for sure, Captain Randle?" Major Elder asked.

"No, Major. This is a low-tech solution whereby we can receive only a confirmation that they reached the surface of the Vemus Alpha. The timer starts and they'll detonate the explosive payload at whatever level they reach," Captain Randle said.

"Is there any way to determine how deep those drills will get before they detonate, Captain?" Major Elder asked.

"It depends on how thick that exoskeletal hull is and when those drill heads come into contact with the hardened alloy of the battle-steel hull of a ship. The drill heads can chew through quite a bit before they'll eventually dull. We've staggered the timers so when they *do* detonate, we can maximize the damage to the ship. Worst case is that the drill-heads are only able to penetrate twenty or so meters before they detonate, sir," Captain Randle said.

"Thank you, Captain," Connor said.

"General, with your permission I'd like to stay by your side," Captain Randle said.

Connor arched a brow while considering. "Did Major Quinn happen to put you up to this?"

"I can neither confirm nor deny that Major Quinn sent me any informal instructions upon his departure from Phoenix Station, General," Captain Randle said with only a hint of a smile appearing over his wide jaw.

Connor snorted. "Alright, Captain. You can help Captain Thorne at Tactical."

"Yes, General," Captain Randle said and went over to the tactical work area.

Connor looked over at the PRADIS output on one of the secondary holoscreens. The Vemus Alpha was still coming steadily toward them. It hadn't changed its trajectory and

Connor couldn't order Phoenix Station to be moved. They would make their stand here. He opened a broadcast channel.

"This is General Gates. By now you've been informed that we're about to begin our engagement with the enemy. We drew the line here on the doorstep to our home. Thousands of people are depending on us. For the first time in human history, we're fighting for something that's unprecedented—our right to survive as a species. On this day we will stand together and in one voice scream into the void. Our enemy will know what we can do—that we will not be vanquished without a fight. This was to be a colony founded upon peace, moving beyond the hundreds of years of conflicts throughout history. None of you deserve to have to fight in this war. None of our families deserve to die at the hands of our enemies. We few, standing here, looking into the mouth of the dragon and showing our enemy what we're worth, are all that stands between us and them, to stop them from killing us all. We stand together. We fight together. And we'll *die* together if that's what it takes. Many of you know who I am, that I used to serve with an elite special-forces platoon. We were legends. But all of you are part of the Colonial Defense Force and are much more than the Ghosts ever were. You fight for something beyond anything we ever did. The Ghosts had a motto, and I'll give it to you. Remember these words as we face our enemy. 'We are the unsung heroes. We are the quiet protectors. We roam through the darkest nights and through the deepest valleys. We choose to stand the watch. No enemy is beyond our power. We are the Colonial Defense Force!'"

The soldiers in the command area cheered.

"Ten-hut!" Captain Randle's voice boomed.

The cheering CDF soldiers became quiet almost instantly as

all of them stood with their arms at their sides and their shoulders back at attention.

"CDF salute!" Captain Randle shouted.

As one, the CDF soldiers saluted Connor. He raised his chin and felt his chest swell with pride as he returned the salute in kind. The soldiers returned to their stations with renewed vigor.

Major Elder leaned toward Connor. "Thank you, sir. They needed that, and, frankly, so did I."

Connor nodded grimly. "Too bad pretty speeches won't stop the Vemus."

"I had no idea that the NA Alliance Special Forces had a motto like that, sir," Major Elder said.

Connor glanced at the major. There was no one on this station who knew the truth.

Major Elder frowned and his eyes widened.

"I'll say whatever I need to so the men and women in the CDF can focus on their jobs," Connor said.

Major Elder nodded. "I understand, sir."

"I know you do. Now, we have a job to do," Connor said.

Connor went back to the command chair. "Tactical, what's the status of the Vemus Alpha?"

"They're within energy weapons range. We were keeping the kinetic weapons in reserve, General," Captain Thorne said.

"I need a firing solution targeting the damaged areas of the enemy ship. Let's see if we can peel back a few more layers and make them bleed some more," Connor said.

"Yes, General," Captain Thorne said. A few minutes passed. "Firing solution ready. Specs are on the main holoscreen, General."

Connor looked up at the screen. "One change to that, Captain. Phoenix Station Main will fire first, then Bravo and Charlie sections."

"Yes, General, updating targeting parameters now," Captain Thorne replied. Connor waited for confirmation from Bravo and Charlie sections.

"Fire!" Connor said.

As the twenty-two-kilometer Vemus Alpha blasted through space, heading for Phoenix Station, a rounded projector swiveled above one of the top sections of the main Phoenix Station group. The magnetic actuators steered the stored-up energy to a wide-open port, and a thick particle beam of protons shot forth in a lance of pale blue light. The proton beam penetrated the Vemus exoskeletal hull before it had to be cycled. Moments later, beams from Bravo and Charlie subsections also cut deeply into the hull of the enemy ship.

"Vemus Alpha taking damage, General," Captain Thorne said.

"Keep firing on them. Ready plasma cannons," Connor said.

They had to keep hitting the enemy ship for as long as they could, and Connor approved the plasma cannon firing solution. Phoenix Station's stabilizing engines went into overdrive to keep them in position. The lights in Phoenix Station's Command Center dimmed as the plasma cannons charged off the main reactor. Next, Connor heard the rapid cadence of magnetically encased plasma bolts being fired into the vacuum. As the bolts traveled, the fusion cores reached a maximum yield in the multi-megaton range. The superheated plasma bolts slammed into the Vemus Alpha. The power draw from Phoenix Station's multiple fusion reactor cores was immense. Connor had the engineers override the safeties so they could run the reactors at critical levels. They needed every ounce of power they could get. Unlike when the Vemus had faced Titan Station, which operated at half the capacity possible, Phoenix Station had an excess of power yield. The reactor cores had been designed for a Barracuda-class battleship carrier and could handle the load.

"Vemus Alpha taking heavy damage, General," Captain Thorne said.

Connor looked at the tactical data feeds. The cyber-warfare AI disseminated and correlated data coming in from all their sensor arrays, giving the CDF the most accurate picture possible of the damage they were doing to the enemy.

"Proton beams are cycling through a down cycle, General," Captain Thorne said.

"Enable Kraken firing solution now," Connor ordered.

Rail-cannons came online. The Vemus Alpha was within kinetic weapons range, which also put Phoenix Station within the known weapons range of the Vemus Alpha. Connor glanced at the latest image of the Alpha. There were immense gashes gouged away from the exoskeletal hull, revealing the dark innards beneath, but it was a blackened section eight kilometers across that seemed to be the soft spot.

"Focus targeting on that dark section off the center," Connor said.

The rail-cannons fired a range of two-to-three-meter projectiles in rapid succession. The long barrels swiveled from side to side, giving the projectiles time to penetrate as deeply as possible before more of them hit. Connor watched as they unloaded Phoenix Station's vast arsenal into the most damaged parts of the Vemus Alpha. He squinted as he tried to make out the details of the visual on the holoscreen.

"Several large pieces of Vemus Alpha's hull have broken away," Captain Thorne announced.

Connor's pulse raced, and Major Elder looked over at him with a hungry gleam in his eyes.

"Don't let up. Keep hitting those spots," Connor said.

"Yes, General," Captain Thorne said.

"General, we're getting multiple reports of weapons overload," Captain Randle said.

"Adjust firing rate down to seventy-five percent and decrease in five percent increments as needed," Connor said.

There were limits to what their weapons could do, but he had to push it. They were breaking the enemy apart.

"Multiple energy signatures being detected on the Vemus Alpha," Captain Thorne announced.

Connor shared a grim glance with Major Elder. Their luck was running out. The Vemus Alpha was about to show them their teeth.

"Incoming enemy fire!" Captain Thorne said.

Connor watched as the tactical holodisplay showed a bright flash of light lancing toward them, and he gripped the sides of his chair as the colossal blast slammed into Phoenix Station with unrelenting force. Connor gritted his teeth, and klaxon alarms blared throughout the Command Center.

"General, we've lost subsection seven. It's showing as completely offline," Captain Thorne said.

Subsection seven held over three hundred CDF soldiers, and their lives had been snuffed out in the blink of an eye.

"Damage report," Connor said.

"Bulkhead doors have sealed off the damaged sections. We've lost twenty percent weapons capability," Captain Thorne said and frowned as new data appeared on his screen.

"What is the status of Bravo and Charlie stations?" Connor asked.

Captain Thorne remained focused on his screen as if he couldn't quite believe what he was seeing.

"Charlie station has been completely destroyed," Captain Randle announced.

Connor gasped and brought up the data feed. Charlie station was completely offline.

"Bravo station is still firing their weapons on the enemy ship," Captain Thorne said.

Connor looked at PRADIS, and the Vemus Alpha was closing in on them. "What the hell are they hitting us with?"

He couldn't think of anything in the NA Alliance arsenal that had such a high yield.

"Tactical, update targeting priority to target their main weapons," Connor ordered.

Connor clenched his teeth. They had to disable those weapons or they were sitting ducks.

"Updates inputted into targeting computers," Captain Thorne said.

The Vemus Alpha fired its main weapon, and a lance of molten plasma blazed toward Bravo Station, burning at two billion degrees Kelvin. The interior of the plasma lance burned hotter than the interior of the sun. The hardened alloy of the battle-steel armor plating didn't stand a chance as the plasma lance sliced through Bravo Station, cutting it down the middle. The Vemus restarted their terrible weapons to finish them off. Plasma lances stemmed from three main batteries on the Vemus Alpha, and they were all pointed at Bravo Station. Phoenix Station Main fired their remaining weapons—which consisted of much less powerful plasma cannons and rail-cannons—at the enemy ship. They pelted the regions around the Vemus Alpha's primary weapons systems. One of them went offline and the plasma lance simply stopped, but it was too late for Bravo Station.

Connor ordered them to go to their own life support. Their battle uniforms were comprised of a thin layer of EVA-suit material, and the thick collars stored an emergency helmet. The

Vemus Alpha retargeted their remaining weapons on Phoenix Station Main. Connor could still hear their own weapons firing, for all the good it would do. Multiple systems went offline as the Vemus Alpha's weapon cut them apart. The stabilizing engines were damaged, and Phoenix Station Main rolled onto its back, exposing its belly for the enemy ship to strike. Another blow of unrelenting force struck the station, and the last thing Connor saw was a brilliant flash of light before everything went dark.

20

NATHAN HAD SCHEDULED the watches so he'd be on duty when Phoenix Station finally engaged the Vemus Alpha ship. The bulk of Lunar Base was located more than a kilometer underground. They'd used the lunar crust as a natural barrier that protected them from the dangers of being exposed on the lunar surface. While the moon did have an iron core that provided a weak magnetic field to protect them from cosmic rays and gamma bursts, it couldn't do anything to prevent the level of destruction he saw occurring on Phoenix Station. Despite the Vemus Alpha taking heavy damage, the enemy ship had closed the distance and then unleashed the full force of its weapons. Nathan and the rest of the CDF soldiers on duty in the Command Center had watched the data feeds flood in until Phoenix Station went offline. Ever since, the CDF staff in the Command Center of Lunar Base had taken to quietly working, with a soft buzz of activity that arose from hushed discussions.

Major Vanessa Shelton entered the Command Center and walked toward Nathan, coming to stand by his side.

"I thought I'd lend a hand, Colonel," Major Shelton said.

Nathan nodded. More than one off-duty officer had found their way to the Command Center, looking for something to do. Nathan certainly didn't want to take any downtime lest all the thoughts he'd been holding at bay threatened to overwhelm him.

"I'm glad you came because I can certainly use your help," Nathan said and shared the holoscreens he'd been working from with Major Shelton. "These are the latest projections of the damage Phoenix Station was able to do to the Vemus Alpha."

Major Shelton's eyes slid over the data as she studied it. Above the data was a three-dimensional graphical display of the Vemus Alpha, and it showed that large chunks of it had been destroyed during the attack. "Those sections toward the rear that are breaking away from the Alpha . . . are those . . .?"

"We think they're ships," Nathan said.

Major Shelton's eyes widened in shock for a moment. "Have these feeds been updated into our passive scanner data?"

"Yes. This is the latest iteration," Nathan said.

Several large ships had detached themselves from the Vemus Alpha's main hull.

"What would you do if you were the Vemus?" Nathan asked.

"There would be a lot of assumptions, but if my objective was to invade this world, I'd be keen to find any hidden defenses that might still be in place. Given how this war has been fought, I'd be expecting it," Major Shelton said.

"I agree. That's why I expect one of those ships to be sent here to look for any CDF presence," Nathan said.

"Well, we've evacuated the surface installations and moved people into the interior of the base. So, they could look for us, but they won't find us," Major Shelton said.

"Are you sure about that?" Nathan asked.

Major Shelton regarded Nathan for a moment. "Colonel, if

you think the enemy is wise to our presence here and an attack is imminent, shouldn't we be preparing to attack them?"

Nathan pressed his lips together. "That's the rub. We don't know what our enemy knows. Until we have credible evidence that suggests otherwise, we'll operate under the assumption that they don't know we're here."

"How much evidence would you need to order an attack, sir?" Major Shelton asked.

Nathan blew out a breath. "It's a fine line to walk. We'll need to maintain Dark-Star status for the time being, even as they insert their forces into orbit around New Earth."

Major Shelton swallowed hard. "Colonel . . ." she began. "Isn't there anything we can do? Phoenix Station weapons did a lot of damage. If we bring our systems online, we should be able to do as much damage, and perhaps even more."

"If we attack now, the Vemus would be expecting it. We need the element of surprise to maximize the damage we can do," Nathan replied.

"If we do that, the Vemus will be able to land an invasion force on the ground, sir," Major Shelton said.

"I know," Nathan said and then held up one of his hands. "When General Gates and I discussed the strategy for Lunar Base's role in defense of the planet, our best bet was to allow the enemy to be lulled into a false sense of security and then strike. It took me a while to see the wisdom of General Gates' thinking."

"But Colonel, if the Vemus reach the surface of the planet, we'd be risking the exposure of everything living on the planet to this viral parasite organism. What if it finds a way to spread itself among the creatures native to this world?" Major Shelton asked.

"Even our scientific experts believe that risk isn't as high as one would expect. The creatures of this world followed a very different evolutionary path. They're likely not as susceptible to the Vemus as we originally thought," Nathan replied.

Major Shelton frowned. "You mean because Earth scientists modified the viral strain?"

Nathan could tell that Major Shelton didn't think much of the gamble. "It's a risk. If we strike at the Vemus now, we'd do some damage, but we'd likely not stop them completely. They'd still get an invasion force onto the planet. Take that as a given. And if they defeat us, the Vemus can land as many of their troops on the ground as they want, knowing we have no more orbital defenses available."

"But isn't that their ultimate goal? Land their forces on the ground? They *are* hunting humans after all, sir," Major Shelton said.

"Yes, but it won't happen as fast as you might think," Nathan said. "First they'll need to assess the planet to find our cities, and that will take some time. All planetary broadcasts have been quiet since we first detected the Vemus presence. If the Vemus *did* somehow trace our communications, it would only lead them to communications satellites that have been powered down and put on standby. So it will take them some time to find Sierra and the other cities on the planet."

"I think I understand better now, Colonel," Major Shelton said.

"Also, if we strike at them while they're focused on getting their invasion force to the ground, they'll be even more vulnerable to attack," Nathan said.

"I agree, but . . ." Major Shelton said and stopped.

Nathan understood all too well. His first instinct was to strike out at the enemy and try to stop them in their tracks, but the fact of the matter was that the CDF couldn't prevent the Vemus Alpha from reaching New Earth. That became abundantly clear as the ship bludgeoned its way through Phoenix Station.

"Colonel, we're getting active comms signals," Sergeant Boers said.

Nathan looked over at the comms station. "From where?"

"Escape-pod frequency, Colonel," Sergeant Boers said.

Nathan felt his insides go cold. "How many pods are there?" Nathan asked, fearing the answer.

"Seven hundred in total, Colonel," Sergeant Boers said.

Nathan looked at the main holoscreen with the PRADIS output. It had been populated with the escape-pod broadcast signatures. Considering eight people to a pod, maximum, there could be over five thousand soldiers alive and in need of rescue.

"What are your orders, Colonel?" Lieutenant LaCroix asked from the tactical work area.

"Acknowledged receipt of escape-pod broadcast signatures. Dark-Star status will be maintained. Send no reply," Nathan said.

"But, Colonel—" Lieutenant LaCroix said.

"You've heard Colonel Hayes. You have your orders, Lieutenant," Major Shelton said sternly.

Nathan watched the main holodisplay grimly as the seven hundred escape-pod signatures were grayed out so they hardly had any impression on the display. Inwardly, Nathan was raging. He wanted to order a rescue mission and get those survivors to safety, but he knew it would be a foolish call.

"Colonel, one of the Vemus ships has broken away from the main group and is on an intercept heading with the escape pods," Lieutenant LaCroix said.

Nathan resisted the urge to rub his hands over his face. "Acknowledged," he said, his voice sounding strained.

A grim silence settled throughout the CDF soldiers serving in the command area. They were being forced to do something that went contrary to basic human nature—abandoning those who needed their help. Though it was in service of the greater objective, that was a cold comfort and Nathan hated himself for it, even if the strategist in him knew it was the right thing to do. If he somehow managed to survive this, would he even be able to look at himself in the mirror?

Over the next few hours, the Vemus Alpha slowly approached New Earth as the news of Phoenix Station's destruction spread throughout the base. Nathan had kept going through the data, hoping to find some indication that there were survivors other than those in the escape pods that had jettisoned. There wasn't any. Phoenix Station was nothing more than a debris field. The escape pods had ceased broadcasting as the Vemus ship came within their vicinity, and Lunar Base couldn't determine whether the Vemus had captured the seven hundred escape pods or simply destroyed them all. The only thing they knew for sure was that they had stopped broadcasting a signal.

Two ships broke away from the Vemus Alpha, heading toward New Earth's moon.

"Passive scans show the ships are Cruiser-class vessels, Colonel," Lieutenant LaCroix said.

Lunar Base was still getting data feeds from robotic scanning platforms they had in orbit around the planet, and they'd been tracking the Vemus Alpha since it crossed Sagan's line and then engaged Phoenix Station at the Lagrange point. The Vemus Alpha had decreased its acceleration, slowing its approach to the planet, while the Vemus cruisers were heading for the moon. The cruisers inserted themselves into a lunar synchronous orbit and were actively scanning the surface where the construction platforms had been.

"Colonel, they're charging their weapons," Lieutenant LaCroix said.

"Acknowledged," Nathan said. "Ops, confirm that those surface installations have been evacuated."

"Zero life-signs, Colonel--," Sergeant Martinez began. "Sir! I'm seeing activity at one of the smaller research and development facilities in sector twenty-seven."

Nathan frowned. "Comms, are their systems still attached to the internal network?"

Sergeant Boers worked through her terminal and nodded. "Yes, Colonel. Comms channel is available."

"Put me through," Nathan said.

"R&D outpost eight. This is Dr. Kendra Robinson."

"Dr. Robinson, you need to power down that outpost and head to your evacuation point immediately. We have two Vemus cruisers inbound," Nathan said.

"Negative, Colonel. We've received a data communication from Dr. Walker's salvage run that claims they've found critical information about the Vemus," Dr. Robinson said, her voice sounding spotty from the low-powered comms channel.

Nathan watched the scope as it showed the Vemus cruisers inbound to the R&D outpost. They only stopped to fire their weapons at the surface installations. "Doctor, you need to listen to me and get your people out of there. The Vemus ships are doing a reconnaissance flyover. They're taking out all surface installations."

Nathan was waiting for a reply when Lieutenant LaCroix suddenly shifted in his seat. "Colonel, I have a surface gun battery being brought online."

Nathan swore. "Find out who it is," he said and then switched back to the R&D outpost comms channel. "Dr. Robinson, confirm that you've heard me."

"We hear you, Colonel. Shutting down the outpost now," Dr. Robinson said.

Nathan closed the channel and glanced at Major Shelton. "Can they make it to the nearby shelter?"

"If they hurry, they can, Colonel," Major Shelton said.

Nathan swung his gaze toward Lieutenant LaCroix. "What's the status of the gun battery?"

"Colonel, they're refusing to shut it down. There's a Lieutenant Robinson who won't comply with your commands. He's switched on the manual override," Lieutenant LaCroix said.

Nathan frowned. "Robinson," he repeated and then his eyes widened. "Ops, get a security detail over there ASAP."

Nathan heard Sergeant Martinez begin speaking to a security detail in the area. He looked up at the screen. "Damn it, there's no time. LaCroix, can you cut the power to that gun battery?"

Lieutenant LaCroix's face became pale. "Sir, he's defending his wife."

"I know that, Lieutenant!" Nathan snapped. "It's them or all of us. Now cut the damn power to that gun battery. Shut it down!"

Lieutenant LaCroix swung his flustered gaze toward his console, and his hands flew through the interface. "Power has been cut off to the gun battery. I've locked out the override and closed the doors."

There was a bright flash on the main holoscreen video feed of the R&D outpost. One moment it was there and the next it was gone. Nathan's mouth went dry and he checked the surface scanners. No one from the R&D outpost had escaped. They were all dead.

"Ops, any change in the cruiser's flight pattern?" Nathan asked.

"Negative, Colonel. They're maintaining speed and heading," Sergeant Martinez said.

That was something at least.

"Ops, let me know when the security detail has Robinson in custody," Nathan said.

There were several surprised glances from the CDF soldiers in the command area. Nathan's brows pulled together sternly. "Listen up. We're at war. Anyone who fails to follow orders will be relieved of duty, brought up on charges of treason, and shot. Is that clear?"

"Yes, Colonel," the CDF soldiers in the area answered.

Nathan nodded grimly and felt a sneer lift his upper lip. But what surprised him was that he would carry out his threat. This was what it meant to survive, and the thought sickened him to no end.

21

MAJOR SEAN QUINN stood on the rooftop of the Colonial Defense Force Headquarters in Sierra. The sun shone brightly over the cradle of New Earth's first colonial city as it stretched out around him. Over a hundred and fifty thousand people had lived here. What had started out as an encampment for a few thousand colonists was well on its way to becoming a full-blown metropolis. He glanced upward, remembering the *Ark* as it had been when it was orbiting their new home. One of humanity's most ambitious efforts, the *Ark* had been the biggest ship he'd ever seen—so large, in fact, that it had been easily visible in New Earth's night sky even with the planetary rings that surrounded the planet.

He'd been among the first to be awakened after their two-hundred-year journey, and those early days of the colony seemed like a lifetime ago. So much had changed. Sean's gaze sank back to the city. The Vemus Alpha dwarfed even the *Ark*. A shiver traveled up Sean's spine, snapping him out of his reverie. He narrowed his gaze as he took in the city through the eyes of a defender. He saw the CDF soldiers setting up multiple defense installations in preparation for an invasion that was difficult for them to comprehend. Mostly, the installations were outfitted with RF mag-cannons whose mobile platforms not only allowed them to track targets in the sky but on the ground as well.

Connor had sent him back to New Earth with orders to defend Sierra. After reviewing their defenses and knowing the Vemus Alpha was on its way here, he wasn't sure how long the city *could* be defended.

To say that his presence was a surprise was an understatement, but when he'd informed the colonial government of his orders, they were met with little enthusiasm. He'd expected as much.

The door to the rooftop opened and Sean glanced over. Captain Juan Diaz strode over to him and saluted.

"We've received news from Phoenix Station, Major. Please come with me," Captain Diaz said.

"Last I checked, comlinks still worked," Sean replied.

Captain Diaz chuckled. "But they lack that personal touch, sir."

"Well, I better not keep them waiting," Sean said and started walking toward the door.

"Connor thinks the world of you, you know," Captain Diaz said.

Sean glanced at Diaz as they were heading back to the Command Center. "Becoming sentimental on me now?"

Captain Diaz chuckled. "It comes with being a father. And I remember seeing the look on Connor's face when he found you in that storage crate."

"He wouldn't have let me come otherwise," Sean replied, remembering how, seven years ago after being denied entry to the new Field Ops Search and Rescue team, he'd snuck into a storage crate bound for the remote training camp. He'd had no idea Connor intended to dump all the equipment and recruits out of the Hellcat transport for a low-altitude drop. Looking back on his actions, he realized how foolish a risk he'd taken. There were so many other ways he could have gotten to the training camp that wouldn't have required the risk of life and limb. Regardless, his life had been forever changed because of it.

Captain Diaz stopped in front of the door to the Command Center and looked at him. He leaned in. "Connor sent you back here to lead," Diaz said.

Sean frowned. "I know, but they aren't listening," he said.

"The CDF soldiers here will follow you. You just need to prove to the rest of them why they *should* listen to you. No one else here has faced the Vemus but you, sir," Captain Diaz said.

Sean remembered Juan Diaz being his superior officer when he was a fresh-faced recruit. Things had changed. Diaz had always insisted that he was only good for command at a certain level, while people like Connor operated at another level entirely. One thing Connor had instilled in the CDF ranks was to respect the uniform. The person who had that rank and uniform had earned it, something those outside of the CDF had trouble understanding. They judged by what they saw, and what they saw was a very young man who had attained a very high rank.

Sean gave Diaz a nod and then entered the Command Center.

Damon Mills, Director of Field Ops and Security Operations, glanced over at him. "Major Quinn, Phoenix Station has been destroyed. Transmitting the latest information from the station's data dump to you now."

Sean's lips pressed together in a white slash, and he used his neural implants to access the data. His internal smart lens projected the reports away from his eyes, so they were easily read by him, and the others around him couldn't see them. Sean quickly went through the preliminary report. The Vemus Alpha's primary weapon had been devastatingly effective.

"They were overwhelmed, but it looks like they did heavy damage as well," Sean said. "Call an emergency session of the city defense committee."

Director Mills relayed Sean's commands. "We can use the conference room over here."

Sean shook his head. "No need. We'll have the call right here. This won't take a lot of time."

"Most of the committee members are already here, and the ones that aren't can join in remotely," Director Mills said.

Sean frowned and peered over at the conference room. He saw his father pacing while speaking with other civilians around the conference table. Sean gritted his teeth and walked over. Damon Mills followed him.

"Why has Lunar Base gone quiet? These reports show that it hasn't used any of its weapons to engage that enemy ship," Parish said.

"We've been over this. General Gates' strategy was to keep Lunar Base in the dark to hide its presence from the enemy," Sean's father said.

"But with Phoenix Station—" Stanton Parish stopped speaking as Sean walked into the conference room. The committee members looked at Sean as if they weren't quite sure what to make of him.

"I see you've heard about Phoenix Station," Sean said.

"Yes, just a few minutes ago. We were just discussing it," Tobias replied.

Sean glanced behind him. "Captain Diaz," he said.

"Yes, Major," Captain Diaz replied.

"From now on, all CDF communications stay within CDF

channels unless I give my express permission for them to be shared," Sean said.

Tobias frowned.

"This includes Field Ops and Security," Sean said before anyone could protest.

"Right away, Major," Captain Diaz said and left the room.

"What are you doing?" Tobias asked him.

"Yes, why cut us out?" Stanton asked.

Sean drew in a deep breath. "Why don't you all sit down," he said and glanced back at Director Mills, who watched him warily. "You too, Director."

The defense committee members looked at his father, who nodded for them to sit. He then regarded Sean for a moment before doing the same.

Sean looked at Stanton Parish. "You're not being cut out. The comms officer didn't follow protocol for CDF briefings. This lapse will be rectified."

"What difference does it make if we read the same briefing that goes to the CDF?" Stanton asked.

"Because you're not qualified to read them. There's a reason that filter's in place," Sean said.

"I beg your pardon?" Stanton said, flustered.

"You heard me," Sean replied crisply. "The status of Phoenix Station is a military matter and should have come to me first. I heard what you were saying when I walked in. Why didn't Colonel Hayes at Lunar Base fire his weapons at the Vemus Alpha? That's what you were pressing for, is that right?"

"It's a valid question," Stanton said.

"It's not what General Gates ordered," Sean replied.

"But he might be dead for all we know," Stanton said.

"Phoenix Station is offline, and the status of CDF personnel is currently unknown," Sean said.

His father cleared his throat. "Don't you mean destroyed?"

Sean's gaze hardened. "I meant offline. Destroyed implies that there are no survivors, which I don't believe until we can do our own reconnaissance of the area. As you're aware, I've been given operational authority for the CDF ground forces." Sean looked over at Director Mills. "Since this is a wartime situation, this includes Field Operations and Security forces as well. I expect you to comply with these agreed-upon orders."

Director Mills pressed his lips together. "When we made those laws, we assumed General Gates would be the person leading the CDF."

Several heads were nodding in agreement.

"He still *is* leading the CDF," Sean replied coolly.

"Sean," his father said, "Phoenix Station is . . . offline. Colonel Savannah Cross is next in the chain of command."

"Let me be crystal clear with all of you. General Gates assigned Colonel Cross to Sanctuary, and he assigned me to command our ground forces. I don't require your agreement with the commands of my superiors in order to carry them out," Sean said.

His father's eyes widened. "What are you going to do? Arrest all of us?"

"No, but I will have you shipped out to Sanctuary on the next available transport. Civilians have no place in this fight. You'll only get in the way of the soldiers," Sean replied.

His father's gaze narrowed angrily. "What about Director Mills? Are you going to remove him and anyone else who gets in your way?"

"Stop this right now!" Sean said, slamming his fist on the table. "I can't afford to waste time convincing you who's in charge. My job is to defend this city from the Vemus forces, not to waste precious time mincing words with all of you."

His father started to speak again.

"I swear, if this is another protest, I'll have a squad of my soldiers escort the lot of you out of here right now," Sean said, glaring at his father.

Director Mills cleared his throat. "I think we all need to take a moment to calm down."

His father took a steadying breath, and Sean looked at Director Mills.

"I'm not going to challenge your authority," Director Mills said and then glanced at the other committee members. "We have laws we all agreed on. One thing I have absolute faith in is that General Gates does nothing without careful consideration. He's sent Major Quinn here on his authority, and I will respect that."

Tobias cleared his throat. "Can you tell us your strategy for defending the city?"

"I think we're forgetting the fact that Lunar Base is there with enough firepower to finish what Phoenix Station started," Stanton said.

"They *don't* have enough," Sean said. "I was there. I saw what was coming for us. Colonel Hayes is following his orders."

"But he could—" Stanton began.

"I know you're scared and I'd be lying to you if I said things aren't going to get any worse. The fact is, we can't stop the Vemus from reaching New Earth. No matter what we do, we simply cannot," Sean said and looked at the defense committee members, giving them a few moments for it to sink in.

Stanton drew in a breath to speak again.

"Enough, Stanton," Tobias said. "We can't defeat this enemy with clever arguments. General Gates doesn't promote anyone who follows orders blindly. The CDF has seen the data and believe that keeping with General Gates' original plan has the greatest chance of success. Let's move on. Major, you were about to tell us about your strategy for defending this city."

Sean swallowed hard. "I've reviewed what's been done to bolster the city's defense here and also in the other settlements. None of you will like what I'm about to tell you."

An ominous silence took hold of the defense committee.

"We've been preparing for the worst. Why don't you tell us what you have in mind?" Director Mills said.

"We can't hold this city," Sean said.

The committee members divided their gazes between Sean's father and Director Mills.

"I don't believe this. After all the work we put in to make the city as defensible as possible, you come in here and say we've wasted our time?" Stanton said.

Sean shook his head. "I didn't say that. And the work that went into the defense of this city wasn't a waste of time. We'll use that against our enemy. I've faced the Vemus aboard one of their own ships. No doubt you're all familiar with the reports from that engagement. We don't have the numbers to meet this invasion force head-on. Connor knew it, and he often said that for all the Vemus's strengths, they aren't the most imaginative fighting force he'd ever encountered. They're powerful and can adapt, but in other respects they're slow to react. In essence, we need to outthink our enemy and be willing to sacrifice everything we've built in order to survive. Anything less won't be enough."

"You have our attention. Now share with us the rest of your plan," Tobias said.

Sean spent the next twenty minutes giving the defense committee the overview of his plan. To their credit, they listened quietly while he laid it out. During that time, Captain Diaz returned and Sean noticed the increased CDF presence in the

Command Center. He hadn't wanted to resort to the use of force in order to take command of the city, but he would if he had to.

"Your plan doesn't include the colonial militia," Director Mills said.

"They're not soldiers. I'm not sure if using them in any capacity is going to help," Sean said.

"People have a right to help defend their homes," Director Mills said.

Sean frowned while he considered. "They do, but I cannot risk the lives of my soldiers on rescuing the militia if they find themselves in trouble. Do they understand the danger involved? At least CDF soldiers have been trained."

"How about as a compromise I suggest spreading the militia amongst Field Ops teams? There aren't enough CDF soldiers to be everywhere. We won't interfere with the work your soldiers are doing, but we need the militia's help," Director Mills said.

Sean knew Mills was right. He needed every able-bodied person who could hold a rifle. He'd love it if they were all trained like the CDF soldiers had been.

"You're right," Sean said, finally. "I just want it emphasized to anyone who remains that there will be no guarantee once the attack begins that we'll be able to get them away from the city. All the bunkers, as well as Sanctuary, will be closed to them. I won't risk sending another transport to any of those locations when the Vemus arrive," Sean said and looked at the others. "Now, this is all I have time for. I can be reached through CDF channels."

"One more question please, Major Quinn," Stanton said.

Sean really did need to go. "What is it?"

"Lunar Base. You didn't say how they'll figure into your plan," Stanton said.

"Colonel Hayes has been receiving the same updates we have

here, and he'll assess the enemy forces and coordinate a strike against them. None of that will affect what we have to do here on the ground. In essence, we're hoping Colonel Hayes will find a way to blindside the enemy. Maintaining communications blackout with Lunar Base is essential in order for that effort to succeed. So, our job is to hold out as long as we can," Sean said.

His answer seemed to satisfy the former governor, and the committee members all left, except for his father.

"I know you have to go, but I need to talk to you," his father said.

"I'll be right outside, Major," Captain Diaz said and left, closing the door.

Sean looked at his father. They were alone. "Where's Mom?"

"She's helping to organize field hospitals throughout the city," his father said.

"There won't be many wounded. The Vemus aren't keen on taking prisoners or wounding us," Sean replied and glanced over at the door.

Tobias came to stand in front of him and put his hand on Sean's shoulder.

"It's been difficult for me watching you grow up. You're making your own decisions, and me questioning them is almost second nature. It comes with being a father. It's an old habit and I'm sorry," his father said.

"We can't be father and son in rooms like this. Not anymore," Sean said.

"I realize that. You're in command. I acknowledge that and promise to do my best not to interfere with it again," his father said.

Sean felt the edges of his lips lift. He hadn't realized it but there was still part of him that craved his father's approval and acknowledgment of the man he'd become.

"I have a request," his father said.

Sean pressed his lips together and frowned. "What do you need?"

"I don't need anything, but I'd like to stay at your side for the duration," his father said.

Sean's brows pulled together. "I can't allow that. I'm sorry."

His father lifted his hands in front of his chest. "I don't mean in combat, but everything else."

"I know what you mean, but I don't think you understand. Every place in this city is about to become a combat zone. I can't do what I need to do and worry about your safety. Can you please understand that?" Sean said.

His father's brows pushed forward determinedly. "I want to fight at your side, son."

Sean's throat thickened. "I know, but I'm going to be where the worst of the fighting is."

"You think that matters to me? You're my son. We may not have always seen eye to eye, but there's nothing I wouldn't do for you. You may be in command of the CDF, but I'm going to stay with you. You can order your soldiers to take me away and I'll still come back." His father's eyes became glassy and Sean felt himself being pulled into his father's arms. "I'm so proud of you. Please don't forget that. I've always been proud of you."

Sean hugged his father, feeling as if a great weight had been lifted from his shoulders.

"I won't order my men to take you away, but you'll have to explain yourself to Mom," Sean said.

His father chuckled. "I've already taken care of that."

Sean frowned. "What do you mean?"

"I mean that the last transport to Sanctuary will have your mother on it. Whether she's conscious for the trip will be another matter," Tobias said.

Sean's mouth hung open. "She'll never forgive you for it."

"At least she'll be alive to be angry. I'll take that over the alternative any day," Tobias said.

Sean nodded. He'd already made similar arrangements for his father. Some things weren't worth the risk.

22

NOAH RETURNED to the mobile Command Center at Sanctuary. They'd received notification that Phoenix Station had gone offline after its engagement with the Vemus Alpha ship. Not a good sign, but Noah knew that the CDF soldiers serving aboard Phoenix Station wouldn't be declared dead until the area was thoroughly investigated. Sean refused to believe Connor had died. Even if massive pieces of the space station had been destroyed, there were still pockets where people could survive. The official CDF update communication had come from Sean, who was commanding the CDF ground troops. Noah found himself looking at Colonel Cross for some reaction to tell him why she wasn't in command of the CDF ground forces.

"I see you looking at me again, Captain Barker. Is there a problem?" Colonel Cross asked crisply.

"No, ma'am, no problem at all," Noah said and turned his attention back to the latest analysis for the power converter. He'd tweaked the controller's sensitivity for the power regulator so that it could handle the greater range of fluctuations that the alien power station was prone to producing. These settings would greatly hinder the converter's life cycle, but he didn't need the equipment to last forever; it just needed to survive a few engagements with Vemus ships if they ever found Sanctuary.

After a few moments, he glanced over at Colonel Cross and she sighed heavily. "Since you can't seem to concentrate, I'll answer the question that's been burning in your mind since I arrived," Colonel Cross said.

"I'm sorry, Colonel. I really am. I'm trying not to think about my wife. She's stationed at Lunar Base," Noah said.

Colonel Cross raised her brows. "There are a lot of significant others serving on Lunar Base."

Noah frowned in confusion for a moment. "Oh, I hadn't realized."

"What? That I'm a woman as well as a colonel? Yes, there's someone important to me up there as well, so you're in good company," Colonel Cross said.

"Does that have anything to do with why you were sent here?" Noah asked and then immediately wished he hadn't. *Idiot,* he thought.

Colonel Cross glared at him and then a bitter half smile crossed her face as her gaze lost most of its venom. "Once again, if General Gates hadn't warned me about you, I'd have you dealt with severely."

Noah looked away, feeling embarrassed. He should have known better, but sometimes his brain just latched onto an idea and refused to let go.

"You know what? Fine, I'll tell you. General Gates sent me to Sanctuary because I'm pregnant and there are regulations against me serving in an active combat zone," Colonel Cross said.

Of all the reasons Noah had thought, Colonel Cross being

pregnant hadn't been among them. He looked at her. "Congratulations, Colonel," he said.

Colonel Cross snorted and shook her head. "I think you're the first person who's said that to me. Thank you."

"I mean it. It's nice to have something like that to think about rather than always . . ." Noah's voice trailed off, and he pointed up toward the sky.

"I'm sure you'll make a wonderful father someday, Captain Barker," Colonel Cross said.

Noah noted the slight bitterness in Colonel Cross's tone. "Does your significant other know about the baby?"

Colonel Cross bit her lower lip and shook her head. "I didn't get the chance to tell him."

Noah perked up in his chair. "I'm sure I can find a way for you to get a message to Lunar Base. I could bury it in satcom—" Noah said.

"No," Colonel Cross said sternly, cutting him off. "We can't take the risk with the Vemus closing in on the planet."

"Yeah, but it would just be another broadcast signal among many. Difficult for them to track, even with an AI tasked with evaluating the signals," Noah said.

"No. And that's an order. The broadcast signals will have decreased now that the Vemus are here. If we keep up the broadcasts, sooner or later even the Vemus will start wondering why we would do such a thing, and it wouldn't take a large stretch of the imagination for them to conclude that we have someone listening on the other end," Colonel Cross said.

"I hadn't thought of that, Colonel," Noah said, conceding the point.

"No one can think of everything," Colonel Cross said.

They heard shouting from outside the mobile Command Center. Recognizing Lenora's voice, Noah sprang out of his chair.

Her shrill voice became even louder through the thin walls of the center. She hadn't taken the news about Phoenix Station well. Noah couldn't blame her and was secretly thankful that, for the time being, Lunar Base was relatively safe from Vemus attention.

Noah hastened outside and Colonel Cross followed him. Off to the side, Lenora swayed on her feet, holding a glass bottle. Behind her, a huge berwolf watched her intently. The creature's large pink tongue lolled out of its blocky head, resting lazily over a row of impressively sized teeth. The tips of retractable black claws that could rend through steel poked out from the brown, hairy paws. Noah recalled that Lenora had cared for the berwolf as a pup and had even named him Bull. The CDF soldiers kept a wary eye on the creature.

"Colonel," Lenora said. Her slurred words and bleary-eyed gaze were indication enough that Lenora had had more than a few drinks before coming here. "They're here! They. Are. Here!" she said, stabbing her finger up at the night sky. "We've spent all that time getting that big cannon to work. Why haven't you used it yet?"

"Lenora, you know why," Noah admonished.

Lenora shushed him with an excessive hiss and a shake of her head. "I want to hear it from her."

"Dr. Bishop, you need rest. Please allow my soldiers to escort you back to your quarters," Colonel Cross said.

Two CDF soldiers stepped toward Lenora, but when one of them moved to grab her arm, a deep growl resonated from the berwolf's massive chest.

Lenora stumbled back away from the guards and toward Bull. "I don't think he'll like it if you try to touch me," she said, scowling at the soldiers and scratching the berwolf behind his ears. "At least *you're* still here," she said to Bull. The berwolf sniffed Lenora's breath curiously. No doubt it hadn't smelled anything like vodka before, or whatever flavored grain alcohol Lenora had been drinking.

Noah walked past the soldiers. "Come on, Lenora. You know we can't bring that weapon online. I know you *know* that."

Lenora glared at him. "Oh yes. All the colonists suddenly find one of my archaeological sites so interesting," she sneered and scowled at the crowd of refugees quickly shuffling away from her. "Oh yes, all of you come cowering here. Half of you thought he was crazy. Remember?" she asked scathingly of the retreating group. "There's no danger coming from Earth. There's no way something like that could happen. You scoffed at his efforts and made him plead for you to give him the tools he needed to defend you all. Now you cower here, looking up at the skies in panic," she said, stabbing a finger up at the night sky. "Now you give him your support, proclaiming he's been right all along. None of you deserve what Connor's given you. None of you!"

Lenora lost her balance and stumbled to the side. Noah stepped forward, ready to catch her if she fell but also keeping a wary eye on the berwolf. He couldn't tell whether the creature was going to attack him or not. For the moment it seemed preoccupied with watching Lenora's drunken rage.

She steadied herself with outstretched arms to keep her balance.

"Lenora, please. They're scared enough without you yelling at them," Noah said.

Lenora looked at him, her long hair in tangles, some of which were in front of her face. She pushed her hair out of the way and Noah saw her glassy, red-rimmed eyes. "How can you side with them? Don't you want to kill the Vemus?"

Noah took a small step forward. "Yes, I want to stop them, but this isn't the way."

"Then why aren't you firing the colossus cannon right now?" Lenora asked.

"Because it won't stop them. It will only alert the Vemus to our presence here," Noah said.

"Good! Then I can grab one of these rifles and put it to good use," Lenora said and looked over at Colonel Cross. "I'm not such a bad shot myself."

"Lenora, please look at me," Noah said.

Lenora blinked slowly as she turned her gaze to him.

"Connor wouldn't want this—" Noah began.

"I don't care what Connor wanted!" Lenora shrieked and glared up at the night sky. "Are you happy now? You got what you wanted. Killed in the line of duty. A soldier's death . . ."

Lenora muttered a few incoherent curses and tripped. Noah caught her in his arms and she pressed her face into his chest, sobbing. All he could do was hold her while she wept. He hadn't seen her since yesterday. She must have found out about Phoenix Station, and he cursed himself an idiot for not going to tell her himself. He should have checked on her. The mostly empty glass bottle clattered to the ground, and he lifted her up and started to carry her off.

"Put her in my quarters. They're closer," Colonel Cross said.

Noah changed directions, heading for Colonel Cross's tent. Lenora kept muttering off and on while he carried her. She needed sleep. He heard the berwolf padding along behind them. Colonel Cross opened the door to her tent and Noah carried Lenora to the small bed inside. He laid her down and pulled a blanket over her. Satisfied that there was nothing more he could do, he left the tent and went back outside.

"You should stay with her," Colonel Cross said.

"But I have to—"

"It can wait. She needs you. You should be here for her when she wakes up," Colonel Cross insisted.

"Thank you, ma'am," Noah said.

Colonel Cross and the CDF soldiers left him, and the berwolf settled down nearby. He grabbed one of the nearest chairs and sat down. The creature would swing its head toward Lenora whenever he heard her moan in her sleep but then would settle back down.

"She'll be alright," Noah said softly and hoped he was right. Lenora had kept so many things bottled up that he should have known something had to give. He crossed his arms in front of his chest and gazed up at the night sky where New Earth's rings cast a soft glow. He never got tired of that sight, but tonight he couldn't take any comfort in it. The Vemus were here and he had no idea how they were going to stop them.

23

THE VEMUS ALPHA had settled into a geocentric orbit around New Earth, and after the cruisers finished taking out the structures on the lunar surface, they returned to the Alpha. The Vemus seemed to have ignored Lunar Base altogether, and Nathan had deployed small scanning drones from one of the comms satellites they had in orbit. The scanner drones were configured to do a single pass by the Alpha and then send the data through an IR channel to repeaters the CDF had placed nearby. Since the IR signal required a direct line of sight to send the data, there was very little chance the Vemus would detect it. If they did, they could only trace the signal to another repeater. In theory, the Vemus *could* be patient enough to track the IR signal, but they would have to be in close proximity to the actual repeaters, which they weren't. The risk was minimal and the CDF needed the data, as it was crucial data for their counterstrike.

Nathan had deployed armed CDF squads to secure all the locations throughout the base that had access to the lunar surface. He hadn't accounted for securing those locations when the Vemus arrived and had nearly been discovered. Less than a handful of people had made the foolish attempt to engage the Vemus, which would have put Lunar Base at risk, but luckily Nathan had more levelheaded soldiers in the area to avert disaster. What really frustrated him was that Dr. Kendra Robinson's death could have been avoided. Struggling to keep the disgust from his voice at the pointless waste of life, he sent out a base-wide update reminding all Lunar Base personnel that the communications receivers were still online and there was no need for anyone to be at the surface installations.

"It's the pressure, Colonel. Makes people do foolish things," Major Shelton said.

Nathan pressed his lips together. "I know. We just can't afford it."

It had been twelve hours since Phoenix Station had gone offline, and he hadn't allowed himself to think about Savannah at all. He'd checked the comms logs from the escape pods and her signature hadn't been among them. The escape pods had ceased broadcasting once the Vemus cruisers entered the area. Unless those CDF soldiers had been able to disable their beacons, it was probable that they'd been captured or killed by the Vemus. Given those options, Nathan hoped they hadn't been captured.

He turned his attention back to the main holoscreen. Despite the massive size of the Vemus Alpha, Phoenix Station weapons had bludgeoned it, rendering near-catastrophic damage. The probe scans revealed that the exoskeletal hull was thickest toward the rear of the massive ship where the engines were buried deep in the cavernous hindquarters. The twenty-two-kilometer ship must have had millions of personnel aboard, perhaps more, but those numbers had to have been seriously decimated. Connor had focused Phoenix Station's weapons on key soft areas that were revealed after the initial HADES IV-B missiles had sloughed off a few layers of the exoskeletal hull. He'd done a lot of damage, but the enemy ship was still flying.

Nathan had brought in his reserve watches and fed all the data they'd gathered throughout the base. He encouraged anyone with any ideas about how they could attack the enemy to bring them to their immediate superior officers, who would then decide whether the suggestion should be sent up the chain of command. Currently, his normal bridge crew, with the additional presence of operations and tactical units, was gathered in the command area.

"We need to hit the Vemus Alpha so hard that they can't recover from it, but we need to be cautious because we can't have that ship crashing into the planet," Nathan said.

Lieutenant LaCroix raised his hand and Nathan nodded for him to speak.

"Colonel, my team and I have run some preliminary firing solutions, but once we commit fully, there's no way we can mask our presence here," Lieutenant LaCroix said.

"Yes, the Vemus will become aware of our presence once we begin shooting at them, so what's your real question, Lieutenant?" Nathan asked.

"Our main objective is to take out the Vemus Alpha, but what about the ships that'll take their forces to the ground? I think we should be trying to prevent that as well, Colonel. What good is a surprise attack if everyone's dead by the time we come up with a plan to engage the enemy?" Lieutenant LaCroix said.

"Any minute now the Vemus are going to send in a landing force. We've seen them use Talon 5s to storm Titan Station, but they didn't use them on Phoenix. Please bring your attention to the main holoscreen. That large scorched area is roughly seven kilometers across, and recent scans show that there are separate ships inside. We think their landing crafts will use that area. How can we stop the landing crafts from reaching New Earth?" Nathan asked as his eyes swept over his staff. "This question isn't just for Lieutenant LaCroix. Once we reveal our presence, there's no going back."

"I have a suggestion, Colonel," Major Shelton said.

"What is it?" Nathan asked.

"We can't let the Vemus land any craft on New Earth completely unchallenged. They're in position, and perhaps they believe they've won. We need to keep them off balance by striking at the landing craft as they make their descent, letting them know they're not unopposed and reassuring the people on the ground that we're still up here fighting for them," Major Shelton said.

"Agreed. Given the distance, what could we use that would reach those targets in time?" Nathan asked.

"We could use our midrange Hornet missiles. They can close the distance quickly, and the Vemus wouldn't have much time to launch countermeasures, Colonel," Lieutenant LaCroix said.

"That could work. Put your team on coming up with a firing solution for that. We'll need to use a LIDAR burst to update PRADIS. Work off the assumption that as soon as we fire our missiles, we return to Dark-Star status. I agree with Major Shelton that if we can get the Vemus to look over their shoulders, it might give us some more time to find the soft spots in their armor," Colonel Hayes said.

An alert came to prominence on the main holoscreen. Several large pieces had broken away from the Vemus Alpha.

"Tactical, those are your targets. Comms, set Condition One throughout the base. Ops, commence LIDAR burst on my mark," Colonel Hayes said.

"Yes, Colonel, ready on your mark," Sergeant Martinez said.

Nathan waited for Lieutenant LaCroix, who, after a few moments, turned and said, "Firing solution ready. Hornets in the tubes and ready, Colonel."

"Ops, commence burst," Nathan said.

On the lunar surface, massive hatch doors opened and actuators pushed up a large sensor array, which sent out a sizeable scanner burst. There was no way the Vemus would miss the sudden activity. The PRADIS scope updated with targeting information.

"Fire missiles," Nathan ordered.

"Yes, Colonel, missiles fired," Lieutenant LaCroix confirmed.

The scanners showed the Hornet missiles leaving their launch tubes, racing toward the Vemus troop carriers.

"Ready second wave of missiles," Nathan said.

Finally, they were in this fight. The first wave of missiles blindsided the Vemus troop carriers, causing the ships to break apart during entry into the atmosphere.

"Colonel, two Vemus cruisers are inbound. They'll be in detection range within ten minutes," Sergeant Martinez said.

"Tactical, do we have time for one more wave of Hornets, with half of them targeting those cruisers?" Nathan asked.

"Affirmative, Colonel," Lieutenant LaCroix said.

"Do it. Fire when ready," Nathan said.

He watched the main holoscreen as their missile tubes were reloaded with the midrange Hornets.

"Firing third wave, Colonel," Lieutenant LaCroix said.

"Retract array and close all missile hatches," Nathan said.

Hornet missiles flew away from New Earth's moon, some darting off toward the inbound cruisers. Nathan watched as the cruisers took out the inbound Hornet missiles. One cruiser escaped unscathed while the second cruiser took multiple direct hits along the prow of the ship, taking out its forward cannons.

"Colonel, the last scans show that some of the bigger troop carriers got through and are heading toward the planet's surface," Lieutenant LaCroix said.

"What're their last known trajectories?" Nathan asked.

"Their trajectories are aligned with colonial settlements. None of the remote emergency bunkers are located at any of those areas, Colonel," Lieutenant LaCroix said.

"That's something, at least," Nathan said quietly.

"Passive scans show more ships heading our way," Lieutenant LaCroix said.

"Ops, I want the gun batteries hot and ready to go, but keep the hatch doors shut unless it looks like the Vemus ships are about to fire on us," Nathan said.

"Yes, Colonel, alerting fire teams now," Sergeant Martinez said.

Major Shelton glanced over at him. "How many do you think got through to the surface?"

Nathan watched the main holoscreen grimly. "Too many. Those troop carriers can hold thousands of soldiers."

"Yeah, but the cities have been evacuated. Only soldiers will be there to greet them," Major Shelton said.

"Maybe I should have used the few HADES IV missiles we have," Nathan said.

"No, you were right to keep them in reserve. Now the Vemus will expend some energy trying to figure out where we are, which buys our soldiers on the ground time to deal with the immediate threat," Major Shelton said.

"Colonel, the last scanner burst came back with some strange detections," Sergeant Martinez said.

Nathan glanced at her, but the sergeant's gaze was locked onto her screen.

"Colonel, I think our scanners detected faint power readings from the Phoenix Station wreckage," Sergeant Martinez said.

"You think? I need more than that, Sergeant," Nathan said.

"It's hard to tell because we had our array focused on the Vemus forces, but what we detected is at the edge of the scanner range. That area is where Phoenix Station was," Sergeant Martinez said.

Nathan looked at the scanner data on the main holoscreen and frowned. He didn't want to start hoping when it was likely to be nothing. "Send in a scanner drone from our Bravo installation on the dark side of the moon."

"Drone away, Colonel. Estimated arrival in ninety minutes," Sergeant Martinez said.

"Very well," Nathan said and continued to watch the main holoscreen while considering their next move.

"Colonel," Lieutenant LaCroix said, "would you and Major Shelton come over to Tactical, please?"

Nathan walked over to the tactical workstation where LaCroix sat with two members of his team.

"The HADES IV-Bs were modified to improve their effectiveness against countermeasures, which made them better able to reach their targets in a long-range engagement. We only have a few of them here on base," Lieutenant LaCroix said.

"That's right—only about twenty. Have you come up with a way to use them?" Nathan asked.

"Since this isn't a long-range engagement with the enemy, we're proposing to consolidate the HADES IVs' payloads, Colonel," Lieutenant LaCroix said.

Nathan narrowed his gaze while he considered it. "You guys came up with this?"

Lieutenant LaCroix shook his head. "No, the idea came up from one of the engineering teams—an engineer by the name of

Kara Roberts. She said—and I'm quoting here, sir, 'I have a way to blow those SOBs out of the damn sky.' She had a few more expletives, but you get the idea."

"So, you want to take twenty of the HADES IVs and combine the payloads into one single missile?" Nathan asked.

"No, Colonel, Major Roberts is proposing that we consolidate them down to four missiles. We cap them with extra armored tips to increase their penetration effectiveness and use countdown detonators since the Vemus can block our command-and-control signals," Lieutenant LaCroix said.

"And you think that will be enough to destroy that ship?" Nathan asked.

"We can't be sure, Colonel, but it's our best shot at doing the most damage against them," Lieutenant LaCroix said.

Nathan glanced at Major Shelton.

"The idea has promise, Colonel," Major Shelton said.

Nathan drew in a deep breath and sighed heavily. "How long until they can be ready?"

"According to Major Roberts, six hours, sir. They need to break down the assembly and transfer the payload to the other missiles," Lieutenant LaCroix said.

"Alright, tell Major Roberts she's authorized to start," Nathan said. "Major Shelton, I need you to go down there and supervise the effort. No use blowing ourselves up while we're trying to save the colony."

"Yes, Colonel," Major Shelton said and left the command area.

Nathan swung his gaze toward the main holoscreen. Vemus cruisers were inbound, and they needed to hold out for over six hours.

24

CONNOR WAS SLUMPED over in his chair with the straps digging into his shoulder as red flashing lights reflected from the smooth surface of the floor. He blinked several times, slowly escaping his stupor. Swallowing the coppery taste of blood in his mouth, he raised his head to look at the main holoscreen. Amidst the flashing alerts was a long list of failed systems. Connor swung his head around and saw CDF soldiers slumped in their chairs. Other soldiers were lying on the floor, their helmets broken. He couldn't tell whether they were alive or dead. Connor unbuckled his straps, rubbed his shoulder, and stumbled to his feet. He turned and approached Major Elder, who had fallen halfway out of his chair, some of his straps having come unbuckled. Connor's neural implants showed that Major Elder was alive. In fact, his life signs were strong.

"John, are you okay?" Connor asked, shaking the man's shoulder.

Major Elder groaned as Connor pushed him upright in his

chair. He opened his eyes and looked at Connor. "I'm still here, General," he said, wincing.

"Just sit tight for a minute and catch your breath. I'll get a medic up here," Connor said.

Major Elder pushed himself up and waved Connor off. "I'll be fine," he said and took in the state of the Command Center.

"Good, let's see where we stand," Connor said.

They started working their way around the command area. The soldiers that had been strapped in their chairs were alive but disoriented. There were more than a few critically injured soldiers lying on the floor, and Connor used his comlink to find Dr. Allen. Fortunately, Dr. Allen had been near the Command Center during the Vemus Alpha attack. The chief medical officer put whoever was standing around to work helping to assess the injured soldiers.

"Ops, I need a situation report. What shape are we in, Lieutenant?" Connor said.

Lieutenant Rawn rubbed his eyes and peered at his personal holoscreen. "General, I'm showing that sections four, five, and seven are completely offline and aren't attached to us anymore. We have critical failures in section six, but the bulkhead doors have sealed and are holding. Maneuvering thrusters are offline. Weapons systems are offline. We have life support and artificial gravity but we're tumbling out of control. We're leaking atmosphere from multiple impact points. Honestly, sir, I don't know how we're still together," Lieutenant Rawn said, his eyes going wide.

"Well let's not start counting our blessings just yet," Connor said.

They had life support for the moment. They needed to get the station stabilized so they could figure out where they were and then figure out where the Vemus Alpha had gone. He glanced up at the main holoscreen, which kept flickering due to power surges.

"Ops, try to reach someone from Engineering. I need to know what the state of our reactor is or whether we're on backup generators. Tactical, is our scanner array intact?" Connor asked.

Captain Thorne raced back to his workstation and opened his console. "Scanners are offline, General. The logs don't show that it was damaged, but with all the systems offline, I'm not sure we still even have the array."

They needed to restore main power and get those systems back online. "Understood, Captain. See if any repair crews can check it out. We're blind until we can get access to that array," Connor said.

Major Elder came back to Connor. "We still have people checking in, but preliminary reports indicate that we're missing a substantial portion of this subsection. Davis, down in Engineering, believes the Vemus Alpha's primary weapon cut right through our armor. The fact that we were out of control and spinning may be the only reason we're still alive."

Connor nodded. "Lieutenant Daniels, do we have any comms capabilities?"

Lieutenant Daniels had a cut on her forehead that one of the medics had just patched up. She peered at her console. "We have short-range comms capabilities, General."

"See if you can detect Bravo or Charlie stations. Don't broadcast right now, but see if you can connect to their systems that are online," Connor said.

"We saw them get destroyed, sir," Major Elder said quietly.

"We saw them go *offline*. There was so much going on that we don't have confirmation that they're gone. *We* shouldn't be here, and I won't count anyone out just yet," Connor said.

Major Elder nodded, considering. "There could be other

sections with survivors, but they might not have any way to reach us."

"That might be a blessing because the last thing we need is to start broadcasting our position. The Vemus Alpha might've passed us by, thinking we were dead," Connor said.

Major Elder frowned. "Why wouldn't they just finish us off?"

Connor shook his head. "I'm not sure. My best guess is that they thought we were no longer a threat, which means they could send a ship back to finish the job or capture survivors."

Major Elder's face became grim. "Not the best position to be in. General, I'd like to assess the damage firsthand."

"That's a good idea. We'll split up. Send me an update via the comlink. We need critical systems back online. Hopefully a few maneuvering thrusters made it so we can at least stabilize our position," Connor said.

"I'll make that my first stop, General," Major Elder said.

They spent the next few hours doing damage assessments, and Connor started to put together casualty reports, as well as lists of CDF soldiers that were simply missing. Connor divided his remaining soldiers into search parties to look for survivors and check ship systems. He left the Command Center to lead one of the search teams. They were still alive but far from out of the woods. For the moment they were on borrowed time.

25

THE ONLY PEOPLE left in Sierra were the ones who were going to fight and those supporting them. The last transport to Sanctuary had left over an hour earlier. Sean's mother had been on it and he was told she was none too thrilled about it. His father had stuck with him ever since they'd learned the fate of Phoenix Station, but Sean was so focused on what he had to do that most of the time he forgot his father was there. They didn't have enough AR-71s to distribute to the militia, but they did the best they could. Some of them were armed with a CAR-74 semiautomatic hunting rifle, and Sean wasn't sure how effective they'd be against the Vemus. Certainly, the smaller Vemus soldiers would be vulnerable to the civilian rifle but definitely not the Vemus Alpha troops. Sean had seen those rise after being torn apart by incendiary rounds from an AR-71. The only time they stayed dead was when there was nothing left to come back to life. Even that wasn't right. The Vemus had remarkable healing capabilities that New Earth scientists were at a loss to fully understand.

Sean knew that fighting the Vemus would be like facing his worst nightmare, except this time he didn't get to escape in a ship. This time the Vemus wouldn't go away. The fighting would be close and he needed them to come into the city. There were only a select few who knew his plan in its entirety. He'd expected more resistance than he'd gotten, but it was no secret that Sean was amongst the foremost experts in dealing with this particular enemy. He didn't feel like an expert—not by a long shot, which was what this whole mission was turning out to be.

Sean powered off the small holoscreen in front of him and stepped away from the comms station. He'd established command units throughout the city so he wouldn't be tied down to one place. His M-Viper sniper rifle rested against the wall beside him. He was one of the best shots in the entire Colonial Defense Force.

Lieutenant Compton shifted his feet and looked at Sean as he turned around. "They're as ready as they'll ever be," he said.

"I just told Delphi and New Haven that they're essentially on their own. I don't know how Connor dealt with this every day for the past seven years," Sean said with a sigh. He felt as if his head was going to burst.

Lieutenant Compton nodded. "It's one thing to take orders and it's quite another to be giving them and making all the decisions. But I'm sure Majors Winters and Roberts will do their jobs."

"They'll hold their respective cities as long as they can," Sean said.

They stood on one of the taller buildings in Sierra, which gave them a bird's-eye view of the city. It was a few hours after sunrise and the Vemus Alpha was in geosynchronous orbit around New Earth. The ship had been there for hours, and Sean presumed it was identifying targets.

"Major," Lieutenant Owens called out to him. "My scope just lit up with a bunch of bogies, sir. We've got incoming."

Air raid alarms began blaring throughout the city and Sean opened a broadcast channel to his gun batteries. "Hold your fire until we have visual confirmation of the enemy. Conserve your ammo as much as you can."

Multiple cracks of thunder boomed throughout the clear sky and Sean peered up, along with everyone else. He felt his brows push forward as he squinted. The sky was full of large, fiery ships that must have come from the Vemus Alpha. The invasion had begun. Behind the ships were several large explosions that tore through the enemy vessels.

"What is that?" Lieutenant Compton asked.

Sean smiled. "That has to be from Lunar Base. Colonel Hayes must've authorized the attack, but he won't be able to attack for long."

"Why not?" Lieutenant Compton asked.

"He's just lending us some support and reminding the Vemus that they're not entirely unopposed. And now they'll have to expend resources in order to investigate where that attack came from—" Sean said and was cut off by the loud sonic booms of enemy ships clearing Lunar Base's attack.

Hundreds of enemy ships streaked down toward Sierra, and the rail-cannon gun batteries began rapidly firing on the approaching ships. Sean watched as the heavy rail-cannons tore into the enemy ships. The high-velocity projectiles were made from a sixth-generation alien alloy they'd found in the abandoned alien ruins on the planet. The components to make the hardened alloy were plentiful and were comparable to what the NA Alliance military would have used.

Some of the enemy ships began to lose control, slamming into each other as they veered off course.

"Owens, start broadcasting the Vemus control signal," Sean said.

"Yes, Major. Broadcasting Vemus disruption signal now," Lieutenant Owens said.

Sean watched as hundreds of ships approached Sierra. They stayed in formation, which meant the Vemus disruption signal was no longer effective.

"Shall I keep the signal going, Major?" Lieutenant Owens asked.

"Yes, keep it going just in case, Lieutenant," Sean said.

The Vemus landing craft never returned fire. They just kept coming despite the damage the rail-cannon batteries were doing. At first, they crashed outside the city, but they were drawing steadily closer.

"The ones behind the front line are breaking apart," Lieutenant Compton said, pointing.

Sean peered at the area, using his neural implants to temporarily enhance his view of the approaching ships.

"They look like pods," Sean said. "They're using drop-pods!" he exclaimed and turned toward Owens. "Alert all commands that the Vemus are using drop-pods with a heavy concentration of troops coming toward the western side of the city."

"At once, Major," Lieutenant Owens said.

"Should we send in the mobile infantry units to bolster the west side of the city, sir?" Lieutenant Compton asked.

"No," Sean said, shaking his head. "They're still coming down. The drop-pods are harder to hit and will only fire their retro-boosters at the last moment for a hard landing. Then, whatever's inside comes out."

Sean's father glanced at Director Mills before looking back at him. "How did you know all that?"

"Connor made sure—" Sean said, then frowned. "He made sure I knew about NA Alliance military tactics," he said, remembering how Connor would randomly drill him on military tactics that Sean wasn't convinced he'd ever use. Sean had thought the bulk of their engagement with the Vemus would be in space. He'd been wrong, but Connor had known better. He'd tried to account for every conceivable attack scenario and had trained the Colonial Defense Force accordingly. How long had Connor been grooming him to lead the CDF ground forces?

Sean watched as the rail-cannon batteries tried to target all the incoming drop-pods, but there were too many of them. He noted that many of the drop-pods were successfully landing in the areas outside the city.

"Comms, send out an alert for infantry teams to target the retro-booster assembly on the drop-pods to prevent their thrusters from working," Sean said.

"Yes, Major," Lieutenant Owens said.

Sean looked at his father. "I'd intended to get you out of here, but—"

"I'm not leaving, son," his father said.

"Fine, but I'm sending you to the east side of the city," Sean said.

Tobias opened his mouth to speak.

"That's not up for discussion," Sean said and glanced over at a nearby soldier. "Corporal, take a squad and escort the governor to the east encampment."

Sean watched as his father was led away. The sounds of the rail-cannon batteries, in their unrelenting barrage against the Vemus invasion force, hadn't slowed down. In fact, now the CDF infantry was firing their weapons at the drop-pods, which added to the sounds of wanton destruction. Drop-pods crashed into the ground and impact craters began to dot the landscape. The CDF soldiers hit the fuel lines, causing drop-pods to hit the ground in flaming wrecks, which became small explosions. Other drop-pods hit the ground without slowing down, the force of the impact shattering the pods and the Vemus soldiers inside them to bits. But still they came, and more of the drop-pods began to make it through to land safely. Some even landed inside the city walls. Upon landing, hatches opened up and large dark figures stalked out of the pods. CDF soldiers stationed on the rooftops above rained fire down on them. The Vemus returned fire, and white stun bolts blazed through the air. Some of the enemy were massive, easily twice as tall as Sean was. Their skin was a deep, dark purple that glistened in the light. Their rounded heads angled to a pointed snout, making them look anything but human.

CDF fire teams worked together to bring them down using kinetic weapons to stall their advance or otherwise immobilize them and then thermite explosive rounds to burn away whatever was left.

Multiple reports came in of Vemus forces gathering outside the city. A large explosion to the west snatched Sean's attention.

"That's not ours," Lieutenant Compton said.

"Order the mobile infantry unit to the west side of the city. Get the Hellcats in the air to give air support," Sean ordered.

He'd held the Hellcats in reserve. The Vemus drop-pods and troop carriers seemed to have stopped. The skies were clear for the moment, but that could change at any time. The high-pitched whine of multiple Hellcats flying overhead filled the air as they streaked toward the west. Updates from New Haven and Delphi reported the Vemus using similar tactics, but the bulk of their forces were here at Sierra. The Vemus had correctly surmised that Sierra would be the most heavily defended.

Carrying his M-Viper sniper rifle, Sean headed toward the barricade wall on the roof of the Field Ops Headquarters, which was centrally located in the city. He squatted down to set up his position and was immediately joined by a few other soldiers. He glanced at the soldier next to him and saw a wisp of blonde hair beneath the edges of the helmet.

"Boone?" Sean asked.

"I hope you're still as good a shot as you used to be, Bling," Field Ops Captain Donna Marten said. She'd been part of Search and Rescue and hadn't left Field Ops.

Sean hefted the M-Viper and rested the barrel on the barricade wall. "Better," Sean said.

Captain Marten arched an eyebrow. "Care to make a wager on it?"

Sean grinned. "Can we get a couple of spotters?" he said.

He'd ordered sniper units to the rooftops of the buildings and could already hear the distinct pop of an M-Viper being fired. They were three kilometers from the edge of the city and taking out a target at that range would be a challenge, but not beyond the capabilities of the M-Viper or Sean.

"Loser buys drinks tonight," Sean said.

"Oh, you're on, Major," Field Ops Captain Marten said.

Finding targets was relatively easy given that the Vemus were so big, and once on the ground, they moved toward the city in a dark wave. Sean peered down his scope, searching for a target beyond the edge of the city, but they moved so fast that he no sooner had a target than it was quickly out of sight. Sean focused ahead of one of the alphas and squeezed the trigger. The high-velocity round blazed toward the target at supersonic speed, and the head of the Vemus exploded like a melon on impact as the large body dropped to the ground. CDF soldiers who were much closer lobbed thermite charges to burn up the remains. Sean updated his nano-robotic ammunition to use incendiary rounds. This would give the CDF soldiers more time to mop up the remains so the Vemus couldn't rise again.

Sean picked another target and squeezed off a round, the incendiary ammunition streaking red through the air to reach its objective. The CDF infantry rotated between using incendiary rounds and regular kinetic rounds, which lasted longer. Sean had ordered them to conserve their ammo, but with so many Vemus storming the city he wasn't sure how long they could last. Field Ops Captain Marten took down at least as many targets as Sean did, probably more. It felt good to see the enemy fall.

Sean wasn't sure how much time had passed, but he started to get an itch in the back of his mind that he was missing something. Backing away from the barricade, he motioned for another CDF soldier to take his place and he returned to the command area where there was a holographic display of Sierra. Computer systems piped in updates from the computing core deep within the building.

Director Mills glanced at him. "What is it?"

Sean frowned. "I feel like I'm missing something. Something important."

The Vemus were primarily attacking certain areas of the city. The drop-pods that landed inside the city were quickly dealt with by the mobile infantry units.

He noted one of the seemingly quiet sectors of the city and picked one at random. "Ops, what's the status of our recon drones in sector three?" Sean asked.

Lieutenant Owens quickly brought up the status of the drones. They had so many deployed that they were grouped and tasked with specific sectors to patrol. The data provided from the drones were too much for any one person to keep track of, which was why they relied on the computer system to alert them to anomalies. Lieutenant Owens frowned. "Major, I'm showing a thirteen percent drop-off in drones reporting in from that sector. The drop-off occurred less than ten minutes ago."

"Who do we have in that area?" Sean asked.

Lieutenant Compton quickly accessed the information on his workstation. "It's mostly Field Ops and militia in that area, but Sergeant Brown is in the vicinity with a squad of CDF soldiers."

Sean opened a comlink to Sergeant Brown. "Sergeant, we've noticed a suspicious drop-off in recon drone activity in your vicinity. I need you to investigate whether there is enemy activity in your area."

The comlink channel opened, and Sean heard the sounds of a battle.

"Sir, we're under heavy attack. We need reinforcements. The Vemus are overwhelming our position!" Sergeant Brown shouted.

Sean looked at Lieutenant Compton. "Alert the reserve Hellcat squadron and send them to sector three immediately." He switched back to the comlink. "Air support is on its way."

"We'll hold out, sir," Sergeant Brown said.

"Why didn't they tell us they were under attack?" Director Mills asked.

"The attack probably came so suddenly that they didn't have time to report it in," Sean said. He studied the map of the city and the troop locations. "Send mobile infantry units thirty-six and thirty-seven to sector three. Do we have any satellite feeds? Can we track where the Vemus landed?"

Lieutenant Owens shook her head. "The satellites were taken out when the Vemus attacked. Backups were supposed to move into position, but none have reported in yet."

Director Mills nodded, finally understanding. "You suspect that in addition to the assault on the city, they landed a few kilometers away."

"It's what I would do," Sean said.

The recon drones failing to report in could only mean one thing. Those drones had been taken out so fast that they'd even failed to send in a destruction signal. Sean accessed one of the cameras on a tall building in sector three. Once it powered on, he put the live feed up for the rest of them to see. Vemus troops were staggering their approach, firing blue bolts of energy at Field Ops and militia soldiers.

"Good god! That's the east side of the city!" Director Mills said.

Sean stared at the video feed. He'd sent his father to that area of the city, thinking it was safer. Instead, it was being overwhelmed by Vemus soldiers. Sean recalled that the Vemus had used blue bolts to overcome the Nexstar combat suit defenses. They were shooting to kill.

The Vemus stormed the area, one group taking out the heavily armed soldiers while another pinned down the helpless combatants and spat a blackish goo onto their faces. They quickly moved on to the next person and did the same thing. The people with the blackish goo on their faces lay on the ground, their bodies going into convulsions that didn't let up.

Lieutenant Owens gasped. "What are they doing to them?"

Sean felt his mouth drop open. "That's how it spreads."

"But the data retrieved from the Vemus ship said the virus was airborne," Director Mills said.

"This is what we saw them do on the ship," Sean said and refreshed the CDF troop placements on the map.

Director Mills' face became pale. "How long does it take?"

"I have no idea. We fled the area," Sean said.

The holographic display showed the reserve Hellcat units moving into position to provide air support. Sean's mind raced and his mouth became dry. It was much too soon to implement the next phase of his plan. He tried to force an idea for some kind of backup strategy, but nothing came.

Director Mills' thick brows drew together in concern. "We can't hold this city, can we?"

Sean swallowed as he searched the map. He gritted his teeth. This was much too soon.

"What are your orders, Major?" Lieutenant Compton asked.

Sean looked around at the CDF soldiers and Field Ops people in the command area. They needed him to be strong. He wouldn't falter now. Connor had picked him to lead and that was exactly what he was going to do.

"We fight. We make them pay for every inch of ground they take from us, falling back to this position," Sean said and used his implants to outline the CDF headquarters. "This will be the secondary rally point. The primary is now highlighted." He looked at Director Mills.

"Those are tunnel entrances," Director Mills said, frowning.

Sean nodded. "They lead out of the city."

"Yeah, but how can you be sure there aren't Vemus forces in those locations?" Director Mills asked.

"Because we'll lure their forces in," Sean answered.

Director Mills studied the map again and then glared at Sean. "You never meant to hold the city."

"Only if it was feasible to do so. It's not," Sean said. "Comms, open package designation Siren-B and send out updated orders now."

"Confirmed. Siren-B package—" Lieutenant Owens' voice faltered, and she cleared her throat. "Orders sent, Major."

The holographic map updated, showing the intended troop movements for the updated orders.

"You bastard," Director Mills snarled. "Why didn't you tell anyone about this?"

Two CDF soldiers positioned themselves between Sean and Damon Mills.

"Because I needed your cooperation," Sean said coldly.

Director Mills glared at him. "I don't believe this. I don't believe you'd do this . . . were even capable of doing this. How many of them are going to pay with their lives for this plan of yours?"

Sean grabbed Mills and slammed him against the wall. "As many of them as it takes to stop the Vemus. That's why Connor put me in charge—because he knew I'd get the job done. Look out there!" Sean screamed and jerked his head to the side. "Just because you suddenly realized the level of sacrifice required so we can survive doesn't make it wrong."

Sean let go of Damon Mills and stepped back.

"I won't stand by and watch you destroy everything we've built," Director Mills said.

"No one will be standing by. The CDF will hold this position until it's done. Field Ops and the militia will escape in the tunnels. Then this city and every single Vemus inside will be blown up," Sean said.

Director Mills flung his arm toward the sky. "What about the rest of them? What are you going to do when the rest of them come down here?"

"I guess we better hope Colonel Hayes on Lunar Base comes up with a good plan. Now that you know, are you going to storm off, or are you going to help? There's more to operation Siren than what you've seen so far," Sean said.

Director Mills balled his hands into fists and sighed, then

looked away in disgust. Sean felt the same way. He hated what he was about to do, but he couldn't think of another way to strike a crippling blow to the Vemus invaders. A lot of people were going to die, but at least others would get to live. Why else would he fight?

26

COLONEL HAYES FROWNED at the three-dimensional holographic image of the Vemus Alpha ship. Everyone else in the mission briefing room remained silent as they studied the same image with the same perplexity Nathan felt. He was glad it wasn't just him, but when his engineers were confounded, that was serious cause for alarm.

"I need options, people. Anything you've got. Let's lay it all on the table," Nathan said.

Major Shelton forced her lips together in concentration, looking at Major Kara Roberts. "Can you go over that one more time, Major?"

"Particularly the part where even with the combined HADES IV missile payloads we'll still be unable to destroy the Vemus Alpha ship," Nathan added.

Nathan watched as Major Roberts sucked in a deep breath. "The explosive force of the additional payload isn't the entire issue. The problem is we can't penetrate the ship deep enough for them to do enough damage."

"When you proposed this idea before, I thought the issue of penetration wouldn't be a problem. What changed?" Nathan asked.

"We got updated scanning data from our recon drones, and the interior of the Vemus Alpha isn't as hollow as we hoped it would be. I'm sorry, Colonel," Major Roberts said.

Nathan shook his head. "Don't be sorry. I'd rather we find out now than after we launched our last missiles."

They'd been about to proceed with the launch of the original plan when Major Roberts stormed into the Command Center, demanding that they abort. Since she was the lead engineer largely responsible for the proposed modified payload, together with the fact that she insisted there wasn't a chance in hell her proposal was going to work, Nathan aborted the launch. Three Vemus cruisers patrolled the area, looking for the lunar base, and their window to launch was rapidly closing.

"We still need to keep moving forward. We managed to hinder their drop-ships, but we don't know how long that will last," Nathan said and switched the holographic display to show the main continent on the planet. "The Vemus managed to land a sizable force at Sierra, Delphi, and New Haven. As far as we can tell, they haven't discovered the bunkers or Sanctuary."

Nathan noticed Major Roberts' shoulders relax slightly at the news, her expression relieved.

"We need to focus, people. We all have someone important down on the planet, counting on us—wives, husbands, daughters, sons, friends, and the list goes on," Nathan said. "Who do you have waiting for you, Roberts?"

Major Roberts swallowed. "My husband, Noah."

Nathan frowned. "Captain Barker? Noah is your husband?"

"Yes, Colonel. The last communication I received from him

was that they were sending him to Sanctuary to work on the power converter for the alien power station," Major Roberts said.

"They have a colossus cannon there. Very powerful. It should give them some measure of protection," Nathan said. He knew of Noah Barker. He was a brilliant engineer. Noah and Kara were the team that had updated the targeting systems of the HADES IV-B missiles. He would've liked to have had Noah here to work with Kara because two great minds are better than one.

He brought the Vemus Alpha ship back to prominence on the holodisplay. "How do we destroy that ship? If missiles can't do it because they can't get deep enough, then what will? Do we send four separate teams to do it? Use drills? Something . . . anything," Nathan said and looked around the mission briefing room, not liking what he saw. A long silence took hold of the room, with no one daring to speak. They were paralyzed by fear and he needed them to snap out of it. "Focus on the solution."

Major Shelton cleared her throat. "If we were to send in teams to storm the Vemus Alpha, they'd need to know the target depth they had to reach."

"We have four bombs, but the trouble isn't with the shape of the Alpha because it's not one big ship. It's made up of smaller ships that have somehow been absorbed into a jumbled mass. If we think of the Alpha as a large asteroid, then perhaps getting our bombs as close to the center as possible would do the trick," Nathan said.

Major Roberts shook her head. "It's not the same. Ordinarily, yes, that would work, but we're dealing with an unknown substance. The exoskeleton grows, and it's the real thing keeping that ship together. So while getting our bombs as far into the ship as possible is a step in the right direction, there's no guarantee it would work."

"What about sending the four missiles into the seven-kilometer hole General Gates blew in there from Phoenix Station? It's already a structural weak point," Lieutenant LaCroix said.

"Maybe, and that's a big maybe because we can't get any recon drones inside there to determine the extent of the damage," Major Roberts said.

"If it *is* a weak point, the Vemus would likely have it guarded," Nathan said.

He agreed with Major Roberts. They needed eyes inside the Vemus Alpha, but he doubted the Vemus would be cooperative about it. They had combat shuttles, but whoever he sent on that mission would likely never return. Nathan knew there would be no shortage of volunteers, but he'd only make that kind of sacrifice if he knew it was worth it.

"Someone has to go take a look then," Lieutenant LaCroix said.

"I'm not sure that would work," Nathan said.

"Why not, Colonel?" Major Shelton asked.

"If we start poking around, the Vemus will know we're interested in that area. If we're going to send a team in, they might as well take the bombs with them and finish the job. The rub is we don't know if the bombs would do enough damage to destroy the ship, and given its proximity to the planet, pieces of the ship could crash into New Earth," Nathan said.

"What if we draw them away from the planet?" Major Roberts said.

"To where?" Lieutenant LaCroix asked.

"Here. If we lure them here and destroy the ship, who cares if it crashes into the moon? Their ship would just make another crater but wouldn't do any real damage to the moon," Major Roberts said.

"How do we get them to come here?" Nathan asked.

"I think you said earlier something about all or nothing. We attack them with everything we have. Reveal our presence," Major Roberts said.

Nathan thought about it for a moment and then nodded. "I think you're onto something," he said and noted the somber expressions in the room. "Look, I don't like this situation any more than you do. Frankly, I'd prefer a solution that didn't end with all of us dying, but if Major Roberts is right and we do this, we'll save everyone on New Earth."

A comlink opened to the mission briefing room.

"Colonel Hayes, please report to the command area," Sergeant Martinez said over comms.

"I'm on my way," Nathan replied.

The comlink closed.

"I invite anyone to come up with a better solution, but I think Major Roberts' idea is the best we've got. We don't have time to endlessly debate this. Time is running out, so if anyone has serious doubts about our way forward, voice them right now," Nathan said.

The Lunar Base staff in the mission briefing room remained silent, if a little pale.

"Alright then. Let's get to work. We're essentially kicking a hornet's nest," Nathan said and headed for the door.

Major Shelton met him at the door. "Colonel, if it's alright with you, I'll stay in here and keep them on task."

"I'll be back as soon as I can," Nathan said.

He walked down the corridor, heading toward the command area. Two CDF soldiers on duty at the door saluted him as he walked by. Nathan entered the command area and walked over to the communications workstation.

"What have you got, Sergeant?" Nathan asked.

"Sir, we've just received a message from Captain Walker,"

Sergeant Martinez said.

Nathan frowned and peered at the message. Captain Walker had left them to search for the salvage team his brother was on. "Update the encrypted channel using what Captain Walker sent us."

"Yes, sir," Sergeant Martinez said. After a few moments, she added, "Relays are up. We're bouncing the signal so the Vemus will have trouble locking on, but it won't last that long."

"Understood," Nathan said and grabbed a headset.

A comms channel opened and he saw Captain Walker's face appear onscreen.

"Colonel, we tried to reach the base when we noticed three Cruiser-class ships orbiting the moon. We assumed they were Vemus, so we came up with this alternative way to communicate," Captain Walker said.

"What's your status?" Nathan asked.

Captain Walker's gaze looked pained for a moment. "We found the salvage team but they were contaminated. All team members have been killed. We encountered Vemus soldiers in one of the large pieces of wreckage."

"I'm sorry to hear that," Nathan said.

"Sir, my brother was able to learn more about the Vemus, maybe even a way to stop them," Captain Walker said.

Nathan's eyes widened.

"Colonel, Vemus cruisers are closing in on our position," Sergeant Martinez said.

Nathan nodded to her and turned back to Captain Walker. "Can you transmit what you've found?"

"We're running out of time. We'll work on getting the data to you—"

The comms channel was severed.

"What happened?" Nathan asked.

"The comms channel was cut on their end, Colonel," Sergeant Martinez said.

Nathan frowned for a moment and then blew out a breath. "Keep monitoring for them."

"Yes, sir," Sergeant Martinez said. "What did they find in the wreckage?"

"Brian Walker was a scientist who wanted to get a living sample of Vemus tissue. He might have discovered something about them," Nathan said and pressed his lips together. "See if you can get someone from R&D up here. Brian's team. Maybe they'll have more of an insight."

Sergeant Martinez said she'd get right on it and Nathan walked over to the tactical workstation where Lieutenant Johnson was on duty.

"What can I do for you, Colonel?" Lieutenant Johnson asked.

"We have a combat shuttle that has important information aboard and we need to get it back to base. Given that Vemus cruisers are in the area, can you think of a way we can get that crew back here safely?" Nathan asked.

Lieutenant Johnson bit his lower lip. "I need a few minutes, sir."

We all need a few minutes, Nathan thought but nodded at Johnson. "The key to defeating the Vemus might be aboard that shuttle, Lieutenant."

"Understood, Colonel."

The Vemus cruisers could move faster and shoot from a far greater distance than a combat shuttle was capable of and he wasn't sure that one lone shuttle could make it safely back to base. He racked his own brain, trying to think of a way to bring Captain Walker in. Nathan gritted his teeth. Nothing was ever easy.

27

CONNOR CHECKED the gray bulkhead door. The repair teams had done a quick patch and then moved on to another part of the station that required attention. It appeared that the partial remains of subsection six was all that was left of Phoenix Station. It had been the centermost area of Phoenix Station where the main Command Center was located, and the reinforced superstructure was the only reason any of them were still alive. They'd been leaking atmosphere in so many places that Connor had tasked every able-bodied person not working on repairs of critical systems to pitch in with patching up the holes. That included him. The lights from his EVA suit made it possible to see what he was doing. He reached inside the supply case and pulled out a repair kit containing liquefied material that could be applied in a vacuum. Once the repair kit material was activated, it quickly adhered and bonded to the surface, filling in the cracks.

Connor gave it a moment to set and then opened a comlink. "That should do it for this area. Try to pressurize the section."

"Copy that, General. You might want to move to the side in case the patch doesn't work," Captain Randle said.

Connor stepped to the side and waited. No need to tempt fate at this point, and besides that, he knew Captain Randle could see him through the camera feed from the nearby recon drone.

"Pressurizing now, General," Captain Randle said.

Connor watched the area he'd just patched and his suit sensors didn't detect any trace of escaping atmosphere. "Looks good from out here," Connor said.

"Same in here, as well. Pressure holding. Dr. Kim will be ecstatic to have his research lab back," Captain Randle said.

Phoenix Station had been home not only to Colonial Defense Force personnel but scientists and engineers as well. Each one of those scientists and engineers believed their work was crucial to defeating the Vemus. While Connor acknowledged the importance of their work, it didn't supersede systems like life support and thrusters. They were still focusing on surviving, and weapons capability was beyond them at the moment.

"That's all the repairs in this area, General. Now please come back inside," Captain Randle said with just a hint of exasperation.

"Understood. On my way back, Captain," Connor said. He packed up his repair case and headed for the nearest airlock. It had felt good to do some hands-on work for a change. The remains of Phoenix Station weren't quite as knocking-on-death's-door as they had been when he'd first awakened after the Vemus Alpha had nearly destroyed them.

"What's the status of the communications array?" Connor asked.

"They should be finishing that up soon, sir," Captain Randle replied.

The airlock doors opened and Connor stepped inside. Once the airlock doors were shut, he disabled his magboots. There was a blast of air as the airlock pressurized and then the interior doors opened. Captain Randle waited nearby. Connor used his neural implants to tell the EVA suit systems to retract his helmet, which then unclasped itself in the front and collapsed into the thick holding chamber at the base of his neck. Connor breathed in the station's air and could still detect trace amounts of smoke. The atmospheric scrubbers were working overtime to make the air breathable, but considering how many people had died, he felt lucky to be breathing at all.

He'd caught a glimpse of all the wreckage from the other subsections of Phoenix Station. Because his EVA suit helmet had excellent optics, he'd also been able to see the wreckage that was in relatively close proximity, but they hadn't made contact with either Bravo or Charlie stations. Connor hoped Captains Mason and Saunders and their crews were still alive.

Connor looked at Captain Randle. "If the communication array is almost up, that means a scanner array should be up soon as well."

"That's affirmative, General," Captain Randle said.

A short Asian man walked out of a nearby room. He looked over at them and smiled excitedly. "General Gates, thank you so much for repairing this section."

"You're welcome, Dr. Kim," Connor said.

Dr. Young Kim regarded Connor for a moment. "You don't realize what we have in this lab. There are samples of different viruses and bacteria we've gathered from New Earth that could be instrumental in our fight against the Vemus."

"I'm glad the redundant power systems were able to keep your samples alive," Connor said and looked up at Captain Randle. The bear of a man chuckled.

They'd been through this a few times. Connor knew research labs had their place, but of all the areas that could've survived the attack on Phoenix Station, he didn't think the research lab rated very high.

"You're still not convinced," Dr. Kim said.

"I meant no disrespect to you or your work, Dr. Kim. It's just that the Vemus Alpha is still out there and we need to find a way to stop them. I'm not sure how your samples of microscopic organisms are going to help us with that," Connor said.

Dr. Kim seemed unperturbed by Connor's answer. "Actually, General Gates, the best chance we have of defeating them is within my lab."

Connor frowned curiously. "Okay, you've piqued my curiosity. Want to explain it to me then?"

Dr. Kim's eyes widened with excitement. "I'd be happy to. If you'd follow me—"

There was an audible comms chime in the corridor they were in and Connor waited for the announcement.

"General Gates, communications and scanning capabilities have been restored. PRADIS is starting to update, sir," Lieutenant Daniels said.

"Acknowledged, Lieutenant. We're on our way," Connor said and looked at Dr. Kim. "Hold that thought, Dr. Kim. I'll be back down here later and you can tell me about what's so important in your lab."

"Of course. I look forward to it, General Gates," Dr. Kim said.

Connor and Randle started making their way toward the

Command Center. A direct path from the section they were in was no longer possible, so they had to circle toward the outer fringes of the wreckage. Connor had to prioritize certain areas, and though they were intact, they had to conserve their power consumption. The overhead lighting had been so badly damaged during the Vemus Alpha attack that there were entire corridors without lighting, but there was limited power available. Repair teams had set up temporary lighting in those corridors.

Connor checked the reports from Engineering as they walked. "Doesn't look like we'll get much beyond emergency power."

"The main reactor is gone, so we're basically running on reserves and the backup reactor," Captain Randle said.

"Looks like one of the hangar decks isn't damaged," Connor said while still reading the high-level reports. "Even if we crammed everyone into the shuttles we have, it still wouldn't be enough to get everyone off the station. We could use the remaining escape pods, but that wouldn't get us back to New Earth."

"One thing at a time," Captain Randle said. "We've got comms and scanners back up."

Connor nodded and hastened toward the command area. When they arrived, they saw that the medics had moved the wounded to another location, but there was blood in some areas that hadn't been cleaned up yet. The main holoscreen was still only showing a partial window, so Connor went to his workstation and brought up his own screen.

"Comms, what's our status?" Connor asked.

"There are still limited broadcast signals from New Earth. But the Vemus attack has begun and these broadcasts are several hours old, sir," Lieutenant Daniels said.

"Ops, what's our current position?" Connor asked.

"We have limited thruster capability, but we've stabilized our position so we're not simply spinning through space anymore. At twenty million kilometers, we're still a long way from New Earth, but we're heading in the right direction, sir," Lieutenant Rawn said.

Connor nodded. "Comms, are there enough communications satellites still up to get a message to Lunar Base?" he asked.

"Yes, there are, General," Lieutenant Daniels said.

"Good. Send an encrypted message to Lunar Base letting them know our current position," Connor said.

If Colonel Hayes was able to, he'd open a direct comlink to their position, which should minimize the risk of the Vemus detecting the signal. He checked PRADIS, but it was still gathering data.

"General, I've received a reply from Lunar Base. They've sent us the coordinates to a specific comms satellite using a nonregulation encrypted channel," Lieutenant Daniels said.

Connor frowned. "Nonregulation?"

"It's not CDF-specific, but it's not NA Alliance military either, sir," Lieutenant Daniels said.

"Alright, connect us using that channel, then. Directly to my screen, Lieutenant," Connor said.

Connor waited a few seconds for the connection to establish and then saw Colonel Hayes on his screen.

"It's great to see you alive, General," Colonel Hayes said.

"You too," Connor replied.

"Before I bring you up to speed, I need you to know that this comms channel will only be secure for a short period of time," Colonel Hayes said and proceeded to inform Connor of what had happened.

"I didn't think the Vemus Alpha was going to attempt a landing on New Earth. The Alliance military couldn't even do something like that with their larger ships, and we all know how big that Alpha is. I think you did the right thing, Colonel," Connor said.

"General, you're pretty banged up. I'd really like to send out a few shuttles to resupply you until we can get a rescue mission organized," Colonel Hayes said.

"We could use those supplies, but we need to focus our efforts on stopping the Vemus," Connor said.

Colonel Hayes's eyebrows wrinkled in grim acknowledgment. "We do have one of our shuttles that was in the debris field when the Vemus attacked. With the Vemus cruisers in the area, we've been trying to find a way to bring it in without alerting the Vemus to our location. The crew was sent to investigate a salvage and recon mission to attempt to learn more about the Vemus."

"What did they learn?" Connor asked.

"We're not exactly sure. The salvage team was lost, but the rescue team was able to retrieve the data and the Vemus samples that were gathered. The lead scientist believed he'd discovered crucial information that would help us defeat the Vemus," Colonel Hayes said.

"That sounds good, but I'm sensing some uncertainty," Connor replied.

"We're dealing with combat shuttle comms. With the Vemus cruisers around we can't even establish a connection to the shuttle long enough to dump the data," Colonel Hayes said.

Connor nodded. "I'm beginning to understand. Who's in command of the shuttle?"

"Captain Jon Walker. He's a good man, but he's just lost his brother, who was part of the salvage mission. It was his brother,

Brian, who made the discovery about the Vemus," Colonel Hayes said.

"Send orders to Captain Walker to bring his shuttle to me," Connor said.

"I was afraid you'd say that, sir, and I'd be remiss in my duty if I didn't warn you about the degree of risk involved. The mission report provided by Captain Walker indicates that the salvage team had become compromised by the surviving Vemus soldiers aboard the wreckage, so we can't be sure that Dr. Walker's claims about his Vemus discovery are really what we hope they are," Colonel Hayes said.

Connor leaned back in his chair and rubbed the stubble on his chin. "We don't have a choice. Order Captain Walker to come here and we'll see what we've got. We can't afford to leave any stone unturned."

"Understood, General," Colonel Hayes said.

They had to close the comlink after that because their time had run out and the risk of a Vemus cruiser discovering the signal would put both Lunar Base and the remains of Phoenix Station at risk. They agreed to reconnect again in a few hours' time.

"At least we haven't lost Lunar Base," Captain Randle said.

Connor looked at Captain Randle. "We're still in this fight," he said. "Ops, inform the hangar bay that we have a combat shuttle on its way to us."

"Yes, General," Lieutenant Rawn said.

Connor looked at Captain Thorne. "Do we have any weapons capability?"

"No, sir. We thought we might have had a few rail-guns and perhaps some point defenses, but those systems are too far gone. Essentially, we're a lifeboat at this time," Captain Thorne said.

Connor gritted his teeth for a moment. He supposed it would have been too much to hope for that they had any serious weapons capability. "Understood. Captain, I want you to continue compiling a list of our assets. I need an inventory of everything we've got."

"Yes, General," Captain Thorne said and went back to work at his terminal.

"Ops, when will PRADIS be back up and running?" Connor asked.

"The scanning array is up. We're running passive scans now and processing the updates we've received from Lunar Base. I can give you a snapshot of the Vemus location within the last two hours, but that's it for now, sir," Lieutenant Rawn said.

The system was taking its sweet time coming back online. He guessed the PRADIS designers hadn't thought of the impact of being cut off from the primary computing core. There were a lot of things they hadn't thought of, so he'd have to be patient. Connor gestured for Captain Randle to follow him. "It shouldn't take the combat shuttle long to get here. I want to meet them when they land."

They headed to the lower decks, and Connor ordered a team of CDF soldiers to meet them in the hangar. Later, Connor watched as a CDF combat shuttle entered the hangar bay. There were gouges on the hull and damaged plating. The hatch on the side of the shuttle opened and a battered crew stepped out. Once they reached the floor, they stood at attention and saluted Connor.

"Welcome aboard Phoenix Station—what's left of it, that is," Connor said.

"Thank you, General," Captain Walker said. "I don't think we could stand being on that shuttle much longer."

A team of medics came forward to check the shuttle crew.

"We followed decontamination protocols, and the samples that were gathered are in the biological containment unit right here, sir," Captain Walker said and gestured to the metallic case in his hand.

"Captain, I understand you've lost your brother. He was on the salvage team?" Connor said.

"Yes, he was, General," Captain Walker said.

"What did he find?" Connor asked.

"We tried to do our own analysis of the data, but we didn't understand it," Captain Walker said.

Connor gestured for one of his soldiers to take possession of the case. "Let's get you and your team cleaned up. Then we can talk."

"I appreciate that, sir, but my brother died for this data. I need to know if . . . I just need to know, sir," Captain Walker said.

Connor regarded Captain Walker for a moment. He clutched the case in a white-knuckled grip.

"Alright. We have a few working labs. Let's head over to them and let those scientists analyze what you've got. In the meantime, the rest of your team will be debriefed and cleaned up," Connor said.

Captain Walker nodded, relieved.

Connor led them out, the CDF soldiers walking behind them. "Not what you were expecting, were they," he said.

Captain Walker frowned.

"The Vemus. Colonel Hayes reported that you encountered Vemus soldiers," Connor said.

Captain Walker's expression hardened. "No, they weren't, sir. I have trouble believing they were once people."

Connor nodded, remembering his own encounter with them. "They might have been people once but not anymore."

They headed toward the biological lab where Dr. Young Kim waited for them.

"I hadn't expected you to return so soon, General," Dr. Kim said.

"Circumstances have changed. Captain Walker here has brought live tissue samples taken from Vemus soldiers. There has already been a preliminary analysis done by Dr. Brian Walker," Connor said.

Dr. Kim's eyes darted toward Captain Walker and then he glanced at the other soldiers. "Where is Dr. Walker?"

"He didn't make it," Captain Walker replied.

Dr. Kim's gaze softened. "I'm very sorry to hear that."

"I have his data. He died for it," Captain Walker said.

"Yes, of course. I'll take very good care of it. Please upload over here," Dr. Kim said and gestured toward the nearest terminal at the end of a long table.

Dr. Kim walked over to the terminal, completely ignoring the case with the Vemus samples. They waited a few minutes while he studied the information. Connor glanced around the lab. There were all sorts of instruments and containers marked as cold storage.

Dr. Kim looked up from his terminal. "This is remarkable."

"We're glad you approve, but we need to know if there's something in there we can use against the Vemus," Connor said.

"Brian said he'd found the key to destroying the Vemus for good," Captain Walker said.

Dr. Kim bit his lower lip and glanced down at the screen. His eyes slid into a look of calculation, as if he were weighing the possibilities, and then he snorted. "I can see why he thought that."

Connor's brows pulled together. "Do you agree with his findings?"

Dr. Kim frowned. "What Dr. Walker discovered was that the Vemus behave like a hive. There's a strict hierarchy," he said and looked at Connor. "I recall your reports on the Vemus included an opinion that they weren't very imaginative."

"That's right. They only seem to react to the immediate threat," Connor replied.

"How can they be a hive? That doesn't make any sense," Captain Walker said.

Dr. Kim shrugged. "Actually, a hive hierarchy is one of the dominant groupings of life. We've seen it on an insect level but also among microorganisms. So it's not much of a stretch of the imagination that the Vemus have this hierarchy as well."

"There's a lot that doesn't add up here. Hives don't work this way. They don't cross interstellar space to hunt humans," Connor said.

"No, they don't," Dr. Kim said. "What we're seeing is a parasitic organism that's in symbiosis with a very specific virus. One cannot survive without the other."

"If there's a hive, then there's a queen. Will the hive die if we kill the queen?" Connor asked.

Dr. Kim shook his head. "I may have oversimplified what the Vemus are. They're hive-like. I need some time to look at Dr. Walker's data and the samples he's collected."

"We're a little short on time. How much do you think you need?" Connor asked.

"This is where you expect me to give you a completely unreasonable timeframe because I'm a scientist who can't see beyond what's directly in front of him. But I assure you, General, I'm well aware of the stakes. Give me a half hour to look things over carefully and then I'll have more answers for you, or at the very least a reasonable estimate," Dr. Kim said.

Connor swallowed hard. "Thirty minutes," he said and left the lab.

Connor walked back into the corridor, his mind replaying what Dr. Kim had said. He really could have used Wil Reisman's help with all this or even Noah's—both were good at finding the devil in the details. He glanced behind him and saw Captain Randle and Captain Walker following him. They were good men, but they weren't Sean. He was surprised by just how much he'd come to rely on Sean Quinn's counsel. He didn't regret sending Sean back to New Earth, but he did wish he was still here with them. Connor closed his eyes and took a deep breath. He thought about Lenora and felt his chest tighten. She certainly had never pulled any punches when dealing with him. He wondered what she'd do if she were here.

Connor stopped walking and leaned up against the wall. "What do you think about what Dr. Kim said?"

"Honestly, sir, this is beyond my expertise. I don't know what to think," Captain Randle said.

"What about you, Walker?" Connor said.

"Brian wouldn't have made the claim that the data he'd found was important unless he really thought it was. He knew he was never getting out of that ship. He'd been infected, along with the entire salvage team. He even stopped the other team members from trying to escape. So if you're asking me whether I believe what my brother said is true, then I do, sir," Captain Walker said.

"The hive theory makes sense, but I'm not sure if that's because I *want* it to make sense. We know the Vemus were using some type of command/control signal for the fleet. We blocked that signal and it severely limited their fighting capability. So there's evidence to support that we're at least dealing with a centralized intelligence," Connor said.

"Sir, how do we go from a disease that spreads among mammals and then, when we try to fix it, it targets humans exclusively? That's what was in the data from the *Indianapolis*. I can understand how the virus spreads, but for it to become some type of collective intelligence, I'm not sure how we can defeat that other than by taking the damn thing out," Captain Randle said.

Connor sighed. "I think you're right. We just need Dr. Kim to confirm it, and hopefully those samples will give us something we can use against them."

Captain Randle frowned. "What's to stop this thing from spreading to creatures from New Earth?"

"There's no way to know for sure. The experts won't say. They'll only say something about life developing on different evolutionary paths. Plus, we know that Earth scientists modified the virus, which made it into something outside of nature," Connor said.

Captain Walker nodded. "I remember my brother mentioning that. But we can't afford to let any of them escape."

"You'll get no arguments from me on that. Let's give Dr. Kim some time and hope he'll give us some good news. In the meantime, we need to come up with a plan to take out that Vemus Alpha," Connor said.

"General, this station doesn't have any weapons capabilities," Captain Randle said.

Captain Walker arched a brow in surprise.

Connor leveled his gaze at them. "Yes, it does."

"We have no missiles or heavy weapons, sir," Captain Randle said.

"You're right, we don't, but I was thinking of something much more dangerous," Connor replied.

Captain Randle frowned in confusion.

"Never underestimate the power of what a soldier can accomplish with the use of only his rifle. There are a few hundred of us left here, and we have the element of surprise," Connor said.

28

SIERRA WAS a war zone and Sean was at the epicenter. Vemus soldiers roamed the streets of the outer city, hunting for them. Sean was in the upper levels of a high-rise building, and the high-pitched whistles and clicks of the Vemus soldiers drew closer as a horde of them closed in on Sean and his team. The combined CDF and Field Ops forces had held the line for as long as they could before retreating. Civilian militia helped with the wounded, running them back to temporary safe zones so they could be transported away from the city.

Sean looked through the scope of his M-Viper rifle and watched a group of Vemus soldiers surround a fallen CDF soldier who was in a twisted heap, covered with a thick black liquid. The soldier squirmed, and for a moment, his face was free of the viscous liquid. He struggled to move his arms but the Vemus pinned him down to the ground. The soldier screamed. Something dark slithered along his body and went into his mouth. The soldier's eyes widened as he tried to cry out. Sean lined up his shot and squeezed the trigger. A lone shot of mercy rang out amidst the gunfire that raged throughout Sierra. The writhing CDF soldier jerked back and then was still. Sean moved away from the window. He'd lost count of how many shots he'd taken like that. Mercy killings. He preferred to think he was easing their pain, but it only slowed the Vemus down. They didn't abandon anyone on the battlefield regardless of whether they were living or not. All seemed to have equal value.

There was a muffled bang from several floors beneath them.

"We can't stay here. They're through the barricade downstairs," Lieutenant Compton said. "There's a Hellcat waiting for us on the roof, Major."

Sean followed Lieutenant Compton up the stairs. The Vemus had ignored the buildings unless they knew CDF were inside. He'd ordered CDF soldiers to remain behind beyond the line of battle to hamper the Vemus soldiers as they pushed forward. They'd conceal their locations and then strike the enemy from behind before escaping to the next building using temporary walkways.

The Vemus seemed conditioned to engage only with something directly in their path, and Sean exploited this weakness for as long as it was effective, but they eventually caught on. The Vemus always did, and in this case it didn't take them long to learn that they had to start clearing the buildings before moving forward. The longer the Vemus engaged the Colonial Defense Force, the more intelligent they became in the execution of their tactics.

Sean ran up the stairwell and heard a Hellcat troop carrier flying overhead. They didn't stop in any one place for very long. He'd tasked the Hellcats with transporting soldiers, removing them from hot zones but keeping them in the fight for as long as they were able. The Hellcats were armed with an M-180 gauss cannon capable of firing thirty-millimeter projectiles in rapid succession. When engaged, the M-180 was capable of mowing down whatever enemy force was in its path. The problem was the damn Vemus energy weapons, which were capable of bringing down even the Hellcats. But the Hellcats could provide air support for a limited time and sometimes that made all the difference for the mobile infantry units on the ground. No sooner would a CDF squad get picked up than they were deposited at another location within the city. The CDF still fought, even knowing they had no hope of pushing the enemy out of the city. Instead, they fought to kill as many Vemus soldiers as they could while drawing them farther *into* the city.

Sean and the others exited the stairwell and followed Lieutenant Compton onto the waiting Hellcat. As soon as he was aboard and the Hellcat pilot was flying away, a CDF soldier raised a rocket launcher to his shoulder and fired it at the building. There was a brief lull in the area before the interior of the building exploded, killing all the Vemus soldiers inside.

In an instant, the hard work of the colonists was ripped to pieces. Sean had stopped telling himself they'd rebuild it all someday. It didn't help. After destroying several buildings, it didn't feel as if there would ever be anything here but death and destruction. A deep-seated fury took hold of him each time a part of Sierra was demolished. They'd killed so many Vemus soldiers, but it was never enough. The brief euphoria at gouging the enemy's numbers was always short-lived. In the beginning, he'd relished the feeling. Striking the enemy down had sparked a deep satisfaction, knowing he'd hurt the things that were there to kill them. Then, bitterness set in at the reality of what they were facing. What good was a victory when they had to destroy their home in order to survive? But still, he would fight. He clutched his rifle—just as all the CDF soldiers had—and kept throwing himself into the fray. Survival required a sacrifice paid for in blood, and the colony as a whole was paying a terrible price.

Sean glanced over to the side and watched as another Hellcat flew toward a rooftop to extract soldiers waiting for a pickup. As the Hellcat approached the rooftop, a large group of Vemus soldiers stormed onto the rooftop of a neighboring building and threw themselves at the ship. The pilot tried to steer the ship away, but some of the Vemus fighters made it on board. Sean raised his weapon and called for help. He aimed and glimpsed the soldiers inside the Hellcat, trying to fight the Vemus soldiers. Deadly blue bolts flashed inside the aircraft. The Vemus had long abandoned the less effective white stunner bolts. The blue bolts could penetrate armor and combat suits alike. Sean was about to fire his weapon when the Hellcat slammed into the neighboring building and crashed onto the street below. Sean ordered the pilot to bring them around so they could search for survivors, but before they could move into position there was an orange flash and the Hellcat exploded. As the Vemus began to turn deadly weapons toward their aircraft, the pilot quickly flew them away.

Sean clenched his teeth and glared at the building swarming with Vemus soldiers. "Sergeant Mitchell, take out that building."

"Sorry, Major, no more rockets," Sergeant Mitchell replied.

Sean blew out a harsh breath and sat down, using his neural implants to sift through the updates from his platoon commanders. The sun was waning in the sky and the Vemus showed no signs of slowing down. Their own equipment worked just fine at night, so it was safe for Sean to assume that the Vemus wouldn't be stopping to rest anytime soon. Did they ever rest?

"Sir, I have a comlink from Captain Diaz. He's on his way to the tower already," Lieutenant Compton said.

"Put him through," Sean said.

A new connection registered with the comlink interface.

"Major, the battle lines are collapsing. The CDF forces to the east are already at the central tower. They were hit pretty hard," Captain Diaz said.

Sean could hear the sounds of the battle on the other end of the comlink. "Understood. We need to hold that tower. I'll send reinforcements there now."

"Sir, I was hoping you would be among the reinforcements," Captain Diaz said.

Sean frowned. They were nowhere near the central tower. He glanced out the open hatchway to get his bearings, and his eyes widened. He'd completely lost his sense of direction. They'd been fighting and moving from building to building while drawing the Vemus steadily toward the central part of the city. A heavy toll had been extracted from the Vemus, but Sean couldn't quite believe that they were already near the central city line.

He looked at Lieutenant Compton grimly. "Order the retreat. All troops are to fall back to the tower. If they can't make it, they're to go to the designated extraction points for pickup," Sean said. "We'll see you shortly, Captain Diaz."

"Understood, Major," Captain Diaz said, and the comlink closed.

Sean went to the cockpit. "Change in plans. Take us to the tower."

"Yes, Major," the pilot said.

They didn't have far to fly. There were still a lot of Hellcats in the air, and when it became apparent that they weren't going to hold the city, certain members of the CDF requested permission to set up a few parting gifts for the Vemus. High-grade explosives were hastily deployed, waiting to be triggered by the unsuspecting Vemus forces. Those explosives would stop the Vemus fighters permanently.

It was then that Sean noticed the smaller Vemus fighters as they reached the tops of the buildings and attempted to glide to the next one. They had skin that stretched from their wrists to their feet. They were much smaller than the average Vemus fighter, at only five feet in height. But for what they lacked in height, they made up in numbers. They were astonishingly fast, but they were also easier to bring down. Sean saw a group of them try to reach the rooftop of a building where the CDF had an M-180 gauss gun nest. The soldiers fired the M-180, cutting the gliding Vemus fighters down, and their small bodies fell to the streets below.

The Hellcat took them to the landing area in the shadow of Sierra's tallest tower. Sean and the rest of the team climbed out and the Hellcat flew off to extract another troop. With his boots on solid ground again he felt weakness deep in his muscles. He was beyond the safety of consuming more stimulants, but it didn't matter. He didn't have time to rest. None of them did.

The landing area was a buzz of activity as soldiers were dropped off and wounded soldiers were taken to the tramway beneath the city. There was only one tramway working. All the other tunnels had been destroyed to prevent the Vemus from using them.

Director Mills walked toward him. His towering form allowed his long strides to quickly cover the distance between them, and his gaze no longer held the bitter disgust it had displayed earlier.

Sean looked at the Director of Field Ops and Security. "Are the trams still running?"

"They are. All these soldiers are being moved there for the final run before we blow the last tunnel," Director Mills said.

"Better make it fast. The Vemus forces are going to make a major push right for this area," Sean replied.

Director Mills frowned and Sean guessed that his father's friend wanted to ask how Sean could possibly know what the Vemus were going to do.

"We'll get it done," Director Mills said.

Sean continued to walk. He needed to get to the Command Center they'd established inside the tower.

"Sean, wait," Mills said.

Sean stopped and looked back at him.

"I'm sorry about before. I should have trusted you," Mills said.

"It's gotta be hard since you've known me since I was a teenager," Sean replied.

Director Mills nodded. "And one who excelled at getting into trouble."

Sean snorted. "We've come a long way," he said and glanced at Lieutenant Compton, who gestured that they needed to get moving. Sean looked back at Mills. "Make sure you're on that last tram. I need someone to get those wounded soldiers to safety."

Director Mills arched a brow knowingly. "And here I thought you just wanted to get me out of the way."

"That too. You're a pain in the ass," Sean said with a half-smile.

Director Mills became somber. "About Phoenix Station . . ."

Sean felt his throat seize up as he fought the emotion. "I wouldn't count Connor out just yet."

Director Mills pressed his lips together. "No, you wouldn't, would you? Connor and I clashed on a lot of things, but I know he was very proud of you. He saw something in you that your father and I both missed."

Sean regarded Director Mills for a moment. "This isn't goodbye, Damon. I'll see you later."

Damon Mills nodded. "Right . . . see you later."

Sean left the Director of Field Ops and Security, keeping a firm grip on his emotions. Thinking about Phoenix Station and the fact that Sierra was a heartbeat from being destroyed threatened to topple his resolve. He hastened toward the tower and took the elevator to the CDF mobile Command Center. He remembered when the tower had been completed, commemorating the colony's sixth anniversary. It was a time when belief in a hostile attack force that was on their way here was starting to wane in earnest. All the preparations they'd made by building Titan Space station, the beginnings of the CDF space fleet, and the missile defense platforms had lulled them into a false sense of security, which Sean hadn't been completely immune to. He'd thought they would have more time. The only people whose commitment never wavered were Connor, Wil, and Kasey—the most senior military officers in the Colonial Defense Force and men who not only had actual combat experience but who had made a career of neutralizing threats that operated outside the normal confines of society. Those men might not have been ideally suited for mankind's first interstellar colony, but they were the best men to see that the colony survived what was coming. Wil and Kasey had been killed during the colony's first battle with the Vemus, and Sean had to admit, if only to himself, the very real possibility that Connor Gates was dead as well. Sean hated that he'd ever had the slightest inkling of doubt that an attack force like the Vemus was coming for them. It all seemed so foolish now with the benefit of hindsight.

The elevator doors opened and the CDF soldiers in the Command Center glanced up, immediately looking relieved that

Sean was there. Sean had seen this same thing many times when Connor walked into a room. There was a certain comfort that came when the burden of command rested on someone else's shoulders and that superior officer was someone like Connor. Sean kept expecting their gazes to shift to the side where Connor would normally have been standing, but they were all looking at him. The soldiers at the entrance saluted him, and Sean returned the salute as he walked past them.

Sean glanced toward the windows, where he saw multiple Hellcats flying in, dropping soldiers off. There were several flashes of light about half a kilometer from where the line of battle was still being fought.

"Major Quinn, I need you over here, sir," Captain Diaz called out from the CIC.

Sean turned away from the windows and walked over toward Diaz, who stood at the command table where the three-dimensional holographic display was focused in on the tower and the immediate surrounding area. Sean grabbed a canteen of water and gulped it down.

"Where do we stand, Captain?" Sean asked.

Captain Diaz regarded him for a moment with concern. "How many stims have you had beyond the recommended dosage, sir?"

Sean gave him a hard look, which he knew wouldn't change the pupil dilation in his eyes that had no doubt given him away. "Irrelevant, Captain."

Captain Diaz frowned but didn't press the matter. Sean knew he was beyond the maximum dosage allowed, but he also knew he could push the limits. He could hear his mother's voice in the back of his mind, scolding him for doing such a thing, but he ignored it. He had a job to do and had no time to worry about how his body would need to cope with the withdrawal symptoms from extended stim usage. If he survived long enough to experience the severe muscle cramping and the inability of his brain to determine reality, it would be a blessing.

"All CDF troops are falling back to this position. The Vemus have been pushing forward much harder than they were before. It's like they become more capable the longer they fight," Captain Diaz said.

"It's only going to get worse. Those bastards can smell blood in the water," Sean said.

Captain Diaz's face became a thoughtful frown. "Interesting choice of words. The last group of scientists we evacuated from here had a theory about the Vemus mimicking the behavior of ocean mammals, particularly predators, which might account for their appearance."

"Does it help us kill them?" Sean asked harshly, the stims barely keeping exhaustion at bay.

Captain Diaz's expression went back to business. "Well, they do seem to follow an alpha in their midst, which suggests they might organize themselves into packs."

"Which is why we've been targeting those alphas. It stalls their attack when we can take them down," Sean said.

"And they're the hardest to kill," Captain Diaz said.

"I don't care where the scientists think the Vemus came from. I only care about stopping them," Sean said.

"What about knowing one's enemy, sir?" Captain Diaz said evenly.

Sean shook his head and grinned. Connor had preached the importance of learning all they could about their enemy. "Point taken, but we really don't have time for a theoretical discussion," Sean said.

Captain Diaz nodded and brought up the Saber failsafe interface, which required Sean's authorization.

"It's a little too soon for that, don't you think?" Sean asked.

Saber failsafe was the CDF code for the self-destruct that would level the entire city.

"This is the authorization for it to be armed. Detonation has to be authorized by you or the next officer in the chain of command in the area," Captain Diaz said.

Sean took a long look at the authorization window that awaited his input. This was his plan for striking a crippling blow against the enemy, so why was it so hard for him to push the proverbial button? Sierra was their home and he hated seeing it destroyed. And what was worse was the fact that there was a Vemus Alpha ship filled with more soldiers, so was there even a point to the destruction? Sean gritted his teeth. Frowning, he looked away from the authorization prompt and sighed. He couldn't worry about the Vemus Alpha in orbit above the planet. The Vemus army in Sierra was what he needed to deal with. Sean used his implants to send his authorization codes, and the Saber failsafe armed. The authorization window flickered away and was replaced with the Saber failsafe status set to ARMED.

"You did the right thing, Major," Captain Diaz said quietly.

"Why does it feel so shitty then?" Sean asked.

"There are no perfect solutions," Captain Diaz replied.

Sean gave him a sidelong glance. "You sound like Connor now."

Captain Diaz snorted. "Who do you think I first heard say it?"

For the next ninety minutes, Sean helped coordinate the strategic withdrawal from Sierra. Wounded soldiers were loaded onto the tram and taken out of the city where ground support vehicles waited to take them to the gathering place. The secret encampment was located in a highly defensible position about a hundred kilometers from the city.

The Vemus pressed the CDF forces back to the tower. The strategic withdrawal of troops worked as long as their lines of soldiers weren't overwhelmed. Each group had to cover the retreat of the previous. There had been a steady stream of CDF soldiers making their way to the tower and then flying out on Hellcat troop carriers. Sean heard the fighting gain intensity down below as the Vemus stormed the landing field and ordered all soldiers in the tower to head to the roof. He glanced out the window and still saw CDF soldiers firing their weapons at the Vemus from nearby buildings surrounding the tower complex.

"We need to get those soldiers out of there before they're cut off," Sean said.

Captain Diaz contacted the Hellcat commander to relay Sean's orders. Sunset had long since passed and they were in the darkest of night—as dark as night could get on a planet with brightly lit rings around it. He saw the glowing points of the Hellcats' engines as they blazed by. There were more than a few CDF soldiers who had stayed behind, doing whatever they could to stall the enemy's advance. The city was being overrun, just as Sean had known it would be. If he'd kept all his soldiers in the city, they might have held it for another day, but the outcome would still have been the same. They would all be dead. The feeds from the recon drones that flew through the city showed Vemus fighters moving into the area, except for the groups that were busy lining up fallen CDF soldiers who were now covered in a viscous liquid that transformed into a dark pod. Something began to move inside some of them. Sean had taken his fair share of shots at them, as well as the Vemus in the surrounding area, but it only slowed down the metamorphosis happening inside the pods.

They headed to the roof and Sean caught the urgent chatter

from the teams still making their way up the tower. Vemus forces were trying to cut them off by scaling the outer walls.

"J-Squad to the edge of the roof. They need covering fire!" Sean ordered.

He grabbed his M-Viper and ran to the east side of the roof, where CDF soldiers slid toward the low walls. The corded safety lines that prevented people from leaning over the side had already been cut away. Sean squatted and quickly crawled toward the edge. CDF soldiers joined him, and he felt someone grab hold of his legs. Sean glanced behind him.

"Give 'em hell, sir!" the soldier said.

Other soldiers quickly moved in and did the same thing, throwing themselves over the legs of the soldiers who were firing their weapons at the Vemus.

Sean leaned over the edge of the thirty-meter-tall tower, which was minuscule compared to the major cities on Earth but was the tallest building in Sierra. He aimed his M-Viper. The light sensor on his scope had already adjusted to the darkness and compensated for it. Sean had a clear view of the Vemus soldiers scrambling up the walls. The creatures' claws gouged into the sides of the tower as they quickly climbed upward.

Sean squeezed the trigger, sending high-velocity projectiles downward and taking the Vemus soldiers by surprise. The Vemus were knocked from the sides of the building. Some slammed into other Vemus soldiers, knocking them off as well. Several floors beneath them, Sean saw the flashes of Vemus weapons fire.

Sean looked behind him and saw Compton. "Make sure they have backup in the stairwell, Lieutenant."

Compton ran off and Sean scanned below, looking for more Vemus to kill. Hellcats flew to the rooftops and CDF soldiers clambered to get aboard. Another Hellcat circled the tower and used its main M-180 gauss cannon to tear into the enemy. The

Hellcat stayed on the move, and the Vemus soldiers were unable to get a clear shot at it.

"Time to go, Major!" Captain Diaz shouted.

The soldier holding Sean's legs down pulled him back from the edge. Sean pushed himself up to his feet, thanking him, and they ran toward the waiting Hellcat. The tower was alive with the Vemus's high-pitched whistles and clicks, and it suddenly seemed like a spoken language that Sean couldn't begin to comprehend. All he knew was that he never wanted to hear that sound again. Sean reached the hatch on the Hellcat and gestured for the soldiers to climb aboard. A squad was covering the stairwell entrance. There were still CDF soldiers running through the door, escaping the hordes of Vemus inside. When the last soldiers came out, the nearest soldier threw a grenade and ran toward them. There was a bright flash as the grenade exploded.

"Your turn, sir," Captain Diaz said, gesturing with his thick, muscular arms.

Sean was about to turn and climb aboard when he noticed a dark shape scramble onto the rooftop. He reached out and grabbed Captain Diaz, shoving him aboard the Hellcat. Sean quickly followed while the Vemus opened fire on the Hellcat.

"Go! Go!" Lieutenant Compton bellowed.

Sean felt something hot singe through the armor protecting his shoulder, followed by intense pain. He cried out, and the CDF soldiers dragged him further into the Hellcat, away from the hatchway. The Hellcat's pilot maximized the thrusters and the troop carrier sped away.

"I'm fine. Let me up," Captain Diaz said.

He pushed his way to Sean's side and looked at his wounded shoulder.

"Get me a medical pack, ASAP!" Captain Diaz said and then looked at Sean. "Just had to be the hero, didn't you? Just lie there for a second. You're bleeding. That damn weapon of theirs cut right through your armor."

Sean gritted his teeth at the pain. "Now you owe me one."

Diaz snorted. "We'll see about that," he said and then glared at the nearest CDF soldier. "What the hell is taking so long? If you move any slower, you might be standing still, damn it!"

A CDF soldier hastened over, carrying a medical pack. Diaz reached inside and grabbed the medi-gun, which carried the treatment for severe burns.

"Alright, bite down. A lot of pain and then nothing at all. You ready?" Captain Diaz asked.

"Stop sweet-talking me and just do it already, Captain," Sean said through clenched teeth.

"You must have spoken to my wife. She likes to take charge, too," Captain Diaz said. He ripped open a sealed canister and shoved it into the medi-gun. "Alright, on three."

Sean didn't hear the rest because Diaz squeezed the trigger and medi-paste flooded the wound. Nanorobotic-filled paste swarmed over the wounded area and Sean's vision swam. He squeezed his eyes shut against the pain and then his shoulder became numb, but he was still gasping as he opened his eyes. He took several deep breaths and looked up at Diaz, who grinned down at him.

Sean climbed to his feet and looked at his shoulder. There was a thick, flexible mesh that looked like an extra layer of skin. He rolled his shoulder and felt a dull ache, but he knew better than to overdo it; his shoulder needed time to heal. At least the pain had lessened.

He looked at Diaz. "I thought you said you'd go on three?"

Captain Diaz smiled, showing a healthy set of pearly whites. "That's just so you'd relax before I got you."

"Thanks," Sean said dryly.

The cool night air came in through the open hatchway in the back of the Hellcat. Sierra was a sea of blazing fires. He could still hear the firing of CDF weapons from inside the city, but it was sporadic and spread out.

"There are men back there," Sean said.

"We can't get to them," Captain Diaz replied.

Sean pressed his lips together and clenched his teeth. The Vemus had taken the city. While they could chance a flyover high above the city, they couldn't risk going down there to extract the CDF soldiers they'd left behind. Sean walked toward the hatchway and watched. He'd gotten the Vemus to do exactly what he wanted, so why did he feel like they'd just lost the battle? The Hellcat raced past the edge of the city and over the dark forests beyond.

Captain Diaz came to his side. "All Hellcats still flying have cleared the city, sir."

Sean drew in a breath and held it, allowing his eyes to take in this last sight of the home they'd built. Buildings were burning, and many soldiers had died in defense of the city as part of their ruse to draw the Vemus in.

Sean used his neural implants to take control of the Hellcat's communications system. He sent out a warning signal to the other Hellcats, then counted to ten and sent the detonation signal for the Saber failsafe. Sean watched as a bright flash lit up Sierra as if a molten sun had just ignited in the middle of the city. He looked away from the bright light, but he couldn't block out the intense sound of the thermal nuclear explosion, which had enough force to level the city and the area surrounding it. One moment Sierra was there and the next it was gone, wiped clean off the face of New Earth. Sean wondered if they would later find a crater where the city had been or if it would just be scorched earth. He forced his gaze ahead, not wanting to look back at where Sierra had been.

The Hellcat was far enough away that they hadn't felt the kinetic forces from the explosion, and they experienced an uneventful twenty-minute flight to the away zone. The Hellcats and ground vehicles that had left earlier had made it to the coordinates. They were far away from the secret civilian bunkers they'd built, which Sean couldn't really think about at the moment.

Diaz came over and sat next to him. "You made the right call," he said.

Sean lifted his gaze and looked at him. "Would he have made the same call?" he asked.

Diaz nodded without even a hint of hesitation. "Connor would have done the same thing."

Sean sighed. "I guess that's something. The question remains: what happens when more soldiers from the Vemus Alpha come down here?"

Captain Diaz swallowed hard. "I'm sure Colonel Hayes and the rest of our forces at Lunar Base are going to take care of that."

Sean wished he had Diaz's confidence, but he didn't say that aloud. No need to spread disharmony in the face of losing their home.

The Hellcat landed and Sean walked down the ramp. The night air was fresh and cool, not at all like the acrid smoke they'd been breathing in Sierra. He glanced up at the deceptively peaceful night sky.

Lieutenant Compton walked over to him. "Major, they need you at one of the tents."

Sean shook his head. "Can't I get a moment, just one moment to get my bearings? Is that too much to ask!"

Lieutenant Compton looked over at Captain Diaz for a moment.

"Sir, it's your father. He's been hurt."

The exhaustion pressing in on Sean suddenly vanished. "Where is he?"

"Medical tent seven. This way," Lieutenant Compton said.

Sean followed the big lieutenant as they ran toward the CDF encampment. Tent seven was only a short distance from the landing zone. He ran inside the tent and saw his mother standing, grim-faced, beside a bed. Confusion and then surprise chased each other across Sean's face. His mother was supposed to be at Sanctuary. How'd she even gotten here? But as soon as the question formed in his mind, he realized his mother had probably bullied her way back. She looked up at his arrival, her eyes brimming with tears. Sean looked down and saw that his father was gravely wounded.

His mother wiped her eyes and walked over to him. "He doesn't have much time," she said.

Sean's mouth hung open. "What happened? Isn't there anything you can do?"

His father stirred at the sound of Sean's voice and opened his one good eye. The other was swollen shut. Sean could see that his father's torso was bloody and bruised beneath the white sheet. He lifted the sheet up and gasped.

"Sean," his father said.

Sean looked at his father and sorrow closed up his throat. "I sent you away from the combat zone. To make sure you were safe . . ."

The painfully grim lines of his father's mouth lifted. "I had to help, son," his father said softly.

The skin around Sean's eyes became tight and his vision started to blur. "You should have . . ."

"What? Gone to safety while other people died? That's not what you would have done."

Sean noted the stubborn gleam in his father's one good eye and recognized a similar view when he looked at himself in the mirror. He leaned closer to the bed. "Thank you."

His father's lips lifted for a moment and then his body arched in pain. He grabbed Sean and pulled him closer. "Survive," his father said in a harsh whisper, and then he collapsed to the bed, his body going limp. He heard his mother cry out and then slam her fist on his father's chest. She began administering chest compressions while calling out for medicine. None of the medics moved and Sean glanced at all the blood on the floor. There was no coming back from such a huge loss.

Sean reached for his mother and she snarled at him.

"He's. Not. Gone," she said, emphasizing each word with a compression.

Sean watched as his mother pounded on his father's chest. "He *is* gone. You need to stop."

Sean gently grabbed his mother's arms as they kept pressing on his father's chest. He brought his other arm around her shoulders, but she just wouldn't stop. "Please, Mom, you need to stop. He's gone."

Sean tried to pull his mother away but she drove her elbow into his stomach. He took hold of her firmly and pulled her back while she cried out, reaching toward his father. Sean held her as she sagged into his arms, weeping. He felt his own tears streaking down his face as everything he'd walled up inside burst forth. He clung to his mother and tried to be strong. It was what she needed. The people around them stepped back, giving them room. Theirs wasn't the only grief being felt that night, but Sean couldn't think of anyone else as his mother sobbed in his arms.

29

THERE WAS a heavy silence across the Command Center on Phoenix Station. Connor had just gotten an update from Lunar Base that Sierra had been destroyed.

"A nuclear explosion," Major Elder said. "We destroyed our own city."

Connor frowned as he reread the report.

"Major Quinn wouldn't have done this without careful consideration," Captain Randle said.

"He's right," Connor said.

"But, General, why would Major Quinn destroy not only Sierra but Delphi and New Haven?" Major Elder asked.

CDF soldiers in the Command Center craned their necks so they could hear Connor's response.

"We obviously don't have all the information, but my guess is that Major Quinn made a strategic decision," Connor said. "They couldn't hold the city, so he did exactly what I would have done—lure the enemy inside and then blow them to kingdom come."

"But General, there are people here who have families there," Major Elder said.

"The cities had already been evacuated and the most recent reports indicate that most civilians are safe at either the secret bunkers or Sanctuary. Look, I know it's tough being in the dark about what's going on back home. I get it. But we still have a job to do. We're still fighting for those same people," Connor said.

Slowly, the Command Center returned to its normal buzz of activity. He knew the war was far from over. With a ship that size, many more Vemus fighters were bound to begin the next stage of the invasion. The question remained: could the Vemus detect the bunkers they'd built, or Sanctuary?

"General Gates," Lieutenant Daniels said, "Dr. Kim has an update for you and requests that you join him in his lab."

Connor thanked her and gave a slightly annoyed glance at the main holoscreen, which was still broken.

"Captain Thorne, you have the con," Connor said.

"Yes, General," his tactical officer replied.

Connor left the Command Center and had Captain Randle send a comlink to Captain Walker to meet them at the lab. Major Elder followed them. Connor kept thinking about Sierra, trying to imagine just how bad the fighting must have been. The report he'd read indicated that the Vemus's fighting abilities had increased throughout the course of the engagement. Connor was familiar with soldiers becoming more adept at their jobs, but this was something different. If the war continued for a lengthy period of time, the Vemus would continue to become even more dangerous. Was this what had happened to the NA Alliance military? They needed to end this war quickly if they were going to have any hope of survival.

Connor walked into the Research and Development Lab. Captain Walker was already there and snapped to attention.

"At ease, Captain," Connor said and looked at Dr. Kim. "I've given you more than thirty minutes. Tell me you have some good news."

Dr. Kim nodded and then gestured one of his assistant researchers toward a clear container on the lab table. Connor glanced inside and saw a small puddle of dark liquid.

"What's in there?" Connor asked.

"It's them," Dr. Kim said. "Or at least it would be if it were to come into contact with humans. Watch."

Dr. Kim accessed one of the transference chambers and put a tiny ball of pinkish skin inside. The ball seemed to quiver. Dr. Kim closed the chamber door, pressed a button, and the ball of skin was deposited inside the chamber. The dark substance that was allegedly a Vemus had no reaction to it.

"That is a living tissue sample created from the DNA of a mouse. Observe how the Vemus sample has no reaction to it," Dr. Kim said.

Connor glanced back at the container. "We already knew the virus was modified to target humans."

Dr. Kim nodded and loaded another flesh-colored ball of skin into the transference chamber. "This was created from human DNA. Though it looks similar to the last sample, I assure you it's quite different," he said and then deposited the second sample into the container.

The dark liquid reacted almost instantly and began to move across the container toward the human tissue sample. It covered it completely. Connor glanced at Dr. Kim and then back inside the container. The Vemus sample was absorbing the human tissue sample and then it just stopped. The dark liquid sank back to the surface, becoming a pasty gray substance. The human tissue sample looked as if it had been only partially consumed.

Connor's mouth hung open in surprise. He leaned closer to

the container, looking for some indication that the Vemus sample would begin to reform, but it didn't. He looked at Dr. Kim, who was smiling proudly.

"Please tell me this is something we can use," Connor said.

"Oh yes, General. We can kill them now," Dr. Kim said with an excited gleam in his eyes.

Connor swallowed. "You need to explain to me exactly what just happened. How this works. Everything."

"Earth scientists had been trying to stop the Vemus for years before they lost everything. You've had these samples for barely an hour," Major Elder said.

Dr. Kim waved them over to the wallscreen. "We've been collecting samples of microscopic organisms from New Earth since we arrived, cataloging them and their properties. What we found was a native virus that breaks down the proteins in other viruses—the very same proteins the Vemus uses to keep itself together. In essence, it sterilizes the virus and starves the parasitic organism. We break the symbiotic chain. We know the Vemus are highly adaptive and that the virus is capable of absorbing the DNA of an infected host. This is then transferred to the parasite that then takes over the host. It introduces new DNA to the host with a set of instructions that causes genes to express at a geometric rate. It's quite literally like being reborn. Think along the lines of a human embryo in its early stages of development."

"And this is possible because we modified the virus?" Connor asked.

Dr. Kim's eyebrows rose. "That's the really interesting part. We already knew the virus the Vemus uses had been modified and we were told it was modified to avoid humans, that it was their plan since they couldn't cure it. This was to buy the people of Earth time to come up with a more permanent solution," Dr. Kim said.

Connor narrowed his gaze suspiciously. "Are you implying that someone deliberately modified the virus so it would target humans exclusively?"

"Once they modified the virus, by its very nature it would take in new DNA to improve itself . . ." Dr. Kim shook his head. "My point is that once they modified the virus, it became a synthetic organism that was designed to behave in a very specific way."

"You mean a weapon. The Vemus are a biological weapon!" Connor said, hardly daring to breathe.

"Precisely," Dr. Kim confirmed.

Connor leaned back and tried to get a handle on his racing thoughts. He clenched and unclenched his fists while he paced.

"But who would do such a thing?" Major Elder asked.

Dr. Kim shook his head. "I'm sorry. I don't know who actually did this. It could have been anyone—government agencies, terrorist organizations, corporate research conglomerates, or some rogue agency. Take your pick, but the evidence is there. The most catastrophic event of our time is of our own making."

Connor couldn't believe it. He didn't *want* to believe it, but it all made sense. "Someone back home seized an opportunity to become more powerful and it backfired on them."

"My guess is that it simply got out of control," Dr. Kim said.

"I don't understand. How could it have gotten out of control? They modified the virus," Major Elder said.

"They must have had some way to protect themselves or thought they had a way to stop it, making themselves into heroes in the process," Connor said.

"They could have done that anyway without obliterating the population," Major Elder said and shook his head.

"Think about it. They found a way to remove any obstacle in

their path, except they underestimated what they'd done. They tried to play God and the whole thing blew up in their faces. This whole thing makes me sick," Connor said in disgust.

They were silent for a few moments while they all digested what Dr. Kim had told them. Connor rested his hands on his hips and shook his head. One of the primary objectives of the Ghosts had been to stop things like this. Human ingenuity, which had spawned their most amazing creations, also came with the threat that the worst part of humanity could also rear its ugly head as well. If so, in a celestial blink of the eye, they would all be gone—just another intelligent, advanced race snuffed out of existence because of someone's blind ambition.

Connor looked at Dr. Kim. "You said we can kill them. How?"

"We can synthesize the virus. I've already spoken to Dr. Morgan. She's a nano-robotics engineer and she believes we can combine the two," Dr. Kim said.

"What good is that?" Connor asked.

"It will make our virus kill the Vemus faster. We can also do our own bit of manipulation to make it seek out the synthetic virus from Earth," Dr. Kim said.

"There has to be more to it than that. You said the Vemus operate like a hive. We've seen them function as if there was a centralized intelligence commanding them. Could you make enough of that stuff to take it out?" Connor asked.

"Most certainly, General," Dr. Kim said.

"How long will it take to make it?" Connor asked.

"We can have a batch ready in about seven or eight hours. Subsequent batches will be much faster as we perfect the process," Dr. Kim said.

Connor frowned as he calculated the time.

"What's the matter, General? I thought you'd have been pleased," Dr. Kim asked.

"We need it a lot faster than that," Connor said and opened a comlink alert message from the Command Center.

"We'll do the best we can," Dr. Kim said.

"You need to. The best way to stop the Vemus is to get aboard the Alpha ship, find wherever the hell this centralized brain is, and kill it at the source using whatever you come up with. You've got less than three hours to do it," Connor said.

Dr. Kim's brows drew up in a worried frown. "Why so little time?"

"Because we just got another update from Lunar Base. Colonel Hayes believes they're preparing for another attack on New Earth. Our best speed in the combat shuttles we have to reach the enemy ship is two hours. You've got one hour to prepare. We can bring whatever equipment you need with us," Connor said.

Dr. Kim's eyes widened. "Me? Go with you?"

"Will that be a problem?" Connor asked.

"We have a mobile lab that we can put on the shuttle, but we haven't perfected the process. I'm not sure we can do what you require in the time we have," Dr. Kim said.

"We don't have a choice. Lunar Base is reporting Vemus scout ships are searching the main continent. It's only a matter of time before they discover where we've hidden our friends and families," Connor said.

Dr. Kim's gaze darted around.

"General," Major Elder said, "why don't I stay behind and help Dr. Kim?"

"I think that would be best," Connor said. "One more thing. We need to send whatever method you come up with for creating this weapon to Lunar Base and they'll broadcast it to the colony."

Dr. Kim frowned in confusion.

"This way, if we fail, at least whoever's left will have a fighting chance. Some chance is better than none at all," Connor said.

Dr. Kim swallowed. "I'll do my very best, General."

Connor nodded and looked at Major Elder. "I'll see you in one hour in the hangar bay."

He left the lab, Captains Walker and Randle following him.

"General, I'd like to be on the away team," Captain Walker said.

"And there's no way you're going without me, sir," Captain Randle said.

"Don't worry, I'm not leaving you guys behind. I aim to bring everyone I can on this. We're going to end this thing one way or another," Connor said.

"Looking forward to it, sir. I'll head to the hangar bay and see about getting the combat shuttles we have ready to fly," Captain Walker said.

Connor and Captain Randle went back to the Command Center. They had a lot of work to do and very little time to get it done. Captain Thorne saluted Connor as he approached the command area.

"Captain Thorne, I need to know what we have left regarding infantry weapons and combat suits. Everything. Do we have enough to equip every able-bodied person left on this station?" Connor asked.

Captain Thorne blinked his eyes a few times while he processed Connor's request. "I need a few minutes to look that up, sir."

"Understood, Captain," Connor said and looked at Lieutenant Rawn. "Ops, I need an intercept course that will take us right to the Vemus Alpha executed at once. Best speed possible."

"Right away, General," Lieutenant Rawn said and began typing furiously on his holo-interface. "Course laid in. Best speed will put us there in five hours."

Connor frowned. Five hours wasn't the best time he could have hoped for, but it was what he had to work with. "Course correction, Lieutenant. Put us in geosynchronous orbit with New Earth. Should be about the same travel time."

"Yes, sir. Course correction updated," Lieutenant Rawn said.

"Very well," Connor replied.

"I have those figures you asked for, General," Captain Thorne said.

Connor went over to the tactical workstation with Captain Randle at his side. "Alright, let's see what we've got."

30

NATHAN HAD HARDLY LEFT the Command Center on Lunar Base, and instead of returning to the mission briefing room, he had his staff join him there. After spending the last several hours planning their attack on the Vemus Alpha, they detected multiple nuclear detonations on the planet where the cities of the colony had been. Delphi had been the first to be destroyed, and within a few hours, New Haven followed. It wasn't until ten hours afterward that there was a massive nuclear explosion at Sierra. He immediately sent an update to Connor on Phoenix Station. Lunar Base had later received an encoded message simply stating that the CDF ground forces were still intact.

Learning that the colony's three major cities had been destroyed was hard to take, but it was Connor who'd figured out what Major Quinn had done. There was brutal efficiency in the plan Major Quinn had employed in his fight against the Vemus. Nathan wasn't sure he could have even conceived it. Though he outranked Major Sean Quinn, Nathan knew the man was a brilliant strategist and he found himself wondering what Sean would do if he were in command of Lunar Base. There were times when Nathan felt his own promotion to colonel had been born out of necessity rather than achievement. But regardless of the reasons General Gates had promoted him, he would carry out his orders and achieve the objectives of the CDF to the best of his ability.

"Tactical, have those Vemus scout ships returned?" Nathan asked.

"Negative, Colonel. They haven't been seen since they entered New Earth's atmosphere," Lieutenant LaCroix said.

Nathan pressed his lips together. They could only guess how long those scout ships would take to locate the civilian bunkers and Sanctuary. The Vemus seemed to increase the complexity of their tactics the longer this engagement went on. If their previous attack had been them asleep at the wheel, Nathan hoped they could take out the Vemus Alpha before the damn thing became any smarter. He'd considered sending a few of their combat shuttles to New Earth to investigate, but they had little chance of escaping detection by the Vemus cruisers patrolling the moon. They were stuck between a rock and a hard place unless they wanted to begin their attack on the Vemus.

"Colonel Hayes, I have a comlink from General Gates," Sergeant Boers said.

"Put him on the main holoscreen," Nathan said.

The tactical readouts disappeared from the screen and were replaced by the head and shoulders of General Gates.

"General, we're showing that Phoenix Station is heading back to New Earth," Nathan said.

"That's correct. We couldn't send an update before this time due to the communications blackout. How stands the battle preparations?" Connor asked.

"We haven't seen the Vemus scout ships since they entered

New Earth's atmosphere, so they probably haven't found our civilian safeholds. We have a strategy to bring the Vemus Alpha to Lunar Base," Nathan said and proceeded to tell Connor their plan for engaging the Vemus Alpha in an all-out assault. Before the attack began, he'd send out four assault teams that would attempt to sneak aboard the enemy ship while it was en route to the moon to plant the bombs they'd made inside.

"That's a good plan and it won't have to change all that much when you hear what I've got to say. But given the time constraint of this communications window, there'll be very little time for explanation or questions. We're sending multiple comms drones loaded with the relevant data that will validate what we're attempting," General Gates said.

"Just say the word and we'll do everything we can, General," Nathan replied.

"I know you will. We'll need to coordinate our efforts because your assault teams won't be the only CDF soldiers on that enemy ship," General Gates said and proceeded to lay out their plan of attack.

Nathan listened, and for the next fifteen minutes, General Gates informed him of the discoveries they'd made using the data and samples collected by Dr. Brian Walker. When he'd authorized Brian's mission, Nathan had had no idea of the potentially profound impact it would have on all their lives. If it worked. The comlink to Phoenix Station closed, and there was a stunned silence in the immediate vicinity of the main holoscreen.

"A way to kill the Vemus," Major Shelton said in a tone that suggested she didn't quite believe it.

Nathan's mind raced. He had so many questions he wanted to ask the general, but he knew there simply wasn't time. He knew Connor had glossed over many of the facts and he also accepted that he didn't need all the facts in order to achieve their objective. They were going to throw everything they had left at the Vemus and there would be no second chance.

"We need to settle down and focus," Nathan said.

The CDF soldiers in the command area went silent.

"Coordinating this attack won't be easy and the battle plan has just become a lot more complicated," Nathan said.

As Nathan began to put the entirety of the plan together in his mind, along with its implications, he faced the grim reality that much more sacrifice would be required if the colony was going to survive. He glanced around the command area at all the CDF soldiers. They didn't realize it yet, but when he caught Major Shelton's gaze and then Lieutenant LaCroix's, he saw that they understood. In a few hours' time, none of them would probably be around to see how their war with the Vemus ended. This had always been a possibility and was one they'd taken steps to prepare for should the worst happen. They still had a bit of time, precious little though it was. There were still preparations to be made, and what remained of mankind depended on the actions they'd take over the next several hours. It was a terrible burden to bear, but they'd do it together—just as they would die together so their loved ones could live.

Sergeant Boers called him over. "Colonel, I just had a comms drone report in from the surface."

Nathan frowned. "Where did it come from?"

Sergeant Boers swallowed. "It's from Sanctuary. There are personal messages from the people there. Sir, I need your authorization to send the messages out since we're officially still under Dark-Star protocols."

Nathan pressed his lips together while he considered. Messages from home could distract his staff from doing what they needed to do. He looked around the Command Center at all the CDF personnel and the scientists who had elected to come here to help with their fight against the Vemus. He had no doubt that some of the commanding officers could deny those final messages from home in order to achieve their objective, but not Nathan. He couldn't do that. He had more optimistic tendencies and believed it was those messages from home that would enable his soldiers to fight much harder because they'd have been reminded of what they were fighting for. He looked down at Sergeant Boers. "Send them on, Sergeant."

Sergeant Boers smiled in relief. "At once, Colonel . . . and thank you, sir."

Nathan gave her a nod and turned to go back to his own workstation.

"Colonel," Sergeant Boers called out to him. "There's a message for you as well. It has Colonel Cross's identification on it."

Savannah? Nathan thought. "Send it to my console, Sergeant."

Nathan went over to his console and put on his headset. The new message flashed in his inbox and he opened it. A video recording file opened, and he took a moment to savor Savannah's beautiful face. She'd let her thick blonde hair down and it surrounded her face like a lion's mane. He felt the edges of his lips curve up into a smile. God, how he wished he could be with her, but they'd chosen to keep their relationship a secret.

He started the video.

"I know the timing of this sucks, Nathan, but I have something to tell you. After we learned what had happened to Sierra and the other cities, I knew you would be neck deep in planning your assault." Savannah's voice cracked and she looked away from the camera. "Damn it, this is a lot harder than I expected, just like I didn't expect you to come to mean so much to me. At first, I thought it was only because we'd both just survived the Vemus attack and were aboard the *Vigilant* together, but it's more. It's so much more," Savannah said and reached toward the camera. Nathan felt as if she were reaching toward him and the breath caught in his throat. "I need you to come back to me. It's so very important that you do because it's not just you and me anymore . . ."

Nathan listened to the rest of Savannah's message, unable to keep his mouth from hanging open. The message finished playing and he leaned back in his chair, blowing out a breath.

"Is something wrong, sir?" Major Shelton asked.

Nathan looked over at her and saw Sergeant Boers watching him too. His heart was racing, and for a few moments he thought of keeping what Savannah had just told him to himself. He smiled. "I'm going to be a father," he said.

Major Shelton's brows drew up in surprise, but then she jumped out of her chair and came over to give him a hug. The news spread like wildfire, and through all the good wishes and congratulations, there were several sympathetic looks from those around him. He understood those looks all too well, given what they were about to do. He was going to become a father. The more he thought about it, the more real it became, along with the looming certainty that he would never meet his child.

Nathan swallowed hard and clenched his teeth to keep himself focused. When he'd authorized distribution of the messages from home, he'd never thought he'd receive the news he had. And now his thoughts went from elation at the thought of becoming a father to a flash of anger at the thought that someone else would be raising his child. He'd authorized those final messages because he thought it would remind people of why they needed to fight. He never would have believed the message he'd receive would remind him of why *he* needed to *live*.

31

NOAH RECEIVED a response from the comms drone he'd sent. The drone had needed to get within the vicinity of the lunar base receivers so the messages the people at Sanctuary recorded could be sent. It had taken a lot of convincing and assurances for Colonel Cross to allow him to send the drone. In the end, she'd sent a message of her own, which he hoped was a good thing. Recording his own message to Kara had been more difficult than he'd thought it would be. He knew what he wanted to say but felt that his message was woefully insignificant when compared with how he was really feeling. Despite his propensity for having long conversations, when it came to what he really wanted to say to his wife, he found that he wasn't as articulate as he wanted to be. He wanted Kara here with him right now—safe, or as safe as either of them could be—and not on some damn moon. That was it, and Noah felt it wasn't too much to ask.

He glanced over at Lenora. Grim lines of grief marred her pretty face. When she had finally awakened, she'd taken to a cold, brooding silence, but the comments she did make indicated she was acutely aware of what was going on around her. Noah hadn't thought it was a good idea to leave her alone so he had insisted she come with him to the mobile Command Center. She drank from a canteen, which was thankfully filled with water. No doubt she was experiencing the mother of all hangovers, for which there was no miracle cure other than simply rehydrating. She hadn't mentioned anything about her behavior the night before and made no apologies either. All night long Noah had sat outside that tent, his only companion the berwolf Lenora had named Bull. He'd finally put his feet up and gotten some sleep. When he'd woken up, Bull was nowhere to be found and Lenora was awake. They went to the mobile Command Center.

Lenora claimed a workstation off to the side and Noah started working from another station nearby. He reviewed the results of the latest simulations and stress tests of the power conversion system, and the changes they'd made had yielded a thirty percent increase in stability. This was a remarkable achievement since they were taking power from old alien technology and converting it into something they could use. The fact that they could do this at all was amazing, but was it enough? They could power the colossus cannon, which fired a powerful lance of electrons that was capable of reaching targets two kilometers away from Sanctuary. What they really needed to do was test-fire the weapon, but that also ran the risk of alerting the Vemus to Sanctuary's location. They had the weapon and a few CDF soldiers, but fighting the Vemus here would be the stuff of nightmares. Sanctuary's location had been picked because they could hide a lot of people, but it wasn't the most defensible position. There were no mountains nearby or natural barriers that would make a ground assault difficult—just an unearthed alien city nestled amidst rolling hills with forests in the distance.

Occasionally the recon drones would find a large herd of

runners, which were long-legged herbivores that averaged close to twenty feet in height and galloped the great plains on their migration trails. The migration drew packs of berwolves, but they left Sanctuary alone. At least there weren't any ryklars in the area. Noah shivered. Ryklars were dangerous and cunning predators that many colonial scientists believed had been genetically altered to increase specific traits. Ryklars responded to certain frequencies and would protect alien sites such as Sanctuary. The ultrahigh frequency stimulated the ryklars' predatory instincts and put them into a heightened state of agitation where they became hypersensitive to their surroundings. Instead of hunting and killing in order to survive, they would start killing far more than they could eat. Prolonged exposure to the ultrahigh frequency even got the ryklars to hunt the colonists. Berwolves, on the other hand, while highly lethal, behaved much more like the predators from Earth. But after being around Bull, Noah was convinced that the berwolves were much smarter than an average dog. Berwolves were stocky like a bear, but they had a strong pack instinct. Colonial scientists believed that even the berwolves had been genetically altered, but not to the extent that the ryklars had been.

Noah leaned back in his chair and looked at Lenora.

"Any idea where he goes?" Noah asked.

Lenora glanced over at him. She sat with her knees folded in front of her chest and had been reading so intently that she probably hadn't heard what he'd asked.

"Bull. Do you know where he goes when he leaves you?" Noah asked.

Lenora shrugged. "He does what he wants and doesn't bother anyone."

She looked back at her screen, glaring at it. Noah had watched her off and on for the past hour and she seemed to go from rigid fury to just wanting to be alone. But being alone at Sanctuary was almost impossible now. Noah knew Lenora hadn't been thrilled at the idea of the CDF designating the archaeological site as a safe haven for the colony, but she'd gone along with it and had worked tirelessly to make sure people were as safe as they could be. Now she looked at all of them as if they were intruding on her own personal space, as if she had claimed the ancient alien city for her own.

"Do you want to get some air?" Noah asked.

"The air out there is the same as in here," Lenora replied without looking up from her screen.

"Alright then," Noah said and stood up. He'd tried. "I'll be outside if you change your mind."

He left the mobile Command Center. The skies were clear and the sun was shining. Even the rings that surrounded the planet weren't as visible as they normally were. By all evidence, contrary to this beautiful day, the cities they'd built had been destroyed over the span of twenty-four hours. Today was an awful, miserable day for the colony. Since the attack on their cities had begun, Colonel Cross had instituted a mandatory curfew, with only small groups of refugees allowed beyond the city ruins at any given time. Not ideal, but it did give the refugees a chance to stretch their legs before returning to the lower levels of the alien city.

Noah glanced back at the brown, prefabricated walls of the mobile Command Center. Through the doorway, he saw Lenora shaking her head at something on her screen and frowned. There was only so much irritated, cold fury he could take from one person, even if that person was family to him. He turned around and walked away.

The mobile Command Center was near the entrance to the archaeological site where the ancient alien city had been discovered. His boots crunched along the well-worn path to the left toward the grassy plains beyond. A group of displaced colonists were heading back to the alien city, and some waved at him as he walked by. After they'd received news that Sierra had been destroyed, only one other communication from the CDF forces had made it to Sanctuary. Noah knew Sean had made it out, but the only thing in the message was that they should remain hidden because the fight with the Vemus wasn't yet done. Of all the things Noah hated most, being in the dark about what was going on was near the top of his list.

He sucked in a breath of fresh air and blew it out. For the span of a single breath, he'd found a moment's peace, and it felt good to stretch his legs. But suddenly, an ear-piercing siren began to wail, catching him so completely by surprise that he actually ducked at the sound of it.

The colonists nearby looked up at the sky in alarm. Noah heard several people shouting, but he couldn't make out what they were saying. A pair of CDF soldiers drove out in an ATV, using the vehicle's PA system to order all of them to return to Sanctuary. The refugees were slow to respond and Noah began shouting for them as well. The nearby colonists looked at him, and upon seeing his uniform, started to head back into the alien city. They were slow to move at first but quickly increased their pace. Noah stayed out on the grassy plains to make sure the colonists were returning to the subterranean levels of the alien city.

The CDF soldiers driving the ATV headed toward him and stopped. "Can we give you a ride, Captain?" one of the soldiers asked.

Noah thanked them. The ATV only had two seats, so he had to hold on from the outside. He stepped onto the running boards and grabbed the handle. The driver pressed down hard on the accelerator and the ATV lurched forward. Noah held on as tightly as he could and they quickly made it back to the city entrance. The last of the refugees were already inside and Noah saw CDF soldiers retreating to the interior of the city. Everyone knew the drill. They had to minimize their presence on the surface to avoid detection by the Vemus. Colonel Cross wouldn't have ordered the use of the siren unless there was a credible threat nearby. That meant there were Vemus ships in the area.

The CDF soldier slowed the ATV down near the mobile Command Center, and Noah stepped off the running board at a jog. They quickly drove away as Noah ran into the Command Center.

Colonel Cross glanced at him as he walked in. "Where've you been?" she asked.

"I went to get some air, Colonel," Noah said and went back to his workstation. "Are they close?"

"Whatever it is, it's at the edge of our scanning range," Colonel Cross said.

A central holoscreen powered up and showed a simplified PRADIS output. There was one ship at the edge of the range, just like the colonel had said, but there was no identification code being broadcast, so they knew it wasn't from the Colonial Defense Force. The unidentified ship wasn't heading directly toward them, but it was going to fly close enough that if they weren't careful, it might detect their presence.

A CDF soldier came into the Command Center. "Colonel, all colonists are inside the safe zones," he said.

"Acknowledged," Colonel Cross said and turned toward Sergeant Yates. "Ops, set Condition One. All CDF soldiers to action stations."

Noah heard Sergeant Yates repeat the order and then send a broadcast to all soldiers stationed in Sanctuary.

"Colonel, should we bring the colossus cannon online?" Noah asked.

Colonel Cross pressed her lips together. "Not right now, Captain," she said.

"When would be a good time?" Lenora asked.

Noah glanced over at her in surprise. She'd been so quiet that he'd forgotten she was there, and he wasn't the only one.

Colonel Cross brought her steely-eyed gaze to Lenora. "Dr. Bishop, I don't think your presence here is appropriate anymore. It would be better if you went to one of the safe zones," Colonel Cross said.

Lenora snorted in disgust. "The Vemus aren't far away. Why not use the cannon we've been working on so hard to shoot them out of the sky?"

The breath caught in Noah's throat. Lenora was completely out of line. He stood up and went over to Lenora before Colonel Cross had her forcibly removed.

"Come on, you can't be here anymore," Noah said and moved to grab Lenora's arm.

Lenora flinched away from him and stood up. She glared at him. "Fine," she said and walked toward the exit.

Noah looked at Colonel Cross, who nodded for him to go after Lenora. He went outside and called out to her.

Lenora spun. "I'm fine. Go follow orders, soldier," she said scathingly.

"That's not fair, and you're out of line," Noah said.

Lenora looked away from him and sighed. "They're coming. We've got to at least defend ourselves."

"We will, and we'll do it the right way, which doesn't involve you questioning the orders of Colonel Cross," Noah said.

Lenora rolled her eyes.

Noah heard Colonel Cross snap an order to someone inside and turned back to Lenora.

"What's the matter with you?" Noah asked.

Lenora jabbed her finger toward the sky. "They're what's the matter!"

Her shouts drew concerned glances from the soldiers passing by. Noah stepped closer to her. "We can't just start shooting at them. There's more than one ship, and if we shoot one down, it'll paint a giant target on us here."

Lenora's brows pulled close together. "I know," she said through gritted teeth and then her gaze softened. "I know. Go back inside. You can't stay out here and babysit me."

"You'd do the same for me," Noah said while backing toward the mobile Command Center doors.

There was a loud whirl of actuators moving something heavy, and Noah's eyes widened. He turned toward the heart of Sanctuary. Jutting out from the ruins was the long barrel of the colossus cannon. It was powering up.

"Barker, get in here!" Colonel Cross shouted from inside the mobile Command Center.

Noah hastened inside.

"We're locked out of the colossus cannon controls," Colonel Cross said.

Noah brought up the command interface for the cannon's weapons systems. He was completely locked out. He tried to take back control, but nothing worked, and he slammed his hands on the desk.

"I'm locked out, Colonel," Noah said.

"Comms, are the soldiers guarding the colossus responding?" Colonel Cross asked.

"Negative, Colonel. They're not responding," Corporal Blanks replied.

"Sergeant Gray, get a team of CDF soldiers down there now
—" Colonel Cross said and stopped.

There was a bright blue flash over the skies above them.
Noah's mouth hung open. Someone was firing the colossus
cannon. He jumped out of his chair.

"I need to get down there to fix the lockout. I can't do
anything from here," Noah said.

There was another bolt of blue-white lightning lancing
overhead. If the Vemus hadn't known Sanctuary was here before,
they did now.

32

The Lunar Base Command Center had become a cauldron of renewed vigor and determination. Nathan was infused by its energy and he also heard it in the voices of those nearest him. He looked at one of the status holoscreens for the base. The smaller satellite CDF locations were home to rail-cannons that were peppered across the lunar landscape. Separate from those were the missile pods that were home to the midrange HORNET class missiles.

"All stations report status green, Colonel," Sergeant Martinez said.

Nathan glanced at the young officer. There was a slight catch to her voice, and she swallowed. "Acknowledged, Sergeant," Nathan replied.

Major Shelton shifted in her seat next to him.

"Tactical, any change in the Vemus cruiser's orbit?" Nathan asked.

"That's a negative, Colonel," Lieutenant LaCroix responded.

The three Vemus cruisers were orbiting the moon on

different elliptical planes that were about to overlap. When his tactical officer alerted him to the possibility of the overlap occurring, Nathan had expected the Vemus to adjust their velocity because the targeting opportunity they were giving him was too good to pass up. They were essentially lining up for him to take them out.

"Let's show them our teeth. Execute firing solution Knock Out," Nathan ordered.

"Executing firing solution," Lieutenant LaCroix said—three simple words that carried with them a huge spike in activity.

Scanners became fully active and fed targeting data to the HORNET missile salvos that were launching from their pods.

"HORNETS away," Lieutenant LaCroix said.

The HORNET missiles were close-range weapons capable of bursts of speed that would crush a human, even with the inertia-dampening technology they had on their ships. Nathan watched as the missile marks on the main holoscreen showed them quickly closing the distance to their targets. The Vemus cruisers hadn't altered course or launched countermeasures.

"Ops, give our guys in the hangar bays the green light for launch," Nathan said.

They needed to get the assault teams away before the Vemus counterattacked.

"Confirm missile detonation, Colonel. Direct hit," Lieutenant LaCroix said.

Nathan watched the main holoscreen as the missiles pelted the Vemus cruisers.

"Tactical, target bravo salvo and task all mag-cannon turrets to target the cruisers. Light them up," Nathan said.

Lieutenant LaCroix confirmed the order. "Scanners show two Vemus cruisers completely destroyed. The third is severely damaged."

A live feed from the high-res optics showed the remaining Vemus cruiser being chewed up by the rail-cannon high-velocity projectiles. Nathan watched with grim satisfaction as the Vemus cruiser exploded.

"Colonel, assault teams are away—" Sergeant Martinez said and stopped speaking in the middle of her status update. Her eyes widened. "Colonel, sensors have detected colossus cannon active fire near Sanctuary."

Nathan's gut clenched. "Are there any Vemus ships in the area?"

"Negative, Colonel," Sergeant Martinez said.

"Comms, have there been any alerts from our CDF forces on the ground?" Nathan asked.

"No, Colonel," Sergeant Boers answered.

Nathan winced and looked at Major Shelton. "It has to be those Vemus scout ships we detected earlier. They've located Sanctuary."

"Colonel, Vemus Alpha is moving out of orbit from New Earth," Lieutenant LaCroix said.

"Put it on the main holoscreen, Lieutenant," Nathan said.

The Vemus Alpha was slowly moving away from New Earth.

"Tactical, ready the next HORNET salvo," Nathan said.

"Yes, Colonel," Lieutenant LaCroix responded.

"What about Sanctuary, Colonel?" Major Shelton asked.

Nathan frowned, trying to think of something they could do to help. "Comms, send an encoded broadcast to CDF ground forces."

It was the only thing they could do. He had already committed his resources to the Vemus Alpha. There were CDF ground forces. They'd have to deal with the threat to Sanctuary.

Three new ships appeared on PRADIS. They came from the Vemus Alpha.

KEN LOZITO

"Troop carrier class ships detected, Colonel," Lieutenant LaCroix said.

Nathan gritted his teeth in frustration. "Target the carriers," he said and watched the PRADIS screen update. The Vemus Alpha was moving faster now on an intercept course right toward them. There would be no hiding from the Vemus. Nathan knew he couldn't stop all the troop carriers from reaching Sanctuary, but he hoped that what they were doing would give them a fighting chance.

"Target all weapons on the Vemus Alpha," Nathan said.

The CDF had built weapons systems all across the lunar surface, and once they went active, they could be tracked by the enemy. Lunar Base was in this fight now. Hopefully, the assault teams were flying undetected, closing in on the Vemus Alpha. They'd have to execute emergency combat landings on the Vemus Alpha, but that was something his teams were prepared for. It was Connor and his team that needed to get inside that massive Vemus ship if they were to have any hope of stopping the Vemus permanently. He couldn't even warn them about the change in plans, but it wouldn't have changed anything. The Colonial Defense Force's final assault on the Vemus was just beginning.

33

A SMALL TASKFORCE of ten combat shuttles had left the remnants of Phoenix Station two hours before. To keep their approach hidden from the enemy, Connor ordered the taskforce to power off their main engines. He didn't want to give the Vemus any reason to suspect the combat shuttles were anything but wreckage from previous battles. Throughout their engagement with the Vemus, they'd proven to be more reactionary when the CDF switched tactics.

"Nothing like putting Sir Isaac Newton in the driver's seat," Captain Randle mused from the copilot's seat in the cockpit of the shuttle.

"There are worse ways to get inside an enemy ship," Connor replied, thinking of when he'd used a storage container to infiltrate a space station. The entirety of the Ghost platoon had been cramped inside that confined space with nothing but a whole lot of waiting to be offloaded.

"Final update from Phoenix Station. The comms drones have

been sent off. They've staggered their departure and speeds," Captain Randle said.

The comms drones contained all of Dr. Kim's findings on the Vemus, as well as what they were about to try. Connor understood the theory that supported the scientist's belief that the Vemus were behaving with a hive hierarchy, but he couldn't help but think there was more to it. The evidence was there to support the scientist's theory, but there seemed to be some missing pieces that Connor couldn't quite wrap his mind around. Primary among those missing pieces was the fact that the Vemus had navigated across interstellar space to find them. They had followed the deep space comms buoy network like a trail of breadcrumbs. A two-hundred-year journey was no easy feat. How had the Vemus survived for that long? Connor was sure that, with time, colonial scientists could answer those questions, but ultimately he just wanted the Vemus gone without a chance of survival. The colonists were the last humans in the galaxy. He was disgusted that part of the reason humanity was in such a predicament had stemmed from an opportunistic human faction. Were humans always destined for such an outcome?

New Earth had been home to an alien intelligent species that had evolved to build a civilization, but the colonists hadn't figured out what had happened to them. They left behind cities and ruins. Colonial scientists had even detected an alien influence over the other species on the planet. Had they reached a point in their evolution where their own self-destruction was assured? Were humans just another species to follow along that seemingly well-worn path to destruction, paved by the intelligent species before them? In the hundreds of years that humanity had looked to the stars with wonder, they hadn't detected any traces of intelligent life.

"The final comms drone is configured to reach Sanctuary's vicinity in seven days," Captain Randle said.

"It's our failsafe in case we aren't successful," Connor said.

"Let's make sure it's not needed then," Captain Randle said.

Connor glance at Randle. They were heading into the belly of the beast. Given that their chances of survival weren't great, Connor was surprised to see a hopeful glint in Randle's determined gaze. He'd seen a similar look in Reisman's eyes right up until Connor left him to die.

"You've got that look again," Captain Randle said.

Connor turned back to the controls. "I was just thinking of Wil and everyone else we've lost during this war."

"Wil." Captain Randle snorted. "I liked him. He always came up with ways to keep you on your toes."

Connor let out a small chuckle. "It was what made him so good at what he did."

A comlink opened to the cockpit from the rear of the shuttle.

"General, it's ready," Dr. Kim said.

Connor sat up in his chair. "Excellent work. I'll buy you a drink when this is over."

"I'll take you up on that, General," Dr. Kim said.

The comlink closed and Captain Randle gave him a sideways look. "Here's what I don't understand. How is whatever the doctor is cooking up back there going to stop the Vemus?"

"I'm sure if you went back there and asked him, he could spend hours trying to educate you on it, but by then the mission would be over," Connor replied.

Captain Randle laughed. "I'm surprised you don't want to know."

Connor shrugged. "The way he explained it to me was that the basic function of a virus is to spread itself. He's just helping to speed that along, which is where the nanobots come in. The process will gain momentum as time goes on."

"Okay, but if the living exoskeleton is what's keeping that Vemus Alpha together, why couldn't we just insert the toxin on the surface and then get the hell out of there?" Captain Randle asked.

"The only way to be sure is to find the collective intelligence behind the Vemus and infect that first. This way, it will spread to all of them while crippling their capacity to fight," Connor replied.

Captain Randle shook his head. "You really think there's a hive queen?"

"Call it whatever you want, but I do believe there's a collective intelligence controlling the Vemus," Connor said.

Captain Randle nodded. "What about the Vemus forces that aren't on the ship?"

"They'll need to be stopped. Every single one of them," Connor said.

A passive scan alert appeared on the combat shuttle's heads-up display. Connor read the alert and frowned.

"Colonel Hayes has begun the attack," Captain Randle said.

"He's early," Connor said while rubbing his chin. "Something must have happened."

He'd kept the combat shuttle's systems on passive to avoid detection, which included the long-range communications systems. He opened the short-range comms channel to the other shuttles. "We need to move faster than originally planned. Start up main engines. We'll use the battle as cover to get aboard."

The other combat-shuttle pilots acknowledged his orders. They were close enough to the Vemus Alpha that they should be able to sneak aboard. Connor initiated the startup process for the combat shuttle's main engines. When the shuttle's engines came online, Connor engaged them and they darted ahead, flying toward the cavernous rear of the Vemus Alpha. Connor had estimated that this was the area where the Vemus Alpha's main engines were located. While not the safest place to fly, he also knew there would be maintenance hatches not far from the engine pods. Colonel Hayes knew the approach vector Connor was going to take, so they didn't have to worry about being caught in friendly fire.

They closed in on the Vemus Alpha, flying in close to the rear section of the hull. The hull of the Vemus Alpha was rough, as if it had been part of a large asteroid. Connor knew the Vemus had absorbed other ships in order to form the hulking mass that was the Alpha. As they approached the cavernous drop-off at the rear of the enemy ship, Connor used maneuvering thrusters to swing the combat shuttle around and then engaged their main engines to slow their approach. Even with inertia dampeners, Connor felt himself pressing into his seat while he used the main engines in a rapid deceleration maneuver. The other combat shuttles did the same, and once they reached the rear of the Vemus Alpha, Connor engaged the main engines in a burst that would take them inside. There was an array of engine pods, some of which Connor recognized from battleship carriers and others that looked like they'd come from civilian freighters used throughout the Sol system.

"How'd they even power all those engines?" Captain Randle asked.

Connor wasn't sure. He knew that, in theory, the reactors that powered NA Alliance military vessels could work for hundreds of years. They just needed a fuel source for their fusion reactor cores. Efficiency was a must for any ship to operate in space, and it didn't matter whether the spacecraft was civilian or military.

Connor angled their approach to avoid the engine pods, taking a circuitous route toward the center. They only needed one point of entry for all of them to board. Connor brought the active scanners online. There was little chance of being detected because they were just outside the inner hull of the ship. Scanning data started to show on the main heads-up display and a map of the hull appeared. He zeroed in on an area that looked promising and slowed the shuttle down. The exoskeletal hull became sparser the farther they went. Bare patches of the original ships' hulls became more prevalent, and Connor felt the edges of his lips curve into a smile.

"I don't get it. Why are there these bare patches here?" Captain Randle asked.

"It's the same as their other ships. They don't fully encase the entire hull with the exoskeleton. Maybe they just don't have the resources to cover it all or they think they don't need to. Regardless, that's where we're getting on the ship," Connor said.

Captain Randle glanced over at him. "You expected this to be here."

Connor nodded. "If it hadn't been, we'd have made our own hole and gotten on board."

Connor highlighted the targeted landing area on the heads-up display and transferred the coordinates to the other shuttles. There was no sign of the Vemus in the area. He deployed the landing gear and brought the combat shuttle to the hull. The landing gear hit the hull and he deployed the anchor bolts that would hold the shuttle in place. He powered down the engines and put them on standby.

Connor and Captain Randle left the cockpit and went to the rear of the shuttle, where Nexstar combat suits waited for them. The assault team already had their combat suits on and were waiting. The chest of the combat suit was split down the middle from the neck to the feet. Connor stepped inside and initiated the startup process. The Nexstar's systems came online and the suit closed up, encasing Connor in a protective shell. He saw Dr. Kim standing off to the side, wearing an EVA suit.

"What do you think you're doing, Dr. Kim?" Connor asked.

Dr. Kim glanced at the other CDF soldiers and then back at Connor with wide eyes. "I just assumed that I was going with you aboard that ship." He had a large metallic cylinder clutched to his chest.

"Is that it?" Connor asked, gesturing toward the cylinder.

Dr. Kim nodded several times. "Yes, this is it," he said in a shaky voice.

"I'll take it from here. Why don't you stay on the shuttle?" Connor said.

Dr. Kim's mouth rounded into a circle. "I can help you," he said.

"You've done enough. We'll take it from here," Connor said.

The warring emotions on Dr. Kim's face cycled through disappointment to stark relief. Connor knew that if he allowed the scientist to come with them he'd be among the first to die. Connor stepped closer to him.

"You've done enough. We wouldn't have this chance without you," Connor said.

Dr. Kim's brows pulled together in a tight frown. "I did nothing but pull together the pieces of other people's work. Brian Walker is the real hero."

"Stay on the shuttle and wait. That's all I need you to do," Connor said and reached out for the metallic cylinder. "I'll take this and ensure it gets where it needs to go."

The scientist reluctantly let go and stood there, unsure of what to say.

Connor turned to the assault team. "Open the hatch."

The rear hatch of the combat shuttle opened and the assault team began stepping off the shuttle.

"General, I just want to . . ." Dr. Kim began to say, and Connor turned back toward him. "I just wanted to say thank you. You're one of the bravest men I've ever known."

Connor gave him a long look and thanked him. "Good luck to you," he said.

As Connor left the combat shuttle, he didn't think he'd ever see the scientist again. He stepped out onto the hull of the Vemus Alpha and gritted his teeth.

"Final gear check!" Captain Randle called. "Check yourself and check the soldiers around you."

There was a flurry of activity as they all did one final check. Connor reached up and cinched the straps of the cylinder hooked to his back a bit tighter, making sure the cylinder was secured to the bracket on his belt. He sure as hell didn't want the damn thing firing off early. Dr. Kim had told him how to activate the nanobots inside.

The other assault teams from the combat shuttles gathered around. They were all heavily armed and were as ready as they could be to face what was inside. Connor sent the team ahead to check the maintenance hatch airlock.

"Sir, there's no manual override," Corporal Manis said.

Connor stepped forward and the corporal moved aside so he could access the panel. He used his old credentials from the NA Alliance military and the hatch unlocked. Connor gestured for the two nearest soldiers to go in first, and Captain Randle stayed at his side while he waited. They went through the airlock in groups.

The inside of the ship was dark and sparse, as if it had been abandoned. A minimal atmosphere registered from the sensors of

Connor's combat suit—hardly enough to breathe in but it had an unusually high nitrogen content.

Once the CDF assault team was inside, they moved deeper into the ship. The dark gray corridors were empty and there was a buildup of a dark substance along the walls. It didn't look like anything he'd seen on the other Vemus ships. Connor figured the maintenance corridor wouldn't see a lot of foot traffic, but he had expected to see some sign that the Vemus had been in here. How did the Vemus maintain the engine pods if they never came down here?

Over the next hour, all seventy members of the assault team cautiously poked around the Vemus Alpha ship, but the exterior of the ship was over twenty-two kilometers across, and they barely scratched the surface. They left the maintenance corridor behind and headed to the main section of whatever this particular ship had been. That was when they began to see a brown sludge adorning the interior walls that was all too familiar to Connor.

"Stay away from the walls," Connor warned.

That brown sludge was the same substance that had begun to absorb Wil Reisman while they'd been aboard the *Indianapolis*. As they went farther into the ship, the sludge seemed to solidify, becoming a hardened substance. The buildup of the brown sludge rounded the edges of the corridor until Connor felt as if he were walking through a large tube.

As they continued, the Vemus Alpha was looking a lot less like an NA Alliance ship, or any ship Connor had been on. He knew from the last time they'd been on a Vemus ship that they couldn't use comlinks because the Vemus could sense them somehow. Their communications envelope was limited.

"General, perhaps we should consider splitting our forces to do some reconnaissance, then meet back up," Captain Walker suggested.

Connor nodded. He'd been thinking the same thing. "I think you're right. Let's split up and meet back here in thirty minutes."

Captain Walker took half the assault team and went off down a different corridor.

"Any idea what we're looking for?" Captain Randle asked.

"Ideally, we'd be seeing more signs of life," Connor said.

Captain Randle grunted.

They came upon another set of corridors and there was a soft amber glow emanating from the exoskeletal walls. There were glowing orbs inside that lined the corridor like shining pearls. They followed along until they came to a tunnel that spiraled down and to the left. The orbs glowed even brighter. CDF soldiers took point on either side of the tunnel, and Connor peered down into the gloom. There was a drop and then the tunnel twisted out of sight. The interior atmosphere had become increasingly humid, according to his combat suit's sensors. Connor leaned forward and took a small step. His foot slipped out in front of him and he went forward into the tunnel. Connor grunted as he rolled, completely out of control. He slid down the long, slimy tunnel floor and crashed into a wall. Connor was gasping, and it took him a few moments to get his equilibrium under control. Everything kept spinning. He pushed himself onto his feet and grabbed his AR-71 assault rifle, which had miraculously stayed by him as he slid down the tunnel. He reached his hand to his back and felt that the metallic cylinder was still securely in place.

Connor looked up the way he'd fallen and cursed. After a few moments, he heard the sounds of something else coming down, so he brought his weapon up and waited. Three CDF soldiers slid down the tunnel like Connor had and came to a stop nearby.

Connor darted over and helped them up. The third soldier was Captain Randle.

"Are you all right?" Connor asked.

Captain Randle sighed and shook his head as if to clear it. "I'll live. I was just about to tell you to get back from the edge when you slipped. I ordered the team to find another way down, then followed you, along with Corporal Mathis and Sergeant Brennan here."

Connor opened an IR channel and tried to reach the rest of the team, but there was no response. Captain Randle turned and looked up the steep slope of the tunnel. The slope angled away from them, so they couldn't see to the top and there was no way to tell how far they'd come down.

"Should we try to open a comlink, sir?" Corporal Mathis asked.

'We can't risk it. The comlink would draw attention to us," Connor said.

"I think we already did that, sir," Captain Randle said and leaned in toward the glistening wall.

Connor frowned. 'What do you mean?"

The orbs inside the walls became brighter and the whole tunnel seemed to light up in an amber color. Captain Randle's helmet was less than a foot away from the wall, and Connor was about to tell him to step back when Captain Randle quickly backed away and glanced at Connor.

"It looks like a swirling mass of liquid is moving beneath the surface. I checked the corridor before we went down and I could've sworn that tunnel wasn't there before."

"Are you saying you think the tunnel just formed?" Connor asked.

"I wasn't sure. I'm sorry, sir. I should've said something sooner," Captain Randle said.

They were all a bit jumpy, and Connor couldn't fault Captain Randle for not speaking up. He started to get the feeling that they were being toyed with.

"Don't worry about it. Let's keep moving," Connor said.

They continued moving forward. The tunnel widened into a vast chamber, and the glowing orbs inside the walls pulsed brighter. Connor looked around the chamber, trying to find another way out but didn't see any near them. They walked into the chamber past massive columns made of the exoskeletal substance.

Corporal Mathis cried out and Connor spun toward him. The CDF soldier was trying to move the legs of his combat suit, which were sinking into the ground. Sergeant Brennan and Captain Randle grabbed his outstretched arms, trying to pull him free. Connor glanced at the floor and saw that the area by their feet had a swirling substance beneath the hardened surface. It was gathering underneath the two men. Corporal Mathis sank to his thighs and screamed in panic, firmly rooted in place. Connor shuffled to the side and squeezed off a few rounds into the swirling mass surrounding the corporal. The slugs penetrated the hardened surface but had no effect, and Corporal Mathis sank past his waist.

"It's in my suit!" Corporal Mathis cried.

Sergeant Brennan started to sink, and Connor saw the area beneath Captain Randle's feet begin to liquefy. Connor yanked Captain Randle backward. Captain Randle tried to grab the sergeant, but he sank too quickly. Within a few moments, the two men were completely submerged, with only the gurgling sounds of the dying men's screams escaping the viscous liquid. Connor stumbled back and pulled Captain Randle along.

"What the hell! How could it just swallow them up like that?" Captain Randle said.

It had all happened so fast that Connor could only react. He'd never seen anything like it.

They ran across the open chamber. "I don't know," Connor gasped. "We have to keep moving or the same thing is going to happen to us."

A shudder worked its way through Connor as they hastened from the chamber. He felt like each step they took would sink them into the exoskeletal substance. The amber glow continued to pulse along the corridor. Connor looked at the ground and there was no escaping the hardened substance. He risked a glance behind them and saw something swirling beneath the glowing surface, as if it were swimming through the liquid. Connor felt his heart pounding in his ears and his mouth went dry as panic gripped him. They came out of the corridor into another vast open chamber. Connor looked up and couldn't see the ceiling. There was only a thick fog gathered about ten meters above him. The glowing orbs inside the walls faded off to either side of them where the fog thickened.

Captain Randle clutched his weapon as he spun around, trying to peer into the gloom. Connor used the combat suit's systems to cycle through a visual spectrum range, and only infrared showed a huge circular shape in the middle of the vast chamber. Thick, rounded cables connected to it. Some he recognized as power cables and others were something he couldn't identify.

Connor moved forward and Captain Randle followed. The lighting in the chamber began to increase and Connor was beginning to make out details of what was with them in the chamber.

"Holy shit!" Captain Randle gasped.

Tall, dark shapes seemed to appear out of nowhere as the fog receded away from them. Their thick dome shaped heads seemed to angle downward aggressively and a harsh blast of air expelled from their mouths startling Connor. He pointed his AR-71 at one, and several of the Vemus fighters shifted their thick legs and clawed feet. The sound of that shift echoed throughout the chamber. There must have been thousands of them in that chamber alone.

Captain Randle's breath came in gasps. He clutched the AR-71 with shaking hands.

"Hold your fire," Connor said.

"Sir, they're going to kill us," Captain Randle said between gasps.

"If they wanted us dead, we'd be dead already," Connor said.

Connor felt a cold shiver rush down his spine as he made himself lower his weapon. He took a step forward and the Vemus soldiers didn't move. A thick amber cord was attached from the lower backs of the Vemus soldiers, went to the ground, and stretched in the direction of the central, amorphous mass in the middle of the chamber.

"There are too many. Too many of them. We can't . . ." Captain Randle muttered.

Connor felt terror grip his chest, but he forced it away. "Wayne, you need to calm down."

Captain Randle turned toward him with wild eyes, moments from panicking. Focusing on him, Connor felt his own fear subside.

"Bull, you can't freak out now. Come on, you've got to keep it together," Connor said.

Captain Randle continued to gasp and then started running. Connor glanced at the Vemus for a moment, but they didn't move or appear to pay any attention to him. Connor ran after his friend, who was heading toward the middle of the chamber. He'd gotten so far ahead that Connor couldn't see him in the gloom. Only a partial image of his combat suit appeared on Connor's heads-up display. He heard Randle grunt loudly, and it sounded as if he'd fallen.

"I'm coming," Connor shouted, hoping Randle would hear him.

Captain Randle screamed and Connor darted toward him. The CDF captain was tangled up in the cords along the ground. Connor squatted down as Randle was trying to push himself to his feet.

"Connor, they're crawling all over me. Get them off me!" Captain Randle said.

Connor tried pulling the cords away, but the ends sought out the fallen captain like snakes. Connor swung his rifle around and started shooting at them. The AR-71's projectiles chewed through the cords, and there was a hiss of vapor whenever they were pierced.

Bright overhead lights flared and Connor could see that he was only three meters from the giant amorphous mass. It was dark gray in color, with streaks of pink spidering across it like veins. Connor froze and his breath caught in his throat. Feeding into the mass were thick power cords over two meters in diameter. For each power cord, there was another cord made from the same exoskeletal material found throughout the ship.

A comlink established a connection to his combat suit.

"Colonel Gates, NA Alliance military," a deep monotone voice stated.

Thousands of high-pitched whistles sounded from the Vemus forces, and Connor felt his knees go weak. The Vemus collective had just spoken to him—using his old rank.

34

Noah raced to the colossus cannon, with Sergeant Gray and a security team following closely on his heels. A blue-and-white lance shot from the colossus cannon, and Noah glanced in the direction the shot had gone. A ship in the distance crashed to the ground and smoke billowed from the wreckage. The massive barrel swung overhead and was priming for another shot. Noah headed for the base of the cannon where the controls were—the only place he could end the lockout.

He heard someone cry out, and as he rounded the base of the cannon, he saw Captain Raeburn Gibson lying on the ground with Lenora standing over him. She had her stunner pointed at Barnes.

The large Field Ops and Security sergeant looked at Noah. Then he regarded the other CDF soldiers and raised his hands. "We had to defend ourselves," Barnes said.

Lenora looked back at Noah. "I tried to stop them, but it was already too late."

Noah nodded and then looked at Sergeant Gray. "Secure the

prisoners," he said and went right for the colossus controls. He didn't have time to consider how Gibson and Barnes had managed to free themselves, but they must have had help. There was a tangle of wires sticking out from underneath the control panel, and Noah clenched his teeth.

Lenora came to his side. "What do you need me to do?"

Noah studied the wires and then looked at the command status of the cannon. It was locked on the Vemus scout ship heading toward Sanctuary.

Lenora reached for something behind the console and pulled out a small metal box. "This is Field Ops issued."

Noah's eyes widened. "Good work. That's causing the lockout. Here, let me see it."

Lenora handed him the box and Noah peered along the edges. Finding a slight indentation, he jabbed his thumbnail in and pried it open. Pain lanced through his thumb as his nail started to tear, but the box opened and Noah used his fingers to force it the rest of the way. He twisted the control chip and it split in two.

Noah opened a comlink. "Colonel, you should have control now."

Lenora took his hand and wrapped healing tape around his thumb. "I'm forever cutting my fingers on a dig, so I always have supplies on hand," Lenora said.

Noah nodded appreciatively.

"Colonel, can you confirm you have weapons control?" Noah asked.

"We have control," Colonel Cross said, finally.

Noah blew out a breath. "Glad to hear it, Colonel," he said and explained how Captain Gibson had taken control of the colossus cannon and that Lenora had stopped them.

"Thank Dr. Bishop for me, but Gibson shouldn't have been

able to take control of the weapon using a secure authentication box," Colonel Cross replied.

"Normally you'd be right, but Gibson removed the hardwired connections that would have prevented it. It's a real mess and will take hours to clean up, ma'am," Noah said.

"No time for that. We need that weapon operational for as long as possible. We've got incoming ships headed right to our location," Colonel Cross said.

"I'll return to the Command Center at once, Colonel," Noah replied.

"Negative. I need you to stay there and keep that weapon working. Is that understood?" Colonel Cross asked.

"Yes, ma'am," Noah said.

"Captain," Sergeant Gray said, "where should we take them?"

Several loud pops from the sky drew their attention.

"Take them to the fortifications near the entrance. Then remove the shackles and give them a weapon," Noah said.

"Sir?" Sergeant Gray asked.

"The Vemus are coming here and we have to defend ourselves. That means we put every able-bodied person who can shoot on those fortifications. Now go," Noah ordered.

Sergeant Gray saluted Noah and took the Field Ops agents away. Lenora started to follow them.

"Where are you going?" Noah asked.

"I'm going to the fortifications. You said they need everyone who can shoot. Well, I can shoot as well as any soldier," Lenora replied.

Noah pressed his lips together and tried to think of a protest he could make so she wouldn't go, but he couldn't. "Stay safe," he said.

"You too," Lenora said and ran.

Noah scrutinized the tangle of wires. The colossus cannon

primed for another shot, and the charged particles in the air made the hair on Noah's neck stand on end. He needed to see the status of the power converter, the console of which was down thanks to his good friend Raeburn Gibson. How much time could they save if they fitted the idiots of the world with shock collars to prevent their stupidity from affecting others?

Noah quickly got to work reconnecting the monitors for the power conversion systems. The weapon would still work without them, but he'd have no way of knowing if the entire weapon system would simply fail on the next shot.

Noah gathered his engineering support teams and stationed them near the power converter at critical systems. He needed to squeeze all the power he could from the old alien power station.

The colossus cannon fired another straight bolt of blue-white lightning surrounded by a blue nimbus. Noah looked up, knowing that the reason they'd put the cannon on such a high platform was to minimize radiation exposure.

Every time the colossus cannon hit its mark, it did devastating damage to the Vemus ships. The beam melted away the exoskeletal hull, wreaking havoc inside, but the Vemus troop carriers were entering the atmosphere almost on top of Sanctuary. Noah heard gauss rifles being fired and knew that some of the Vemus had made it to the ground.

Noah managed to keep the colossus cannon firing for an hour, then it failed. In the end, it wasn't the power converter but the alien thermal core taps that had completely melted away due to the severe overload of the system. The heavy barrel of the colossus cannon sank down as the mechanized support structure lost power. He'd been so focused on converting the power for the colossus cannon that he hadn't even thought of the effects the sustained power output would have on the old alien technology. Now that it had failed, it seemed painstakingly obvious and something he should have noticed. But he wondered if he could have done anything about it if he had known.

Noah ordered all his teams to the fortifications near the entrance of Sanctuary. There was nothing more they could do here. As he ran out of the heart of Sanctuary, he didn't pass many colonists. Colonel Cross must have had anyone who couldn't fight moved as far from the fighting as possible.

One of the first things Colonel Cross had the CDF soldiers do when she'd first arrived at Sanctuary was set up fortifications that could be quickly assembled if the Vemus were to discover their location. Noah hadn't given it much thought when she'd done it, but as he reached Sanctuary's entrance, he couldn't have been more thankful that Colonel Cross had prepared them for battle.

Noah was quite familiar with the sounds most CDF-issued weapons made when they were used, but it was the sounds the Vemus made that instantly grated on his nerves. He'd seen the video recordings of the Vemus from combat suit cams, but they sounded different now. The ear-piercing whistles made him clench his teeth.

Noah raced for the nearest fortification and found Colonel Cross looking at drone feeds.

"Put me to work, Colonel," Noah said.

Colonel Cross glanced at him and the people he'd brought with him. "We only have civilian hunting rifles left. Grab them and get up on that wall."

Noah grabbed the CAR-74 semiautomatic hunting rifle that was a common weapon for people who worked remotely, as well as Field Operations. While he knew the CDF had more powerful weapons, there hadn't been enough to circulate to everyone. He raced down the fortification wall and found Lenora wearing a CDF-issued helmet and firing her own CAR-74.

Noah took up position next to her, peeked over the wall, and wished he hadn't. There were thousands of Vemus fighters on the field. They fired their white stunner weapons that would completely disable a person if they were hit with it. Noah aimed his rifle toward the nearest Vemus soldier and fired a shot, taking him in the chest. The Vemus hardly slowed down. Noah fired off a few more rounds at it, hitting it on its large, rounded head. Gritting his teeth, he found another one and kept firing his weapon. He noticed that CDF soldiers were interspersed throughout the fortification and were firing incendiary ammunition at any Vemus that went down. Death by fire was the surest way to guarantee that the Vemus stayed down.

"What are you doing here? Don't you have a cannon to keep working?" Lenora asked between firing her weapon.

"I missed you," Noah said.

White bolts slammed into the fortification walls near them, and Noah jumped.

"You're the only family I've got," he said.

Lenora smiled and punched him in the arm. "Don't get sentimental on me now."

They continued fighting and the Vemus drew steadily closer. They kept coming over the nearby hills, and he had no idea how many of them there were. Runners had come by and dropped off ammunition blocks, but Noah was almost out again.

The Vemus fighters surged forward in an all-out run. Sanctuary's defenders tried to keep them at bay, but the Vemus kept moving forward. They could no longer get a clear shot to incinerate the fallen Vemus, and they rose again. Noah kept firing his weapon as panic seized his chest. He just wanted them to stop. He wanted it all to stop.

Lenora cursed. "I'm out!"

"So am I," Noah said.

Twenty meters away the Vemus fighters vaulted over the walls, overwhelming the CDF soldiers there. Noah grabbed Lenora's arm and started pulling her in the opposite direction.

"No, they're over there too!" Lenora said.

Noah looked behind them. Vemus fighters were storming the fortifications and there was nowhere for them to go. The way the Vemus moved, there was no way they could outrun them.

The Vemus finally noticed them and Noah's mouth went dry. He held onto Lenora. "Don't look at them," he said, but Lenora wouldn't turn away. She screamed angrily and flung her empty rifle at them.

To his left, Noah saw something moving toward the Vemus fighters and was shocked to recognize packs of berwolves racing toward them. They tore into the Vemus fighters and overpowered them in a rush. Noah watched as Vemus bodies were tossed into the air and then were torn apart by the berwolves' powerful jaws. Noah wasn't sure whether the berwolves were vulnerable to the virus. Most colonial scientists didn't believe that the creatures of New Earth would be, but there was no way to be sure.

A scarred-faced berwolf padded over to them.

"Bull!" Lenora cried.

Noah watched as more berwolf packs entered the battle. A sonic boom sounded above, and soon after, seven more Vemus troop carriers came into view.

"We have to get out of here. More are coming," Noah said, knowing how futile it was.

The Vemus were regrouping after the berwolf assault. Noah was watching the approaching Vemus troop carriers when a salvo of missiles streaked across the sky and slammed into them. Flaming wrecks crashed to the ground.

A broadcast signal registered on Noah's comlink as CDF Hellcats flew into the area.

"This is Major Quinn. We saw that you have an infestation of Vemus soldiers and we thought we'd help out," Sean said.

Noah smiled and pumped his fist into the air. He had never been so happy to see a Hellcat in his entire life. The CDF Hellcats made another pass and began mowing down the Vemus on the battlefield. Meanwhile, CDF troop carriers landed behind the fortifications and dropped off reinforcements. Noah was choked with emotion and happy to be alive. He and Lenora picked up two fallen weapons and headed back to the fortification walls. They were still in this fight after all.

35

THE VEMUS ALPHA closed in on New Earth's solitary moon even as weapons of the Colonial Defense Force tore into its hull. The Alpha's primary weapon cut deep gashes into the lunar surface, taking out CDF installations.

Nathan looked at his two main holoscreens. At least no more ships were leaving the Alpha. They'd stopped as many as they could, but he knew a small number must have gotten through.

"Comms, has there been any reply from our assault teams on the Vemus Alpha?" Nathan asked.

"Negative, Colonel. We just had a partial broadcast," Sergeant Boers said.

He shared a look with Major Shelton. The partial broadcast they'd received earlier could be taken as a sign that the assault teams had successfully delivered their payloads and were moments from detonation.

"Colonel, the last plasma cannon has been taken out. Their next shot will be at our location," Lieutenant LaCroix said.

"Comms, send out the evacuation codes for all base personnel," Nathan said.

The ground shook beneath his feet as it had done every time the Vemus Alpha fired its primary weapon. They'd fired everything they had at that weapon and they just couldn't disable it. The CDF soldiers in the Command Center began evacuating the area. They'd try to survive in one of the underground bunkers they'd built.

"Aren't you coming, Colonel?" Major Shelton asked, her voice shaky.

Nathan kept studying the holoscreens that still showed sensor data coming in. He'd sent the detonation signal for the assault team's payload shortly after receiving the partial broadcast. Nothing happened. They could have set the bombs to use a timer, which couldn't be overridden by a detonation signal from Lunar Base, assuming the signal could even penetrate the Vemus Alpha.

"Colonel, there's nothing more you can do here. We have to go," Major Shelton said.

Nathan had done everything he could but it didn't feel like enough. Nonetheless, he began to back away from the command area. He didn't want to leave, not with the Vemus Alpha still out there, but Major Shelton was right. They had no more weapons and the Vemus knew their location. They'd been systematically taking out all CDF installations.

"Please forgive me," Nathan muttered and turned away from the main holoscreens.

He followed Major Shelton out of the Command Center. They ran to the nearest transit tube, which was almost full of CDF soldiers.

"It'll be a tight squeeze, but we'll get you in," said a soldier near the entrance.

Major Shelton went in first and Nathan followed. As the doors shut behind him, they were squished together like sardines. There was a loud pop and the elevated capsule they were in shot away from Lunar Base. The magnetic tracks had no friction, and aside from being pressed up against each other, Nathan could hardly feel the movement. Thrusters fired as they reached their destination bunker. The doors of the transit capsule opened, and once they started to get off, Nathan finally released the breath he'd been holding in. The lights in the area dimmed.

"Emergency power activated," a monotone voice said.

The main facility of Lunar Base was gone. Now all they could do was wait, hope, and pray.

36

CONNOR FELT an immense vibration from the exoskeletal floor and something rippled beneath him, heading toward Captain Randle.

"Stop!" Connor shouted.

Captain Randle tried to squirm away from the swirling mass under the ground.

"He will be brought into the collective. A soldier he will remain, but better," the voice said.

Captain Randle was pulled under the ground, and Connor screamed. He clenched his teeth and swung around, bringing his AR-71 up. The amorphous mass of the Vemus collective didn't react at all. With Connor's comlink activated, he began receiving broadcast updates from the lunar base assault teams. The bombs had been planted.

"No, he won't," Connor said. "He'll die, just like you will."

"You resist. Just like before."

Connor frowned. "What do you mean, before?"

Something glowed inside the Vemus collective. He imagined

the gray mass was one huge infected sack of living tissue, and if he fired his weapon, the infection would ooze out of it.

"Your weapon will not harm me. I am everywhere," the Vemus collective said. The entirety of the vast chamber pulsed in rhythm with the words spoken. The glowing orbs flared brilliantly from deep inside the exoskeletal-encased cords. They went beyond sight, and Connor suspected that they went throughout the entire Vemus Alpha. The Vemus collective was the ship.

"You're nothing but a disease," Connor sneered.

How could a disease achieve anything resembling sentience?

"They used to believe as you do. They thought to stop us, but we are the same."

"What are you?" Connor asked.

"We're humans who've taken an evolutionary leap," the Vemus collective replied.

Connor shook his head. "That's impossible. You can't be human."

New network connections became available to Connor through his combat suit's system. Then a data dump began to download to his suit computer.

"Why have you come here?" Connor asked.

The Vemus collective didn't respond. Instead, words began to appear on his heads-up display.

::*Biological imperative.*::

A series of images flashed on Connor's internal heads-up display—mission briefings to research subheadings for things Connor had never heard of before.

"It won't succeed. There are bombs planted all over this ship," Connor said.

"We have the measure of your weapons. They will not stop us," the Vemus collective said, once again speaking aloud.

Connor glanced at the AR-71 in his hands and let it fall to the ground. Reaching behind his back, he moved to the side, next to one of the exoskeletal cords. Another ripple moved through the floor toward him, and he slammed into the cord. He braced himself against it and the shuddering movement beneath his feet stopped.

"You could just leave. You came all this way and for what? There aren't very many people here," Connor said as he moved away from the cord.

"Humanity is the imperative," the Vemus collective replied.

Connor swallowed as an image appeared on his heads-up display showing an NA Alliance soldier with his weapon pointed straight at him. The name *Col. Gates* appeared on the HUD overlay.

Connor's eyes widened. "What's this?"

Memories blazed through Connor's mind like wildfire. The image was from his last Earth mission. Everyone who'd been witness to it was dead, or so he'd thought. The Ghosts were gone, and there was only one other person who'd been standing in front of him.

"RJ!" Connor hissed. His eyes widened as he realized that buried within the Vemus collective was the leader of the Syndicate—a powerful group that operated above governments. They'd wanted to control everything and establish dominion over all people. The Vemus organism must have given them the opportunity.

The horde of Vemus soldiers behind him seemed to move all at once.

"You cannot harm us, and you will never leave this place," the Vemus collective said. "Your weapons are not strong enough to stop us, nor will you ever kill us—"

"I just did," Connor said quietly, holding up the cylinder

that was attached to the canister on his back. Four large-bore penetrators were still deployed from one end, each dripping with thick amber-colored liquid. Connor watched the blackened area around the spot he'd shoved the injector into spread rapidly. The New Earth virus, coupled with the nanobots, spread away from Connor like a black wave. The Vemus soldiers still attached to the collective started convulsing violently, and the soldier nearest him fell to the ground, unmoving. Connor turned toward the giant mass and watched with grim satisfaction as it seemed to sag into itself. He heard the fleeting, high-pitched whistles of the Vemus stretch into an elongated tone that soon faded to nothing.

"General?" Captain Randle groaned.

Connor spun toward the call. The cords that had held Captain Randle had slipped off of him, and the CDF captain was trying to claw his way out of the murky liquid. As Connor ran over to Randle, his feet were sloshing through the exoskeletal surface. He barely made it to the captain before his legs could hardly move through the stuff.

"I'm here," Connor said.

Captain Randle turned toward him. "My comlink is online. The other team—"

"I know," Connor said.

The Vemus exoskeletal walls weakened, going from a hardened surface to a liquid form. A large section sloshed to the ground, upsetting the rest, and the glowing orbs within went dark.

The only lighting came from their combat suits.

"What happened? Did it work?" Captain Randle asked.

Connor stopped trying to struggle against the thick, viscous liquid and simply stood there. He looked over at Captain Randle and saw that his combat suit had been severely damaged by the Vemus exoskeletal sludge.

"It worked," Connor said and glanced at the timer for the bombs the assault teams from Lunar Base had planted.

"My suit is going offline. You should leave me behind. You might be able to get away," Captain Randle said.

"Like hell I will," Connor replied.

"But General," Captain Randle protested.

"We're about to die. You can use my first name, Wayne," Connor said.

"Well, don't stay on my account, Connor," Wayne said.

"You're not that pretty," Connor replied. He doubted he could crawl out of there anyway.

Wayne snorted. "I'm no Lenora Bishop, but I do like what I see when I look in the mirror."

Connor shook his head. "You would," he said, and his throat thickened. He closed his eyes, not wanting to watch the timer anymore. Instead, he pictured Lenora's beautiful face and long auburn hair with the rays of the sun casting her silhouette in shining brilliance. He wished he could be with her right now. He'd gladly live the rest of his life apologizing for the fool he was.

He slipped beneath the liquid surface of the Vemus exoskeleton as the New Earth virus broke it down, and he looked over at Wayne's darkened suit. The damage must have killed his power.

"Wayne!" Connor called.

There was no response, and Connor tried to wave to get his attention, but Wayne didn't move at all. His body just sank in the murky sea of liquefied Vemus exoskeletal material. He screamed to Wayne and there was no response. Wayne was gone. His vision blurred. This was it. He was going to die . . . alone. He felt a wave of panic seize his chest. Connor gasped for breath and glared at the sight around him. He was surrounded by the dark bodies of dead Vemus soldiers, sinking into their watery grave. They'd once been people and he hoped they were at peace.

Connor cringed inwardly as a flash of regret blazed through his thoughts, and he didn't try to stop them. Instead, he let all his regrets have their due. The darkness closed in all around him and he felt an overwhelming sense of loneliness. He didn't want to die here. He flailed his arms, trying to work his way through the murky liquid, but nothing worked. He just continued to sink among the still forms of the Vemus soldiers. Connor swallowed and glanced at the timer. Squeezing his eyes shut, he finally surrendered to the inevitable.

COLONEL HAYES LEANED BACK and closed his eyes. A cool breeze blew through the open doors of the mobile Command Center at Sierra's CDF encampment on New Earth. As the tension melted away, he sagged into his chair and his breathing became deep and regular with the allure of sleep. He'd found himself leaning over, succumbing to some much-needed sleep three times already, and by the fourth, he just gave in. There'd hardly been a moment's peace in the two months since the Vemus Alpha ship had been destroyed. Fragments of the ship had bombarded the lunar surface, and the careful cleanup operations he'd been overseeing for the past few months were starting to catch up with him. He'd slept when he could sneak it in, and he felt himself drifting away now. Would anyone notice if he just rested his head on his desk? Perhaps he could just lie down on the floor.

A woman's voice cut through his slumber like a cleaver, and an instant headache came over him, snapping him awake.

Nathan winced, hearing her walk into his office. He cracked an eye open and glanced at the doorway.

"We do have a bed you can sleep in," Savannah said.

"I know, but if I take the time to go there, I'll just wake myself up," Nathan said softly.

Savannah snorted. "So, you don't want to join me for my four-month checkup with Dr. Quinn?"

Nathan's eyes snapped open, startled. "I thought that was tomorrow," he said and quickly stood up.

"It *is* tomorrow," Savannah said.

Keeping the days straight had become increasingly difficult when he hadn't had a day off in so long that he couldn't remember the last one. "I don't know how Ashley does it."

"Her appointment as governor is temporary. She'll serve out the remainder of Tobias's term, but she'll always be a doctor at heart," Savannah said.

Nathan arched his back and stretched. He glanced at the small swelling of Savannah's midsection and smiled. She was only just now starting to show her pregnancy. "Are you sure you don't want to wait to find out if it's a boy or a girl?"

Savannah arched a brow. "What? Is it suddenly five hundred years ago?"

"Well, technically it's a little over four hundred and twenty, but since we spent two hundred of those years in . . ." Nathan's voice trailed off and he raised his hands in front of his chest. "I was just asking."

Savannah stepped closer to him. "Does it really matter if it's one or the other?"

Nathan smiled. "No," he said.

"Good answer," Savannah purred and kissed him.

They left the mobile Command Center and he told

Lieutenant LaCroix to continue monitoring the teams they had out in the field.

They stepped outside and Nathan's eyes widened. He was still waking up and his brain wasn't quite functioning yet.

"What is it?" Savannah asked.

"If today is your appointment, that means we should also be getting the results for the survivors," Nathan said.

"Colonel Quinn is already there," Savannah said.

Promoting Sean Quinn to colonel was something Nathan had pushed for recently. Sean had been doing the job since Connor had put him in charge of the CDF ground forces. Being the war hero of Sanctuary, he had a loyal following that starkly rebuffed anyone who questioned Sean's decision to blow up Sierra. Nathan had reviewed the reports and also supported Sean's decision. Given the overwhelming enemy fighting force they were facing at the time, it was the best choice to ensure their survival. It had taken CDF forces weeks to hunt down all the remaining Vemus that had made it to New Earth. Once the Vemus collective had been destroyed, they seemed to lose some of their fighting capabilities, including their highly adaptive fighting abilities. Scientists were still theorizing about how the Vemus connection worked. They wanted to collect samples for study, which Nathan had steadfastly refused. All Vemus and remnants of equipment modified by the Vemus were to be destroyed. No exceptions. Nathan was the most senior officer of the Colonial Defense Force, so the decision was made by him. On the one hand, he understood the scientists wanting to know exactly what had happened on Earth to spawn the Vemus, but on the other hand, the colony had just miraculously survived something that had claimed billions of lives, so why tempt fate? He wasn't convinced there was a real benefit to studying the Vemus, and some stones were better left unturned.

Nathan and Savannah took an ATV to the CDF secure location outside the encampment a hundred kilometers from where Sierra had been. With the threat of the Vemus lessening as the days passed, colonists were being transported from the bunkers to the encampments near the decimated cities. The "clean" nature of the fusion bombs used to destroy the cities allowed for immediate reconstruction, and temporary housing had already been established for the surviving colonists. They were starting over, but the colony had paid a terrible price for the privilege. Nathan suspected that some of the new structures would incorporate a way to reverently honor the sacrifice of all those who had died in the war against the Vemus.

They went through the security checkpoints to enter the CDF base and drove to a secluded, heavily guarded warehouse. The driver of the ATV stopped near the entrance and Nathan and Savannah climbed out.

Standing outside the warehouse was a short, muscular CDF captain Nathan had come to know recently.

"Colonel," Captain Diaz said and saluted Nathan and Savannah. While Savannah's pregnancy had prevented her from service aboard Phoenix Station, she was still part of the CDF and a ranking officer, the same as Nathan.

Standing next to Captain Diaz was an older Asian man.

"Captain," Nathan said and turned to the other man. "Dr. Kim. Thank you for your discretion in this matter."

"I only hope that after all this time we get some good news," Dr. Kim replied.

Dr. Kim had been with Connor's assault team and had stayed behind on a combat shuttle. During the battle, when the CDF bombs were about to detonate, Dr. Kim had flown the combat shuttle away from the Vemus Alpha. He'd waited as long as he could, but Connor and his team hadn't returned.

It was Dr. Kim who'd detected the active combat suit signals from among the wreckage of the Vemus Alpha. CDF rescue operations had recovered nearly sixty CDF soldiers from the wreckage, including General Gates. Some of the CDF soldiers had been encased in the Vemus exoskeletal material and were in a state of being absorbed into the Vemus collective when the toxin had been released. There was nothing they could do for those soldiers. They weren't quite dead, but they weren't fully alive either. They were a biological contagion and had to be destroyed, so when the survivors had been discovered, Nathan had ordered it kept secret. The families of those soldiers already believed their loved ones were dead, and to reveal what had really happened to them would have been cruel. But for Connor's body it was different. His combat suit was perfectly intact, with only some minor damage, but the suit itself had been directly exposed to the Vemus collective. Nexstar combat suits were designed to keep their wearers alive through the harshest conditions. When exposed to a prolonged harsh environment, it would administer medicine that reduced the consumption of life support. The best way to achieve this was to put the wearer of the suit into a temporary coma.

Nathan had had Connor's body quarantined and made the knowledge of his survival confidential. Only a select few knew the CDF general was alive, but whether he was free of the Vemus was another matter entirely. They'd kept Connor in a medical coma while in quarantine. Ashley Quinn had injected nanobots into his system to evaluate Connor's cellular structure. They needed to know whether his suit's exposure to the Vemus had left him infected. The evaluation had taken weeks, and today they would find out whether they would lose one more friend to the Vemus.

They went through another security checkpoint. Even the

CDF soldiers serving in this facility weren't aware that their commanding officer was being held in quarantine, fully sedated.

Dr. Quinn stood at the medical capsule, speaking with her son.

"You know him. If we wake him up and he suspects he's been infected, he'll take matters into his own hands," Sean said.

Ashley glanced at Nathan as he and Savannah walked into the room, navigating among the monitoring equipment that was connected to the capsule. Captain Diaz and Dr. Kim followed them inside. They were the only people who knew Connor was alive.

"Today is the day," Nathan said.

Ashley looked at Savannah and gave her a warm smile. Then she turned back to Nathan. "I was just explaining to Sean that no matter what these results show us, there's no way to know for sure whether Connor's exposure to the Vemus will have lasting effects, or even latent effects."

"And I was saying that when we do wake Connor up, we'd better be sure of the results or he might do something rash," Sean said.

"He's right," Diaz said.

"So what are you suggesting?" Nathan asked.

"That we don't make any snap decisions once we get the results," Ashley replied.

"I think it's time we find out the results of the test," Nathan said.

When they'd decided to run the full spectrum of tests, with the nanobots essentially examining every part of Connor's body, they'd used a lockout protocol that required all six of them to be present to get the results.

Ashley went to the capsule and opened the console. She inputted her own authentication and stepped aside so the rest of them could do the same. Nathan went last, but before he inputted his credentials, he whispered a silent prayer that the results would be positive.

CONNOR FELT a jolt and then something tugged him from a bottomless sleep. He became aware of the deep void he'd been in and felt as if he were being pushed through a doorway to the frigid outdoors. He felt a tingling pain in his hands and feet. There was something hard in his throat and he heard the sound of muffled voices speaking. Connor tried to cough as his throat muscles worked to expel the hard rod from his mouth. Then he felt the tube in his throat slowly being pulled out. He winced and coughed weakly, spitting out a foul-tasting liquid as someone helped roll him to his side.

"Just take it easy for a moment. You've been in a medically induced coma."

He recognized Ashley's voice and did as she said. Connor lay on his side and took a few breaths.

"Where am I?" Connor asked, his voice sounding hoarse.

"You're on New Earth," Ashley said.

Connor opened his eyes and blinked several times before his vision began to clear. The bed began to lift him into a sitting position so he was more upright and that helped clear his head. He looked around and saw Ashley standing near him. He glanced behind her and saw Sean, Nathan, and Savannah. There was a clearing of the throat to his left and he saw Dr. Kim standing there, smiling.

"Either you're all dead or I'm alive," Connor said.

Ashley smiled at him. "You're alive," she said.

Sean gave him a measured look. There was a hardness to his

gaze that Connor recognized as something that came with the burden of command.

"Is someone going to tell me what's going on?" Connor asked.

"Barely awake for a minute and he already wants a mission report," Diaz said and grinned.

"The Vemus are gone," Sean said.

Connor tried to remember his last moments on the Vemus Alpha. "Were there any other survivors? Wayne Randle was with me."

Sean shook his head. "No one else aboard the Vemus Alpha survived."

Though Sean met Connor's gaze, he had the impression there was something they weren't telling him.

"You all suck at poker," Connor said and frowned. "Am I infected?"

There was a deafening silence in the room and their expressions became somber.

"According to the nanobots, there are no biological contagions in your system," Ashley Quinn said.

Connor gave her a level look. "But there's no way you can be sure," he said.

He looked at Dr. Kim. "What do you think?"

Dr. Kim sighed. "There's strong evidence that supports your continued health. But there's also a lot we don't understand. We only figured out how to stop the Vemus. We're not adept at detecting whether someone is infected."

"Well, if I were infected, wouldn't symptoms start to show by now? How long have I been in a coma?" Connor asked.

"Yes, they would," Sean said. "And you've been in a coma for two months."

Connor took a moment, considering. "So monitor me. Have

the nanobots continue to monitor me for as long as it takes until we're sure. Any deviation and we'll deal with it then."

Sean's eyes widened and Connor watched as he glanced at his mother.

"They were worried you'd find a more permanent solution to the problem that involved you removing yourself from the equation," Ashley said.

Connor's mouth hung open as he looked around at all of them. Then he started to laugh—a chuckle at first and then a full-on, hearty bellow of a laugh.

"Maybe at one time I might have, but . . ." Connor shook his head. "No," he said and frowned at the thought. "No, definitely not."

He swung his legs off the bed and stood up. Ashley was closest to him, and he reached out and pulled her in for a hug.

She hugged him back and then pushed him away. "You need a shower."

"Where's Tobias?" Connor asked.

A pained expression showed on Sean's face. "He died fighting the Vemus."

The momentary elation he'd felt diminished. "I'm so sorry," he said.

Ashley gave him a nod and he finally noticed the pain in her eyes. She was still grieving. Sean met his gaze and Connor leaned on the bed.

"Alright, tell me the rest of it," Connor said.

For the next few hours, they brought Connor up to speed about what had happened since the Vemus Alpha had been destroyed. More than a few times he found himself glancing at Nathan. If there was anyone he'd appointed to the right post, it was him. Connor suspected there was much more they hadn't told him. He had the distinct impression they were pacing him in regards to how much information they were sharing.

"General, we'll need to tell everyone you're alive," Sean said.

Connor pressed his lips together. "That would be good, but you shouldn't call me that anymore."

Sean frowned. "What do you mean?" he asked and glanced at Nathan.

Connor shared a look with Nathan. "I can't be the general of the Colonial Defense Force."

"There is ample evidence that you've not been infected. The colonial government would certainly approve it," Sean said and glanced at his mother.

Connor looked at Ashley. She'd been his friend since he'd woken up from stasis all those years ago. "I know, but I'm resigning my commission."

Their reactions ranged from complete surprise from Sean, to relief from Nathan, and then to intrigue from Ashley. The others in the room had varying degrees of the same.

"But—" Sean began.

"Any one of you," Connor said, pausing to look in turn at Sean, Nathan, and Savannah, "are more than capable of taking command of the CDF. I'm going to take some time off."

There was a loud snort from Diaz. "Take time off? I didn't think you even knew how to say that, let alone do it."

Connor smiled. "I'm going to start right now, assuming I'm free to leave this place."

Nathan stood ramrod straight and saluted Connor. He was quickly followed by Savannah and then Sean. Diaz renewed his stoic features in an instant and followed suit.

Connor's throat thickened, and he returned their salute.

"I'll handle all the formalities of your . . . retirement," Ashley said with half a smile. "And there's a Hellcat that will take you anywhere you'd like to go, but I do suggest you put on some clothes. You can find them over there."

Ashley pointed to a metallic footlocker by the wall and the others left the room while Connor put on some fresh clothes. He walked out of the room and Sean was waiting for him.

"I can't believe you're going to just walk away from all this," Sean said.

"I'd like to think of it as walking toward something. The CDF is in good hands. You've exceeded all my expectations and I have no doubt that you'll continue to do so," Connor said. What he didn't say was that he needed to put a lot of distance between himself and the CDF. They hadn't shown up yet, but Connor knew that the ghosts of those who were no longer with them would be felt in earnest before long.

"Thank you, sir," Sean replied.

"Your father was really proud of you," Connor said.

The skin around Sean's eyes tightened. Connor knew that, with time, the grief wouldn't sting quite so much as it did now. There was no shortage of that going around, judging by the somber expressions of those around him.

Sean escorted him out of the secure warehouse. The CDF soldiers had been dismissed so Connor's return wouldn't become public knowledge just yet. Ashley had assured him that they'd wait a few days to announce his miraculous recovery.

Sean walked with him to the Hellcat and went right for the cockpit, taking the pilot's seat.

Connor arched an eyebrow at him.

"You've been in a coma for two months. I'm not going to let you fly one of our Hellcats. Just tell me where you want to go," Sean said.

"I retire just a few minutes ago and you don't trust me anymore?" Connor asked.

Sean calmly waited for Connor to tell him their destination. Connor did.

THE HELLCAT LANDED at a remote site about as far away from the colony as they could get. Scorched craters could be seen from the sky, marking where the battle had been fought at Sanctuary. Connor saw the wrecks that had been the Vemus troop carriers, and Sean filled him in on the battle here. One day he'd return to Sierra, but right now he just wanted to be here.

"There'll be a supply run here in a day or so and I'll make sure there's a package for you," Sean said.

"I expect your mother will want me to return to the encampment in a few days for the formal announcement," Connor said.

"They might want to make you governor," Sean said.

Connor winced. "I hope not," he said.

"Good luck, sir," Sean said and made a show of looking past Connor. "You're going to need it."

Connor walked down the hatchway and stepped onto the ground. The hatch closed and Connor watched as Sean flew the Hellcat away. There were a few temporary structures, and the archaeological team had gathered outside. There were a few CDF soldiers there with them and one noticed Connor's approach.

Connor smiled as Noah walked over to him, grinning. "You're alive!" he said in a tone that sounded as if he couldn't quite believe it.

"They had me under lock and key for a while," Connor said.

Noah shook his head in disbelief. "I don't believe it."

Connor looked around at the people, searching.

"She's not here. She's in the dig site. They found a new

chamber . . . well, one of the refugees did. I'll take you down there," Noah said.

Connor followed Noah into the alien city. There weren't many people there, but the few they passed gave Connor strange looks, as if they thought they recognized him from somewhere. They went down into the central city, and he heard Lenora's voice.

". . . and now that the refugees are finally gone, we can get back to our work here. We're a bit shorthanded with the new chamber, but the data archive we found should help us figure out who used to live here," Lenora said, speaking to a small group of people who looked over at Connor and Noah as they approached, and Lenora turned around.

Connor just stood there, taking in the sight of her. Her long auburn hair was tied back and her hands had dirt on them. She must have been digging. From the corner of his eye, Connor saw Noah motioning for the others to leave them alone.

"I heard you were looking for an extra pair of hands," Connor said.

Lenora narrowed her gaze. "It's been months and you show up now as if nothing has happened?"

She stalked toward him and then stopped. "You . . ." she hissed. "You're still alive?" she said accusingly.

"I was in a coma. They only just brought me out of it today," Connor said.

Lenora's mouth opened and she licked her lips. "That's crap. Ashley would have told me if you were alive," she said and walked away from him.

Connor sprinted after her. "I swear to you, it's true. They didn't know if I'd been infected."

Lenora rounded on him and shoved him away. "If you've come here to tell me you're dying, I swear I'll shoot you myself."

Connor shook his head. "I'm not," he said and then repeated himself. "They found me in some wreckage and kept me in quarantine."

Lenora glared at him. "And you thought what? You'd come back here and we'd patch things up until the next crisis?"

Connor had known she'd be angry with him, but the level of fury in her eyes wasn't what he'd been expecting. "I had to see you," he said.

Lenora held up her arms. "Great, you're alive. You've seen me. Now leave me alone," she said and started walking away.

Connor stepped toward her and grabbed her arm. "I'm sorry," he said.

Lenora snatched her arm away from him.

"I should have listened to you sooner. I'm sorry for leaving, for not being able to let it go. For everything," Connor said and reached out, taking Lenora's hand. "You were the first person I wanted to see when they woke me up and you were the last person I thought about when I thought I was going to die on that ship. You might hate me now, but I'm not leaving. I don't care how long it takes. I'm staying."

Lenora pursed her lips. "What if I've already moved on? Would you still wait?" she said.

A momentary doubt seized Connor's chest, but then he pushed it away. "Someone once told me I'd make a good archeologist," he said and stepped closer to her, "so I thought I'd work with the best."

Lenora snorted and her lips curved upward. He pulled her into his arms. There was no one else.

"It'll take years to become the best. A lot of work. A lot of time," Lenora said.

"Time is the one thing I *do* have," Connor replied.

Lenora shook her head. "You've got an answer for everything."

"Not everything. Just this," Connor said.

He knew the colony would carry on despite the heavy toll that had been paid for their survival. Throughout his whole life he'd been restless, always moving from place to place. He'd struggled to know where he fit in, and he'd found a home in the military. When they learned of the threat to the colony, he'd reacted in the only way he knew. He was familiar with that life, but now he was ready for something new with the woman he loved. He didn't know what was in store for him and he'd lost count of the many chances life had given him, but he was determined to make the most of this one.

THANK YOU FOR READING LEGACY - FIRST COLONY - BOOK THREE.

If you loved this book, please consider leaving a review. Comments and reviews allow readers to discover authors, so if you want others to enjoy *Legacy* as you have, please leave a short note.

The First Colony series continues with the 4th book.

FIRST COLONY - SANCTUARY

ABOUT THE AUTHOR

Ken Lozito is the author of multiple science fiction and fantasy series. I've been reading both science fiction and fantasy for a long time. Books were my way to escape everyday life of a teenager to my current ripe old(?) age. What started out as a love of stories has turned into a full-blown passion for writing them. My ultimate intent for writing stories is to provide fun escapism for readers. I write stories that I would like to read and I hope you enjoy them as well.

If you have questions or comments about any of my works I would love to hear from you, even if its only to drop by to say hello at KenLozito.com

Thanks again for reading *First Colony - Legacy*.

Don't be shy about emails, I love getting them, and try to respond to everyone.

Connect with me at the following:
www.kenlozito.com
ken@kenlozito.com

ALSO BY KEN LOZITO

Made in the USA
Lexington, KY
05 April 2019